SWAMP SPIES

A Miss Fortune Mystery

NEW YORK TIMES BESTSELLING AUTHOR
JANA DELEON

MISS FORTUNE SERIES INFO

If you've never read a Miss Fortune mystery, you can start with LOUISIANA LONGSHOT, the first book in the series. If you prefer to start with this book, here are a few things you need to know.

Fortune Redding – a CIA assassin with a price on her head from one of the world's most deadly arms dealers. Because her boss suspects that a leak at the CIA blew her cover, he sends her to hide out in Sinful, Louisiana, posing as his niece, a librarian and ex–beauty queen named Sandy-Sue Morrow. The situation was resolved in Change of Fortune and Fortune is now a full-time resident of Sinful and has opened her own detective agency.

Ida Belle and Gertie – served in the military in Vietnam as spies, but no one in the town is aware of that fact except Fortune and Deputy LeBlanc.

Sinful Ladies Society – local group founded by Ida Belle, Gertie, and deceased member Marge. In order to gain membership, women must never have married or if widowed, their husband must have been deceased for at least ten years.

Sinful Ladies Cough Syrup – sold as an herbal medicine in Sinful, which is dry, but it's actually moonshine manufactured by the Sinful Ladies Society.

CHAPTER ONE

I STUFFED MY HIJAB INTO A TURQUOISE TOTE BAG WITH giant sunflowers on it and stepped out of the bathroom. Harrison was looking out the window of our hotel room at the Strait of Hormuz. It would have been a beautiful view if we'd actually been on the vacation we claimed to be there for, but nothing about our trip to Khasab was what it seemed.

He looked over as I stepped out and grinned. I already knew what had amused him. The turquoise palazzo pants, white-and-turquoise-striped full-sleeved tunic, and white sneakers weren't exactly my normal dress, and the giant sunflower tote was the icing on the cake. But when in Rome— or in this case, when in the Middle East—it was best not to draw attention to yourself. Just being an American tourist had enough people looking. I wanted to make sure that if they looked twice or simply too long, I didn't appear to be anything other than what I was supposed to be—the pretty wife on vacation with her husband. It was a role Harrison and I had played before, and we knew how to do it well.

"The view is gorgeous," I said as I walked over, "and the

bathroom is really clean. I give it my picky traveler seal of approval."

My way of conveying that my sweep for bugs in the bathroom didn't produce anything.

Harrison nodded. "The bedroom and lounge are as well."

"And the 'aunts'?"

Harrison grinned. "No complaints."

I relaxed a bit. Although it was an upper-end tourist hotel, you couldn't be too careful, especially when you were former CIA traveling under fake identities and your real identity could get you a visit to a prison—the kind of visit you might not return from. Even though the Khasab government wouldn't necessarily have a problem with us being there, we were problem-adjacent. And most people had a dollar amount where all ethics and morals could be compromised.

So Harrison and I were Mr. and Mrs. Williams, taking our elderly aunts on a bucket-list vacation they'd requested. Ida Belle and Gertie were there under their own passports, as they wouldn't set off any alarms. Even if someone did a deep dive and turned up their military service during Vietnam, no one would ever find out they were spies. As women, they'd be assumed to have played an administrative or medical care type role. And the reality was, they were overwhelmingly overlooked and underestimated because of their age. It was one of the only things I was looking forward to when I got older.

"Are they changing for the walk?" I asked.

Harrison nodded. "We'll stop by the marina before they close, settle up for the rental, and get the keys. That way, we can head out before dawn tomorrow morning. Our cover is good, but the fewer people who see us leaving, the better."

I nodded. We'd purchased diving equipment in Dubai and would carry it onto the boat in a duffel and rolling ice chest, but fewer people observing our passage was optimum. "Anything else tonight?"

"Just dinner. And try to look like you're having fun."

I frowned. "That might be the hardest role I have to play."

Harrison put his hand on my shoulder. "We're going to find him and bring him home. You know I don't make promises that I can't keep, but I'll promise you this—we're not leaving the Middle East without Carter."

It had been five days since Colonel Kitts had shown up on Emmaline's porch and told us that Carter was MIA. He was supposed to have served on the mission in only a consulting capacity, but at some point, circumstances had changed. It was the thing I'd feared the most as soon as he told me of his decision to assist the Marines and the Force Recon unit he used to be a part of. I knew that if a situation arose where Carter felt becoming part of the insertion would save lives, he wouldn't hesitate to do it.

I knew that because I was the same way.

The Marines wouldn't provide any details. No surprise there, as it was a matter of 'national security.' But the instant the colonel drove off, I called all my contacts and got them working, starting with my former boss at the CIA, Director Morrow.

It paid to have friends in high places.

Within two hours, I knew everything the Marine Corps wasn't going to tell me and had assembled a team and was hard at work on an extraction plan. Harrison and Mannie were part of my intel and were also determined to be part of the solution. As much as I didn't want my friends taking the risk, I couldn't deny that their help would be invaluable. Mannie's connections would be key to getting us into Iran unseen, and all the years Harrison and I worked together meant we were already on the same wavelength when it came to our roles on a mission. I couldn't ask for a better right-hand man for this.

Short of death, there was no way I was going to be able to leave Ida Belle and Gertie behind, so we'd booked them as a family affair. And to be honest, their presence made our vacation there seem credible and, most importantly, innocuous. Ultimately, the Strait of Hormuz was as far as they'd be going, and they'd remain on the 'safe' side near Oman, but they were eager to play whatever role was necessary. I could tell this had shaken them far more than either cared to admit.

It had shaken me as well.

The door to the adjoining suite opened and Ida Belle and Gertie stepped into the living area, looking as out of place as I did with their wardrobe choice. Gertie, who'd had to leave all her questionable fashion calls behind, looked practically obscure in a plain blue cotton skirt down to her feet, white T-shirt, and white Keds. Ida Belle, on the other hand, looked dressed up in tan slacks, blue polo shirt, and brown loafers.

Harrison grinned at her. "You look like you're off for your first day at private school."

"Private school for *boys*," Gertie said. "I tried to talk her into a skirt, but you know how that goes."

"I don't want to risk flashing a calf at someone," Ida Belle said. "I know we're supposed to be lying lower than corpses here, but when you're around, I always end up running. A skirt could be a potential prison sentence in the wrong circumstances. And 'wrong circumstances' is your middle name."

"I thought 'that was a fluke' was her middle name," Harrison said.

"There's a very long list," Ida Belle said.

"Whatever," Gertie said. "I'm crazy but not insane enough to Gertie in the Middle East. Can you imagine Celia over here, though? She'd get chased by a camel, fall down, flash the whole city, and then there would be another conflict, probably named after her."

"Desert Moon," Ida Belle said, and we all laughed.

"Let's get going," Harrison said. "We've got an errand to run, then we all need to have a good dinner and get some rest. The next twenty-four hours are going to be critical. We need to be on top of our game."

I nodded. But I already knew that I wouldn't be able to sleep a wink until Carter was safe.

———

EARLY THE NEXT MORNING, IDA BELLE AND GERTIE STOOD in the cabin of the boat, staring at me, their expressions a mixture of hope and extreme worry. I couldn't blame them. I was probably reflecting the same look right back at them, even though everything had been planned in intricate detail, right down to the minute. We couldn't make direct contact with Mannie because all conversations were at risk of interception. So all movement had been assigned very specific windows of time. And everything had to go off perfectly, or the entire mission would fail.

"Everyone knows their role, right?" I asked.

"Gertie and I remain anchored here and fish," Ida Belle said. "If you haven't returned by tomorrow evening, we bring the boat back to the marina after closing and leave it in the slip, go back to the hotel, order up room service for all of us, and pretend everything is normal until we hear from Mannie."

Gertie made a face. "Then we proceed to worry-eat waiting for you to show up, and if that doesn't happen, the next morning we head out to shop, claiming the 'lovebirds' wanted to sleep in. This might be the only time in my life I'm not looking forward to eating or shopping."

Ida Belle took my hand and squeezed it. "*Your* job is to bring Carter back."

"That's the plan."

And then I did something outside the norm... I hugged them both. Long and hard.

"Thank you," I said. "If anything goes wrong—"

They both started shaking their heads.

"I'm former CIA," I said. "Things *can* and *do* go wrong all the time, so let me finish. If anything goes wrong, I want you to know that the best years of my life were because I came to Sinful. And they all started with meeting you. I love you guys."

Gertie sniffed. "We love you too."

Ida Belle nodded, her eyes misty.

"In my office safe, there's some letters. If things go sideways, pass them out. There's also a will."

"We'll take care of everything if it comes to that," Ida Belle said. "What about you, Harrison?"

"Cassidy and I lined up things back when we moved in together," he said. "And she knows what we're doing here— more or less. We said what we needed to say before I left. But...you'll look out for her...if..."

"Of course," Ida Belle said. "She's family."

I checked my watch and felt adrenaline course through my body. It was time.

"They should be in position," I said to Harrison. "You ready?"

We crossed our arms and clasped our hands together, as we had before every mission we'd done, and everything shifted. Our minds, bodies, and emotions fled our domestic existence, and once again, we became the highly skilled weapons we'd been trained to be.

We headed onto the deck, already clad in our wet suits, pulled on our air tanks, and positioned ourselves on the side of the boat. I gave Ida Belle and Gertie one last look and a thumbs-up before falling back over the side. The Gulf floor was twenty meters, but we'd be going even deeper just as soon as we acquired the equipment Mannie's friends left for us.

The diver propulsion craft, or DPCs, were secured to the remnants of a ship. We released them and clipped the straps to our gear, then fired them up and headed for deeper waters. Our destination was across the Strait of Hormuz and would take a little less than an hour to traverse, which was just short of the range on the DPCs and our oxygen tanks. We had to watch our gauges and make sure we stayed exactly on course. Even a slight deviation could put us too far off course to make it to our target.

Which would be dire because we'd be surfacing in Iran-controlled waters.

I was grateful that I'd kept up my physical fitness after leaving the CIA. Granted, I wasn't at the same level now as then, but if I hadn't been diligent with my strength training, the DPCs would have been hell on my core and upper body. And all the running had kept my oxygen requirements low, which was needed to not expend my tank before we arrived at our destination.

At the forty-five-minute mark, I signaled Harrison and we slowed. Somewhere above us was the fishing boat that would transport us into Iran. He pointed up, indicating he was ready to surface, and we began our ascent, careful to maintain the correct speed to avoid decompression sickness, or 'the bends' as divers called them. I'd had them a time or two when surfacing correctly hadn't been an option, and I wasn't anxious for a repeat. Besides, the necessary recovery time wasn't factored into our schedule.

As we drew closer to the surface, I could see the outline of a vessel about twenty feet away. We adjusted our rise to breach closer to the boat. Our eyes locked as we covered the last few feet to the surface, and I knew we were both thinking the same things. What if it's not our ride? What if the fishermen, who were members of a rebel group, decided to trade us for a bigger paycheck from the enemy?

It had happened before.

But when we broke the surface, the first thing I saw was Mannie, decked out in the loose-fitting pants and long-sleeved shirt that were common dress for men in Iran. One of the fishermen sent straps down for us to secure the DPCs to be hauled in, and Mannie reached over the side and pulled me onto the deck. I hurried into the cabin, and Harrison followed closely behind. The boat engines fired up almost immediately, and we headed for shore.

Mannie closed the door and pointed to the duffel bags on the counter that contained our supplies. We stripped out of the wet suits and covered our faces, necks, hands, and wrists with skin bronzer to help boost our tans, which had faded since the previous summer. Then I headed for the tiny bathroom and exchanged my wet bathing suit for dry undergarments, tan slim-fit pants, and matching tank and T-shirt. When I popped back into the cabin, Harrison had ditched his swim trunks for pants and tee in the same shade of tan.

We'd both dosed our hair with dark brown wash at the hotel in Houston the night before our flight, so I popped in a pair of brown contacts to complete my transformation. Then we donned an outer layer of clothes like what Mannie was wearing—Harrison in predominantly navy and me in black with tiny purple lines. Our hijabs were navy and black as well, the dark colors chosen specifically to hide any of the bronzer that rubbed off on the material before it dried.

The additional steps taken to conceal our identities would help us move through the country without notice. Even our

Farsi was good enough to pass a sniff test by the average citizen as the regions had different dialects, so something slightly different wouldn't be questioned. Not that we had plans to test our ability in the city. The real threat came once we left the populated areas and went into the mountain ranges heavily guarded by the Iranian military. Vehicles were often stopped for no reason whatsoever and although we'd played these roles before, it had never been personal.

Failure was not an option.

Once we were suited up for our mission, we took a seat at the table so that Mannie could bring us up to date on everything before we docked. He already had a map of the area laid out on the table.

"Carter is being held in a compound here just inside the mountain range." Mannie pointed to an area that was supposed to be uninhabited.

"And the rest of the unit?" I asked. "Director Morrow said there's been some chatter—unverified as of yet—but it didn't sound good."

"We intercepted that chatter and were initially of the same opinion as Morrow." Mannie said. "But I got intel an hour ago that an operation is underway near a suspected compound farther up the coast. I can't say more."

I nodded and my spirits lifted a little. If an operation was in process, maybe they could get to the other members of the unit.

"Any rescue plans for Carter?" I asked.

Mannie gave me a frustrated shake of his head. "The Marines are being exceedingly tight-lipped about the situation with Carter. I have to assume their intel is as good as mine, but if they're planning a rescue, it's locked down so tight, not even a whisper is reaching outside the base. Will you have trouble if you cross paths?"

I shook my head. "There are certain ways to identify ourselves as CIA. Morrow gave me what they're using now. They won't like it if they run into us—they never do—but it won't be a problem."

"Morrow's putting a lot on the line," Mannie said.

"He is. But Harrison and I are gifted at plausible deniability. And my contact with Morrow can't be traced. We'll take his involvement to the grave."

Harrison nodded. "Once a spy, always a spy."

"Well, let's get you two back to being a PI and deputy and Carter back to sheriff," Mannie said. "You'll hitch a ride from the docks with the fishermen's transport guy. He makes one delivery at the far end of town, then his next takes him right past your drop-off point. If you get stopped, he'll claim he's training new people for the route, but with any luck, any soldiers or police who spot him will recognize the vehicle and leave you alone. He drives this route several times a week."

"So it looks like a couple hours' drive," I said as I scanned the map and pointed to what looked to be the best point of egress from the road. "Is this where he's dropping us off?"

"Yes. It's a couple miles to the compound and no road."

"We wouldn't be able to use it even if there was one," I said. "We'll need to approach from the ridgeline. We have to assume there are cameras."

Harrison nodded. "As soon as we're dropped off, we'll ditch the top clothes and blend with the terrain. How many men?"

"We suspect ten but can't be sure. No one has had eyes on them long enough to determine who's come and gone, and they could have some long-term personnel stationed there." Mannie gave me a grave look. "I don't have to tell you how dangerous these people are. They're terrorists and arms dealers. Rumor has it some of them were Ahmad's men."

"My former bread and butter," I said.

"Also the reason you were sent to Sinful," Mannie said. "They know who Carter is as far as military position and rank go and have their suspicions as to why he was in Iran, but so far, we haven't heard any chatter connecting him to you."

I let out a breath of relief. That was excellent news. Being Force Recon alone was enough to put a high price on his head, and no doubt, they'd pegged him as the unit leader, which was why he was being held separately. But if they found out he was in a relationship with me, that would make him even more valuable. And as soon as they realized they weren't going to get anything out of him, that's exactly what they would do—sell him to the highest bidder.

"Do these fishermen know?" I asked.

Mannie shook his head. "I'm sure they have their suspicions, especially given that a female operative still isn't the norm. And they know me from before, so I'm sure they're wondering about the connection. But they don't know anything beyond that."

"As long as no one connects Carter to Fortune, we'll be good," Harrison said.

Mannie peered between the blinds. "We're approaching the dock. I need to get you two into a crate. That's your transport until you're out of the city. We're going to pray that they don't get stopped in the city for a random inspection or if so, that they only inspect the crates on the rear of the truck. I'm afraid it's not going to be the most comfortable ride or the best smelling."

"We've had worse," I said.

"After you retrieve Carter, get to any of the five pickup zones I indicated," Mannie said. "I have men standing by at each of them."

"What's the extraction plan?" I asked.

Carter wasn't exactly traveling with a passport and couldn't risk a visible exit, even from a neighboring country and with the proper documents.

"You two will reverse the process with these same fishermen and head back to Khasab to finish your 'vacation.' A different boat will take Carter and me as far as they can into the Gulf of Oman, then we'll dive. There's a US submarine patrolling there that I'll be able to contact. I'll take him aboard and the Navy will get him to a US base. I don't know which one, but it doesn't matter. They'll keep him for debriefing and any medical care needed, then he'll be sent back to American soil."

"And if he's not in any condition to make the dive?" I asked. It wasn't something I wanted to think too hard on, but prisoners of war were rarely treated well, especially special ops. And especially when the enemy wanted information they refused to give.

"I have a mini-sub. He won't have to lift a finger."

Harrison's eyes widened. "Do I even want to know how you acquired that? Because I know the Navy didn't lend you one. And they don't come cheap."

"Big and Little decided to 'partner' with Fortune a long time ago. They're happy to use their considerable connections and resources to aid those of us on the ground...or in the water. And the sub can be sold afterward, so it's just a temporary reduction of holdings."

Harrison shook his head. "You know this relationship all of you have is not normal, right?"

Mannie snorted. "What relationship in Sinful is?"

"You sure you don't want to come with us?" I joked. "I mean, stuffed in a fishy crate for a ride through a hot desert, then walk for miles in sand-covered mountains while remaining out of sight. We'll probably get to shoot guns, kill some bad guys, then hike back out of there. It sounds like a good time."

Mannie smiled. "If you were swimming there, I'd already have my wet suit on. But I think I'll leave this part of the mission to those with the skill for it."

He stepped toward me and surprised me by giving me a hug. "You come back alive. Otherwise, I'll have to answer to Ally, and she's fierce for a little thing."

He released me and extended his arm to Harrison to clasp. "You too, brother."

Harrison gave him a single nod. "Count on it."

CHAPTER TWO

THE RIDE FROM THE DOCK AND OUT OF TOWN WAS AS uncomfortable and smelly as I'd expected, but we barely noticed. We were silent most of the ride, and I knew we were both praying that we got clear passage out of town, that we could breach the compound, and that Carter was still there and viable for rescue. I used those words when I processed the mission—words like 'viable'—because I didn't want to consider the words that made it personal. The words that could bring an unexpected and extremely important aspect of my life to a premature, jolting end.

I knew Harrison had the same thoughts as me. He and Mannie were the only ones who knew the score as well as I did. I was already thankful for the friends and connections I'd made that allowed me to conduct this mission, but I was also battling my own internal feelings, starting with anger. Anger that the Marines had asked Carter to go into the field. Anger that their screwup—and there had to have been one—had allowed him to be captured. Anger at Carter for agreeing to become unit leader. And finally, anger at myself for being angry at him.

It was a lot to process.

During my time with the CIA, I'd never experienced that range of emotion because I didn't have people I loved waiting for me to return. I certainly didn't have people I loved depending on me to save their lives. So many of my cases in Sinful had crossed over into that personal territory, but nothing compared to this. To now.

When the truck rolled to a bumpy stop, I assumed we were at the delivery site on the edge of the city. I heard the men shuffling the crates behind us and about twenty minutes later, we were back in motion. It took another fifteen to get far enough outside of town for the driver to pull over, and then we waited for him to give us the okay before popping out of the crate.

The hot desert air was refreshing compared to the closed fishy atmosphere in the crate. Even with tiny gaps in the slats, little air had circulated through the container. The driver signaled us into the truck for the long drive ahead of us. Several times, we passed soldiers on patrol, but the driver just waved and no one indicated they wanted him to pull over. We reached our destination without incident, and I felt both relief that we'd made it this far without issue and tension knowing what was ahead.

We thanked the driver before stripping off our native wear and collecting our gear. I ditched my contacts, and we pulled on goggles and masks to protect our eyes from sudden bursts of blowing sand. Then we headed into the vast landscape. The driver didn't stick around, and I didn't blame him. He had been very well paid—enough to retire—but he'd risked his and his family's lives helping us. It was a lot to put on the line, even for an ally.

Harrison and I easily spotted the tire tracks leading into the mountain and set off at a good clip far enough away that we could duck behind a dune if we saw a vehicle approaching. We took turns scanning for any sign of life, but all was quiet when we reached the base of the mountain range.

We ducked in behind a small rise and rehydrated while we reviewed our map and surroundings one more time. The winds in the desert shifted things, sometimes dramatically, so it was a process we'd repeat often. We couldn't afford to be off mark. Every second that Carter remained a hostage was one they could decide he wasn't worth keeping and sell him. Or they could start another round of torture. So far, they hadn't discovered his connection to me, but that wouldn't hold forever. And once they did, his value would shoot up and an auction would begin.

"It looks like the route we picked is still viable," Harrison said. "We'll have decent protection if we follow along this lower line."

I nodded as I lifted my binoculars to scan the mountains in front of us. We'd reassess as we went, of course. The big unknown being what level of security they had for the compound. Cameras were easily avoided if you spotted them soon enough, but a good sniper was much harder to navigate. No one knew that better than the two of us.

"Let's get to it," I said and headed up the rise.

Every minute counted.

———

I PEERED OVER A SMALL DUNE AT THE BUILDINGS BELOW. There were several small structures surrounding one larger central one. Based on the firepits and cooking utensils in front of the smaller buildings, I pegged them as where the men lived. The larger structure held arms and whatever else they were dealing in. Including Carter.

"Only one camera pointing this way," Harrison said. "And it will be easy enough to avoid if we take a straight line down to the back of that building directly below us. But it means crawling to maintain coverage."

"Not like we haven't done it before. I count six men, but there's more housing than that."

"We have to assume they're all occupied, especially with Carter here."

"We'll have to pick them off as we go," I said. "Can't clear the path from a distance."

"No. That would send them scrambling, and I'm going to bet they've got more firepower than just those AKs they're strapping."

I looked over at Harrison. This was it. That final moment of 'safety' before we put ourselves right in the thick of it. Never had mission success been more important than it was right now.

"Thank you, Harrison. If I don't get a chance to say it later…"

"You would have done the same for me."

"Yeah. I would have."

"Then let's go get Carter and get back to our real lives."

We got down on hands and knees and gripped our rifles in our right arms until we made it fifty yards from the compound. Then we shifted lower, lying on our stomachs, rifles across our forearms. A sniper crawl was slow going but necessary to avoid detection while also being ready to fire. This was the part of a mission where speed wasn't an objective, even though the sense of urgency was steadily increasing.

We made it to a boulder just outside the compound perimeter without incident and watched as two men patrolling walked by smoking and chatting. The nearest structure was twenty yards away, but there was no way to determine whether it was occupied except by entering it. I pointed to it and Harrison nodded. As soon as the men on patrol disappeared around another building, we hurried from our hiding spots and ran.

I hadn't spotted cameras inside the perimeter, probably because they had placed them on the outside structures to monitor the mountains and because they had men patrolling inside the compound. I hadn't spotted a sniper either, but if they were any good, you wouldn't know they were there until the bullet tore through you. I knew that the closer we got to that center building, the more the security would ramp up.

Along with the danger.

But our lucky streak continued. The structure was empty, and the side door provided the ability to get a look at three sides of the building Carter was being held in without being seen. There was a door on the right side, but no windows at all. I had no reason to believe the wall we couldn't see would be any different. So the only option for entry was through the doorway.

Cameras were located on each corner of the building, which was no surprise, but also made it impossible to get into the building unseen. As soon as we came into view, one of the men would sound the alarm. We had to be fast and accurate, because there was no way we were getting out of here without a gunfight.

"Should have tagged those two guards to better our odds on exit," Harrison said. "We can make it in. But we're going to have to shoot our way out."

"We figured that would be the case."

"Yeah. But the big unknown is what Carter's condition is. I know he's a tough son of a bitch, but even tough guys have limits. We're probably going to have to clean the entire place to get him out of here, because I don't see any of them retreating."

I nodded. "I came prepared to clean."

"It's your mission. You take the lead."

I said a quick prayer covering all the necessaries—that Carter was in the building, that he wasn't badly injured, that Harrison and I made every shot count—then I slipped out and bolted for the building.

I heard Harrison charging behind me as I rushed to the doorway and men shouting behind us somewhere. There was no time, or point in trying, to sneak inside, so I hit the door with my shoulder and then dropped and rolled. A bullet whizzed past me, and I heard Harrison squeeze off a round behind me. I popped up and took out another man who'd just stepped into what appeared to be some sort of meeting room.

There were two hallways leading away from the room. We couldn't afford to split, so I chose the narrow one, figuring the larger one was used to move crates of weapons. I heard shouting behind me as I ran down the hallway, scanning the rooms as I went. I made a sharp left turn at the end and that's when I saw it—a door with bars over an opening at the top.

That was it!

I knew I wouldn't be able to knock this one down myself, but we'd anticipated this. By the time we reached the door, Harrison had already pulled a small explosive from his pack. It took only seconds to attach it to the door near the lock, and then we hurried back and covered our ears before it detonated.

The explosion shook the entire building. Our masks kept us from choking, but we both covered our goggles with our arms to help keep them clear and kept our arms in position until we could no longer feel debris falling on them. Through the haze, I bolted through the now-open doorway. In the center of the room a man was slumped over, taped to a chair. His back was to us, but I would have known him anywhere.

Carter!

I rushed over, my heart pounding. Were we too late?

Then he looked up at me and smiled.

"What took you so long?"

His face was swollen, both eyes blackened, and there was dried blood stuck to his lips that had run down onto his chest. His smile was lopsided because of the swelling, and one eye was almost completely closed. I pushed down my overwhelming rage and focused on the mission. Finding Carter alive was only one of many huge hurdles we had coming our way fast. His arms and legs were taped to the chair, and I immediately set about freeing his arms while Harrison worked on his legs.

"Is anything broken?" I asked as I worked.

"My nose and probably some ribs," he said. "Hurts like hell to breathe. What's the exit plan?"

"We were spotted coming in, which I assume you gathered already. It's a shoot-out to get out of here. Any idea on the number of men?"

"Seven or eight, maybe. How far do we have to retreat?"

"Couple miles through the mountains, on foot. When was the last time you ate?"

"I don't know. What day is it?"

I cursed and the tape finally broke. He moved his arms in a circular motion, then massaged them, trying to get circulation back into his forearms and hands. Then Harrison and I helped him stand and gave him a couple seconds to make sure his legs were going to steady.

"You good?" I asked.

"Sixty percent, maybe?"

"Your sixty percent is probably better than their hundred," Harrison said.

"It's going to have to be," Carter said.

I handed him a pistol from my backpack. "We'll pick up an AK off one of the dead guys on our way out."

Carter reached out, pulled down my mask, and kissed me hard. "I knew you'd come. I didn't want you to, but I knew you would. Harrison, I would kiss you too, but I don't think it would be appreciated as much."

Harrison grinned and threw an arm around him in a quick bro hug. "Let's get the hell out of here."

Carter managed goggles and a mask on his battered face, and we began our escape, with me in the lead and Harrison at the rear. We encountered no one in the hallway or the side rooms, and I stopped when we reached the end and peered into the front room. There was a chance someone would be positioned there, although if I were the enemy, I would be waiting outside to pick us off as we exited. But if these men were basic criminals with no snipers in the bunch, we had the advantage.

I didn't see any movement in the front room, so I motioned to Harrison, who slipped around the opening and made a dash for a stack of crates on the right side. Immediately, automatic gunfire followed him, and he made a dive for cover. But he'd accomplished what we needed. He'd drawn out the gunman.

I fired a single round and after a spray of rounds at the ceiling, opposing gunfire ceased. Harrison sprinted to the next set of crates and peered into the room where the gunman had been hiding.

"It's clear," he said and popped out with the gunman's AK, which he passed to Carter.

"Fortune and I will clear the path," Harrison said. "You cover."

Carter gave him a grim nod. He wasn't happy playing backup, but he knew his current physical limitations wouldn't affect his aim. Our best chance for getting out of here was Carter staying back. Harrison and I took up position on each side of the exit. The nearest cover was one of the buildings being used as living quarters, but we had to assume that's where more men were positioned, waiting to fire when they caught a glimpse of us. We needed to get past the outside buildings so that we could make a run for the mountains. Once there, altitude would give us the advantage over anyone on foot.

I pulled a grenade from my backpack and removed the pin, then tossed it outside, toward the nearest structure. The blast would eliminate anyone inside and cause everyone to duck long enough for us to get out of the building. We'd just have to pray the smoke was thick enough that they couldn't pick us off and that they valued their own men enough to prevent random open fire.

As soon as the blast shook the ground, Harrison ran out, Carter and me right behind. Bullets whizzed around my head, slamming into the side of the building as we went. When we reached the side of one of the closest structures, gunfire had ceased, and the smoke was still thick enough to risk a dash to a building on the outside perimeter. When we were ten feet from the entry, a shadowy figure leaned out of the doorway and took a shot. Harrison fired at the same time and the figure dropped, his round passing over Harrison's head. Harrison never even slowed —he just jumped over the dead man and we followed him inside.

Another shower of bullets hit the side of the building, and I gave silent thanks that they had built the bunkers out of concrete blocks, even though the lack of windows made picking off the enemy much harder. I peered out the doorway and another wave of bullets exploded on the wall just inches from my head.

"Where is the next cover?" Carter asked.

"There's not any," I said. "These buildings are in a giant ring around the building you were held in. The only thing after them is the mountains."

"How far?"

"A hundred yards to the nearest dune."

Carter shook his head. "The only way out of here is if none of them are standing."

"I know. The two shooting at me just now are in the structure to our right."

Harrison pulled a grenade from his pack and positioned himself at the edge of the doorway. Then he pulled the pin, flipped around the side of the doorway, and chunked the grenade right in front of the entry to the other building. A second later, the blast shook the ground and dust filled the air as the walls of the building collapsed.

Another round of bullets hit the side of our building as Harrison ducked back inside.

"Those came from that building to our left," I said. "But even with your throwing arm, you're not going to reach it."

"I guess you didn't bring a grenade launcher," Carter joked.

"Ha," I said. "Ida Belle wouldn't let me borrow it. We need to draw them out. A grenade won't create enough smoke for us to make a run for the dune, and I'm not a fan of turning my back to people with automatic weapons anyway."

"I'll pop around," Harrison said. "It might draw one or two of them out enough for you to get off a good shot."

He crouched, ready to spring around the opening, when a huge explosion rocked the side wall of the building and it collapsed. Thank God the roof collapsed with it and had fallen at an angle, creating a barrier between us and the men who'd launched the explosive at the building.

"I guess it was too much to hope that they didn't have explosives," I said. Dust filled the air around us, making it impossible to see more than a foot in any direction. But we had to get out of there. Another round would collapse the entire thing on top of us.

"Can we blast out the back wall?" Carter asked.

I shook my head. "I don't have anything small enough to take out the wall but not us. Not from the inside."

A round of rapid fire burst out in the open area between us and the main building and I squinted, trying to make out anything in the haze. I saw shadows moving through the dust but couldn't tell where the shots were coming from. The only thing I was certain of was that they weren't being fired in our direction, which made absolutely no sense.

A second later, an explosion rocked the building that the shooters were in, the blast so big that it sent chunks of concrete onto the roof above us. I glanced at Harrison, who shook his head. What the hell was going on out there? I prayed we hadn't just stepped into the middle of a turf war between arms dealers.

I heard a clank on the back wall of our building, and a man's voice yelled, "Take cover!"

We all hit the ground, covering our head and ears as the blast ripped through the back wall of the building. I looked up as a man stepped through a giant hole in the wall. His hands and forearms were so dark anyone would have assumed he was born that way, and he was dressed like the men in the compound, his face and head completely covered, except for his eyes, which were shielded by sunglasses.

But I still would have known him anywhere.

"Hurry!" he yelled.

I jumped up and rushed for the opening, Harrison and Carter right behind me. When we reached the next building, we stopped behind the back wall.

"Those in charge were already on their way when you entered the compound," he said. "They travel with a lot of security, so we're talking a matter of minutes until you're completely outnumbered. And they've got the road you entered the range on covered. You'll have to go straight across the mountains to a secondary location."

I glanced over at the two ATVs next to the building. "Can we take those over?"

He shook his head. "No. The passage is too narrow. But I know something that will work. Follow me."

We hurried after him as he made his way to the last building on the west end of the compound, and I saw the corral on the side with three horses.

"How are you bareback?" I asked Carter.

"Excellent," Carter said.

"Go!" the man said. "I'll clear the rest of them."

"What about you?"

He grinned. "Don't worry. The men on their way here now are expecting me, and no one who saw me help you will be talking by the time they get here, and I'm not fleeing the country, so I have more options."

I stuck out my hand and he glanced at it, then pulled me in and gave me a single squeeze before he hurried off without so much as a backward glance.

"Who the hell was that?" Harrison asked.

"My father."

Both their jaws dropped, but there was no time to talk about Dwight Redding's second debut from the grave. We took off for the corral and grabbed the bridles hanging on the fence posts and quickly threw them on the horses, who were dancing around, ready to run away from all the noise and dust. Harrison opened the gate and we all jumped on the horses and set off in a dead run for the mountain.

I leaned over, close to the neck of my horse to help maintain my balance as we ran. Another explosion sounded behind us and then rounds of rapid fire. I had a flicker of a moment when I started to worry, but then I remembered who I was worrying about. Talk about a waste of energy.

Dwight Redding had more lives than a cat.

CHAPTER THREE

THE HORSES CARRIED US THROUGH THE MOUNTAIN PASS with no issues and much quicker than we could have managed on our own. We'd had to duck under rock shelves a couple times to avoid a helicopter, but so far, we'd only spotted one. We'd also lucked out with the weather. As soon as we'd hit the base of the mountains, a sandstorm had developed, effectively erasing our tracks. It couldn't have worked better if it had been planned.

Our pickup guys were thrilled to take the horses off our hands, and I didn't blame them as the quality of the animals was stellar. Then they quickly got us hidden in the back of a cargo truck and we were on our way to the coast. Since we'd come directly across the mountains, the ride wasn't nearly as long as the first one, and it gave Harrison and me a chance to fill Carter in on everything we had arranged.

"Next time the Marines need someone to plan a mission, I'm giving them your number," he said, shaking his head. "You did more in a matter of days than we managed in weeks."

"We're free agents," I said. "Trust me, it wasn't quite as

easy when we were CIA. The red tape there isn't quite as bad as the military, but it's still a time suck."

"Free agents with a military-grade budget," Harrison added. "I'm afraid you're going to have to make nice with the Heberts. They really went the extra mile on this."

Carter nodded. "I'm nice. I've always been nice. But the fact that they managed to acquire this equipment so quickly is not going to improve my side-eye."

Harrison grinned, then looked at me. "Speaking of the side-eye, what the heck is up with your father? Does he have a tracker on you?"

I shook my head. "There's a reason he's considered the best spy the CIA has ever had."

Harrison snorted. "Yeah, because even the CIA can't find him."

"You know the military is going to want to debrief you," Carter said. "And they *will* debrief me. What story are we going with?"

"According to our passports, Harrison and I never left Sinful, so you can go with whatever you'd like. My suggestion is a war between arms dealers broke out, and you were hauled out by one of the men, thinking he'd cash in on a sale. Instead, you dispatched him on a boat and after that, some fishermen found you drifting and unconscious and turned you over to the Navy. Your memory is a bit fuzzy after you dispatched the guy in the boat."

"So no mention of arriving in a multimillion-dollar mini-sub?" Carter asked. "Or knowledge of the exact location of a US submarine?"

I shrugged. "Mannie will have a cover for you that leaves us out of it. But the less we know of each other's business, the better."

Harrison nodded. "Can't be compelled to talk about things you don't know."

Carter shook his head. "The whole thing is unbelievable. I can't thank you enough. I wouldn't be able to if I lived a thousand lifetimes."

"All the thanks I need is a promise from you to never agree to do this again."

"You can count on that. I think I'm more scared to face my mother than I was those arms dealers."

I nodded. "I would be."

When we arrived at the dock, Mannie lifted the rear door on the cargo truck and grinned at us.

"It's great to see you guys," he said. "Ready to get back home?"

Carter stepped forward and stuck out his hand. "More than you can imagine. Thank you for everything. I know this couldn't have happened without you and the Heberts. But I hope I'm not going to get you into hot water with the Navy."

Mannie shook his head. "Some of my buddies get credit for the recovery of a high-value target. They're already counting the accolades, so don't worry about me. Like Fortune and Harrison, I was never here."

"Do you know anything about my unit?" Carter asked.

"Green Berets got them all out," Mannie said. "They're back on allied soil."

Carter's shoulders slumped in relief. "Thank God."

"Now, let's do the same for you," Mannie said.

We said quick goodbyes, and Harrison and I hurried onto the fishing boat that had brought us in. Carter and Mannie ducked onto another fishing boat docked right behind ours. We all headed straight into the cabins and the boats immediately left the dock. One of the fishermen stepped inside and pulled water and sandwiches out of an ice chest.

"You eat?" he asked.

I thanked him in Farsi, and he smiled and gave me a nod before heading out.

Harrison held up his bottle of water and I clinked mine against it.

"Another successful mission down," he said.

"Hopefully, our last."

———

IT WAS LONG AFTER DARK WHEN WE SURFACED, THE LIGHTS from the boat casting a dim glow around it. Ida Belle and Gertie must have been on the back deck waiting for noise because they were both leaning over the side as we came up, the tension in their faces and bodies so clear. The last communication they'd had with us was when we'd gone over the side of the boat that morning, and as impossible as what we'd just accomplished had been, I knew that sitting here doing nothing had a level of difficulty all its own.

"We got him," I said as soon as I yanked out my mouthpiece, not wanting them to worry a second more than they had to.

"Praise the Lord!"

"Thank God!"

They both yelled at once, and Ida Belle looked upward with her hands pressed together in a prayer arch and I knew she was giving thanks. They helped us haul in the tanks and we climbed onto the boat, both collapsing on the bench seats, then Gertie thrust a prepaid cell phone in my hand.

"It's got signal," she said. "Barely, but it's there."

I nodded and sent a short text to Walter.

Having a great time. See you soon.

We'd prearranged communication before we left Sinful,

and I knew that Walter was at Emmaline's house, praying for this specific text to come through. The one that meant Carter was alive and we'd gotten him out of Iran.

Glad to hear it. Everyone says hi and they miss you.

I smiled and showed Harrison the text, knowing that the normal statement reflected nothing at all of the celebration that was taking place there right now. I could picture Walter and Emmaline crying and hugging and smiling as if we were standing right there. Then they'd notify Ally, Cassidy, Ronald, and Blanchet that it was over.

Ida Belle and Gertie helped us pull off our gear and then ordered us to stay put while they brought out towels and bottled water.

"We've got plenty to eat inside," Ida Belle said, "but I figure you two need some time to decompress, and not just because of the dive. Do you want to head in?"

"If you're comfortable navigating back to the marina tonight," I said.

Ida Belle raised one brow.

I laughed. "Then absolutely, positively yes. I hear a hot shower and a comfortable bed calling me. We'll dump the diving gear overboard on the way. And as soon as I feel like moving again, we'll head inside and tell you all about it."

Gertie leaned over and gave me a hard squeeze, then did the same to Harrison. "I've never been so worried in all my life. And that's no small statement given the things I've been up to."

I smiled as I watched her and Ida Belle enter the cabin. A couple seconds later, the boat engines fired up and the magnitude of the day finally hit me. Because he knew exactly how I felt, Harrison gripped my shoulder with one hand and squeezed. I nodded, feeling tears form as the adrenaline started to exit my body.

"I can never thank you enough—"

Harrison shook his head, cutting me off. "You would have done the same for me. You're more than a partner, more than a sister. I don't know how to explain it."

"I get it."

"But if it's all the same, I really hope this was the last time we have to partner up like this. I know Sinful is the home of crazy, but it's nothing like what we did today."

"High stakes. High risk," I agreed. "But we are officially retired from the spy business. I promise."

"What about your dad? What's his deal?"

"Ha. I don't have a clue."

"You didn't seem surprised that he was alive."

"I had a feeling he didn't die in that explosion. I think unless I'm looking right at him when he goes, and I can check his pulse myself and cover the grave, I'll probably never believe it."

"Me either." Harrison shook his head. "He said the arms dealers on their way would expect him to be there, which means they think he's either one of them or a client."

I nodded. "He's infiltrated somewhere. The big question is who he's working for."

"Surely not the CIA. They think he's dead, right?"

"Maybe. The only thing I'm certain of is that they wouldn't tell me if they knew differently. And I can't say that I blame them. The truth is, he's a bigger asset to the CIA than he is to me as a father, and they both know it. Today being an exception that I don't expect to repeat."

"If it makes you feel any better, I think we would have made it out without him."

"So do I, but not as easily, and maybe not without injury. Carter is worse off than he indicated. He tried to hide it, but I'd bet he's got some damage to his knees, the nose and ribs

34

are definitely broken, and I think his shoulder is dislocated. His rifle stance was off. If we'd had to hike out, fighting for every inch..."

Harrison nodded. "But we didn't. And everything that's wrong will heal."

"I'm still giving extra thanks when I say my prayers tonight."

"Goes without saying."

I smiled. "We better head inside and give those girls the whole story before they explode."

Harrison grinned. "I've had enough explosions for one day."

———

WHEN WE GOT BACK TO THE HOTEL, I SHOWERED AND scrubbed until the majority of the self-tanner was removed. Then I fell asleep before I even hit the pillow, and I slept hard. I was still in good shape, but I wasn't in mission shape, and the physical strain was only half of what I'd had going on that day. Before we got back to the dock, I'd gotten a text from Walter on the burner phone that read *Emmaline says to please get her a handmade scarf.*

That meant they'd heard from Mannie through other channels and Carter was safely on the Navy sub. I had no idea how long they'd try to hold him for debriefing, but at least he was safe and someplace where he could get medical care.

Mannie would retrieve the DPCs Harrison and I had left tied to the shipwreck and sell them along with the mini-sub. There was a healthy underground market for military equipment, and I had no doubt he'd have the Heberts' money back in their bank accounts before he set foot in Sinful. I had no idea how he'd gotten into Iran in the first place, but I assumed he'd be able to exit equally quickly.

We had one more day booked in Khasab but planned on cutting things short and heading back to Dubai to catch an earlier flight. Gertie was all set to play injured—a role she knew well—which would explain our early departure just in case anyone wanted to give it the side-eye.

I sat up and stretched when I awoke, my muscles aching a bit. I'd taken magnesium, potassium, and Aleve before I'd crashed, but it was going to take a couple days for the stiffness to disappear entirely. I figured I might as well help it forward and headed for another hot shower. I'd barely finished dressing when I heard a soft knock on my door and Gertie poked her head in.

"How you feeling?" she asked.

"A little stiff, but otherwise, like a million bucks," I said.

She stepped inside, nodding. "I slept like the dead. I don't even think I snored."

"You did," Ida Belle said, stepping into the room behind Gertie. "Trust me on that one. They probably heard you back in Sinful."

Gertie waved a hand in dismissal. "You brought your headphones."

I grinned. "You guys want to grab some breakfast before we head out of here?"

"Definitely," Gertie said. "All this worrying has given me a case of the munchies. I went through half our minibar snacks last night after we got back."

Ida Belle snorted. "You went through half the minibar snacks because you went through half the minibar liquids."

Gertie raised one eyebrow. "Says the woman who ordered room service champagne."

"We had celebrating to do, and those tiny bottles weren't

going to hack it," Ida Belle said, then gave me an apologetic look. "I poked my head in to invite you, but you were already out."

I laughed. "That's okay. We can have a big celebration with plenty of snacks and champagne just as soon as we're back home. Maybe I'll even throw a dinner party—reason known only to us, of course—and get Molly to cater it. My way of thanking everyone who made this possible."

Gertie sniffed. "I think that would be wonderful."

"Don't you start again," Ida Belle said. "You've cried more in the last week than you have in the hundred or so years I've known you."

"I've worried more in the past week than I have in those *forty* years you've known me."

Harrison poked his head in from the living room. "Hey, you ladies going to stand around gabbing all morning or are we going to get something to eat? I'm starving!"

We headed for the hotel restaurant, which had an excellent breakfast service, then when we'd consumed enough food to regret it later, Gertie glanced at her watch.

"Do I have time to run to the market and pick up some souvenirs?" she asked. "That text from Walter reminded me that there *are* some handmade scarves that are perfect for Christmas gifts. They're all wide and long. I saw this red-and-gold glitter one that I was thinking I could wrap around me for Jeb to open on Christmas."

Ida Belle gave her a pained look.

"You have time," I said. "The next available flight wasn't until six this evening. But remember, you're going to be injured —that's why we're leaving early."

"I'll limp on my way back to the hotel. At least a chunk of the flying will be overnight. Sixteen hours is a long time to be in one seat, even first class. Okay, anyone else interested in shopping?"

We all shook our heads and Gertie grabbed her purse and headed out.

"At least we don't have to worry about what's in her handbag here," Ida Belle said. "I started to flinch when she pulled her purse on her shoulder and then remembered."

I watched as she exited the hotel. "Maybe one of us should go with her..."

Ida Belle frowned. "Yeah, that's a good idea. I'll do it. You and Harrison still need recovery time."

She jumped up and hurried off. I took care of the breakfast bill, and then we headed back to our rooms to start packing. To keep up appearances, we'd hauled a decent amount of luggage with us, but it was mostly still packed. Still, I figured by the time Ida Belle and Gertie got back, Harrison and I could have everything ready to go. We'd just toss Gertie's purchases in her suitcase and head for checkout.

I had just shoved the last of my toiletries into my suitcase when I heard yelling outside. Harrison stepped in my room, looking worried.

"Isn't that the direction of the market?" he asked.

"Crap!"

We both ran to the sliding door and hurried onto the balcony and spotted a camel running wild through the market —sending displays up in the air and people diving to avoid being trampled.

The camel had a passenger. Gertie!

CHAPTER FOUR

SINCE WE WERE IN A SECOND-FLOOR ROOM, I DIDN'T EVEN bother with running back inside for the stairs. I just vaulted over the railing and landed behind a well-placed bush. I heard a gasp behind me and glanced back to see a lady on the porch before I sprinted for the runaway camel. A man ran ahead of me, clutching a broken halter, explaining everything except the part where Gertie had ended up on a camel to begin with.

I jumped over two fallen tables of clothing and as I drew up beside the camel handler, I grabbed the halter and lead from his hand. I heard him yell but didn't care. I turned up the afterburners and cut off the charging beast in between aisles. I tossed the lead around his neck and dug my heels in, praying he'd respond to the lead and stop. Otherwise, he was just going to keep running with Gertie and potentially trample me.

But the rope on his neck sent him immediately back to calm. He dropped his neck and stopped so suddenly that Gertie flew off and over his head, landing in a crate of fish. Seabirds immediately began to circle overhead and dive in for the scattered buffet. As the fishmonger ran around, waving his arms in the air to try to stop the birds from flying off with his profit, I dashed over to help Gertie out of the fish crate, then hesitated when I got a good whiff of it.

"I've got it," she said as she pushed herself to a standing position.

Then she took a single step, slipped in the fishy water, and went sailing back into the crate again. Ida Belle and Harrison ran up beside me and we all stared, none of us wanting to compromise our morning showers. After all, she didn't appear to be injured.

She pulled herself out of the crate and this time, she elected to crawl until she reached dry ground. We still kept our distance as she pulled herself upright with a pole and then looked over at us with a huge grin.

"What a ride!" she said. "Those camels can really go."

The camel handler approached, leading the now docile animal. "Much apologies," he said, pulling money from his pocket.

"You paid to ride a camel?" I asked. "Good God."

I motioned to the fishmonger. "Give him the money for the fish."

The camel handler smiled and approached the fishmonger with the money, pointing back at me, and he gave me a thankful nod.

"Now let's get the hell out of here before someone posts a video of me catching that camel," I said. "It definitely wasn't a normal tourist move."

"You can always tell them you're from Texas," Harrison joked.

"At least I don't have to fake an injury," Gertie said, looking far too pleased with herself. "My ankle is already starting to swell."

"I swear, I stopped to look at a wallet for just a matter of seconds and she was gone," Ida Belle said. "You intended to do this the whole time, didn't you?"

Gertie grinned. "It was my last chance. Although I really did want some scarves."

"You can pay double at the airport," Ida Belle said. "Serves you right."

———

IT WAS A TIRED AND STIFF BUT HAPPY CREW THAT STEPPED off the plane in Houston, ready to hit the bathroom and a restaurant while waiting on our connecting flight to NOLA. But apparently, the military had other plans. As soon as we exited the gate, airport security picked us out and invited us to join them for a private chat. I couldn't imagine what we'd done to upset the airline, but when they motioned us into a room and Colonel Kitts was standing there, I knew.

"Can we make this quick?" I asked. "I've got a lady with an injured ankle here, and I'm really tired. We don't want to miss our connecting flight."

Colonel Kitts swelled up his chest. "I could have you court-martialed."

"A civilian on vacation? Good luck with that."

"You're no civilian. You're retired CIA."

"I'm *resigned* CIA. You should learn the difference, because it means there's no insurance or pension you can threaten me with."

"I know all about you, Agent Redding, *and* your father. Did he help with this?"

"My father is dead."

"You claimed he was dead before."

I pushed beyond frustration and straight into mad as hell.

"And do you know why I claimed he was dead? Because the CIA and the military confirmed it—to a teenager—and then I never heard from him again. So even if he is still alive, what in the world leads you to believe that he'd be in contact with me? He abandoned me as a child, with government cover-up, and thought nothing of it, despite being the only parent I had left. Why on earth would he waste a second of worry on me as an adult?"

Clearly Kitts didn't like logic, because his jaw clenched. "I won't have a CIA agent interfering with military actions."

"*Civilian* and don't you mean 'inaction'? Because you had zero plans to rescue Carter. But go ahead and pursue a case against me. I'm sure the public would love to know how you bungled *your* mission and risked the lives of soldiers, one of whom isn't even active duty and wasn't supposed to be on the ground."

I heard the door behind me open, and Morrow's voice sounded off.

"She's 100 percent correct. Face it, Kitts, the real problem here is that someone else did your job and did it better than you could have. The only words that should be coming out of your mouth are *thank you*. So if you can't manage those, then I suggest you take your leave before my department launches its own investigation into why your mission failed so miserably and took unnecessary risks with the lives of your men."

"If it weren't for me," I said, "you'd be explaining to Carter's mother why her son was dead. As it is, she's going to get him back battered and tortured. And that's all on you."

Kitts's face turned red as he stepped toward me, and I knew any pretense at maintaining military manners was officially over.

"Do you know who I am?" he asked. "I can make your life a living hell."

"You mean like the hell those men went through? Those

men you were too incompetent to rescue yourself, so the Green Berets had to bail you out?"

I took a second to breathe, just getting started. Kitts had threatened the wrong civilian.

I stepped right up to his face and continued twisting the screws. "I assume since you're here harassing me that you haven't bothered to see or talk to Carter. If we'd been even an hour later, no one would have ever talked to him again. So you can take your rank and your threats and stuff them all the way up your rigid, incompetent ass."

Ida Belle and Harrison gasped. Morrow's jaw dropped. Gertie laughed.

Then Harrison joined Gertie, then Ida Belle, and finally Morrow cracked a smile. Colonel Kitts whirled around and stomped toward the door. He'd lost the battle, but I had no doubt he intended to continue the war.

"Oh, and Colonel," I said, "it's really not a good idea to challenge people who can kill you from three thousand meters. That's a viable threat, by the way, unlike all your blustering."

He slammed the door behind him, and Morrow sank into one of the chairs at the table, shaking his head. "I hate to say it, but I enjoyed that," he said. "He's the most impossible, pompous man I've ever dealt with on the military front, and given my thirty-plus years with the CIA, that's saying a lot. He *can* make trouble for you, though."

"I wish him luck," I said. "I wasn't making an idle threat about airing his dirty laundry. It's obvious that mission should have never happened. The fact that Carter was asked to step in at the last minute was a big enough indication that things weren't right."

"He's an old fool," Morrow said. "Probably wanting one more feather in his cap before he retires. But he might have finally overplayed his hand. A foul-up this big is going to bring an investigation down on him, but that investigation is likely to fall out on you."

I shrugged. "No one can prove we were there. The only people who left the US are Ida Belle and Gertie."

"On paper," Morrow said, "but this is an airport. There are cameras everywhere."

"So Harrison and I traveled under false documents. So what? It's dangerous for us to be in that realm using our real identities, and Ida Belle and Gertie had a bucket-list requirement to meet. If anyone wants to pursue that in court, I'll be happy to go there with them...and with the truth."

"If they launch an investigation, no one is going to believe that vacation story."

I smiled. "See, this whole civilian-detective thing has been legally enlightening. It's not about what they believe. It's about what they can prove. And even if everyone in Khasab had their phone camera on and pointed at me, they can't prove I got any farther in the Sea of Oman than a fishing boat."

I frowned, the implication of Morrow being here just hitting me. "Why are you here, anyway? Your name has been left clear of everything. Now Kitts will be aiming at you too."

"That's my word against his, and I had another reason for coming. A *documented* reason." He blew out a breath. "There's been some other chatter, and I need to get in front of it. I don't want to ask but I have no choice. It's going to come up, and I'd rather you hear it from me."

"What is it?" I asked, already knowing what was coming.

"Is your father still alive?" Morrow asked.

"No idea."

I wasn't lying. I only knew that he was alive when we'd fled the compound. I had no assurance that was still the case.

"This chatter—where is it coming from?" I asked. "Because Colonel Incompetent asked me the same thing."

"You know I can't say, but if I find out anything I'll let you know."

I shook my head. "If my father is alive and wanted me to know it, he'd just be in my kitchen one morning when I went down to make coffee and disappear again before I could even pour him a cup. But just like I told Kitts, considering he never made me aware of his existence when I was a child and could have actually used a father, I can't see any reason for him to do so now."

Morrow gave me a pained look. "He thought he was a better parent for leaving you with me."

"Keep telling yourself that. It might even be partially true, but we both know that the only true love Dwight Redding ever had was the job."

Morrow looked down at the floor and nodded. When he looked back up, he sighed. "Go catch your connecting flight. I know there are some people back home that probably haven't slept a wink, waiting on you to get home."

The reunion at baggage claim in NOLA was a lot different from our greeting at the gate in Houston. Walter, Emmaline, Cassidy, Ally, and Ronald were all there, rushing to hug us all. Everyone but Walter was crying, but I did see his eyes mist when he clutched Ida Belle. Emmaline held on to me for a long time, whispering in my ear. Carter had been allowed to call her and he was being debriefed. He had insisted that he be sent home immediately after and held for no longer than absolutely necessary. He hoped to be back in Sinful within forty-eight hours.

She didn't mention his physical condition, and I figured he hadn't told her because he didn't want her to be upset or worry. She'd do enough of that when she set eyes on him because those bruises were going to be even uglier by the time he arrived home. And my guess was he'd have an arm in a sling and be moving very deliberately with those damaged ribs.

We wrapped up the hugging and crying by the time the bags arrived and then hurried outside and into the vehicles, beyond ready to get to our own homes and showers. As we got close to town, I saw a boat display on the side of the highway, complete with a bass boat perched on top of a tall pole, advertising a sale at Sinful Marine.

"That's new," I said.

Walter nodded. "Rumor is someone made a mistake on the order form and added an extra zero to the inventory request, so instead of getting one new bass boat in, they got ten. Inventory sitting costs money, so they need to move them. Apparently, there was a fight in the parking lot yesterday over the one with blue stripes. They only got one blue striped one and two men were itching to buy it."

"Who won?"

"Neither of 'em. A roughneck went in and bought the thing while they were carrying on outside. Word is he got it financed and had signed on the dotted line before those two wore themselves out."

I grinned. "Do you know how great it is to be back to normal?"

Walter snorted. "Do you realize what you just called 'normal'?"

"Yeah. Home."

CHAPTER FIVE

GIVEN ALL THE TRAVEL, CELEBRATION, GENERAL overstimulation, and what might have been the longest shower in the history of mankind, I slept like the dead. At some point during the night, Merlin tried to convey his dissatisfaction with my disappearance by tapping me on the forehead with his paw, but I just turned over and kept right on going. When I finally opened my eyes, the sun was streaming in, and I could tell it was closer to noon than sunrise. I yawned and stretched and threw the covers back, my body already feeling better now that I was back in my own bed.

Merlin groused as he climbed out from under them and I laughed.

"Sorry, buddy. I guess you're past ready for your breakfast." I headed downstairs, Merlin trotting ahead of me. "No pretending you're starving or lonely. I know better."

Ally had volunteered to stay at my house while I was gone. She'd claimed that the bakery would keep her busy during the day, but she needed something to concentrate on at night or she'd lose her mind. I didn't figure feeding Merlin and letting him in and out of my kitchen was going to cut a big chunk out of worrying time, but I also knew she needed to feel she was contributing. And since the spoiled cat got up to mischief when he was unhappy, it worked out well for everyone.

Ronald had volunteered to tend to my landscaping. I didn't have the heart to tell him that my 'tending' amounted to paying someone to plant and fertilize, and making sure the sprinkler system was on. I knew Emmaline and Walter would keep each other in check, as much as they could, and Tiny was perfectly fine being spoiled at Emmaline's house.

Andy Blanchet, a retired sheriff who was filling in for Carter while he was away, was running herd over Sinful. I'd recently worked a case with him and had gotten to know him well during the investigation. I knew the town was in good hands, even with all of us out of pocket.

Big and Little Hebert were the only other people who had any idea what we'd been up to, and since they'd been in it up to their necks—at least financially—I knew they were probably better apprised of everything that had happened than anyone else. But as soon as I'd finished a pot of coffee and at least two of those muffins that Ally had left on my kitchen counter, I would head over to thank them again in person. We couldn't have been successful without their support. Their money and Mannie's invaluable connections had given Harrison and me the opportunity we needed, and I would never forget it.

I fed Merlin while I waited for the coffee to brew and was just pouring my first cup when I heard someone knocking on my back door and realized I hadn't unlocked it yet. It had to be Ronald. Ida Belle, Gertie, and Ally had a key to the front, and Mannie just appeared in my kitchen like Houdini. I grabbed my cup and headed over to the door to let him inside.

He grabbed me in a hug, as though he hadn't been at the airport the day before, and I had to work a bit to keep coffee from sloshing on my hand.

"I just had to come over and see you again in person," he said. "I went to sleep last night so relieved and happy, and then I had this ridiculous and awful dream that I'd imagined your return. Of course, I knew that wasn't true, but I couldn't stop dwelling on it. So here I am, and I will give you my new Gucci handbag if I can have some of your dreadful coffee."

I raised one eyebrow. "You're letting handbags go at a serious discount these days. And my coffee isn't dreadful."

He rolled his eyes. "It comes out of a can, for goodness' sake. It's already ground. It's like bleaching your hair with drugstore peroxide. If you have a few bucks to your name, you just don't do it."

We sat at the kitchen table, and I put one of the muffins on a plate for him.

"Is this keto?" he asked. "I'm trying a new thing. My spandex is starting to give me the side-eye."

"Ally made them, so I'm going with no."

"Well, why didn't you say so? Carbs and sugar don't count when Ally did the baking."

"As long as your spandex agrees."

He took a huge bite of the muffin and sighed. "I mean, it *is* stretchy. I guess the ladies haven't made it over yet."

I shook my head and looked at my phone for the first time that morning. "Wow, 10:00 a.m. No wonder Merlin was playing badminton with my forehead. I haven't slept that late since... Well, I can't remember."

"You needed it, honey. The four of you looked positively beat, but you were the worst."

"Thanks."

"I'm not trying to insult you. But it was clear that the mental strain had worn on you as much as the physical. I know you can't give details, and I think this might be the one time in my life I don't want them, but just know that if there's anything I can do to help all of you get back to normal, I'm available. Mani-pedi appointments, massage, a good blowout, because that desert is hell on hair, and that correction rinse I gave you didn't work completely. I can still see some of that dye on your roots—"

I held up one hand before he made it to shopping for a new wardrobe or something worse, like bikini waxing. "I appreciate it, but after a mission, I tend to avoid the general public. It's how I decompress."

He frowned. "This is one of those introvert/extrovert things, right? I've been reading on them so I won't be so judgmental and worn out by people who aren't like me."

He waved a hand in dismissal. "Who am I kidding. I'll stop judging when I'm cold in the grave. Maybe. I wonder if ghosts judge."

"Do you plan on becoming a ghost? I thought the angel wardrobe would be of more interest, given the wings and all."

"White really isn't my color. I wonder if you can dye those wings. Or maybe a couple well-placed sequins."

"You should talk to Gertie. I'm sure she already has some ideas."

"That woman is full of ideas about fashion—most of them awful—but I have to give her credit for knowing what she likes and rushing forward with it despite popular opinion."

I grinned. Given that Ronald was currently decked out in a hot pink tuxedo with glittery gold vest and furry white boots, I could see where he would feel that way.

"Everyone decent?" Gertie called out from the front door.

"Everyone was before you got here," I yelled back.

"Very funny," Gertie grumbled as she shuffled into the kitchen.

She wore a red sequined robe, matching flip-flops, and of all things, was using a red sequined cane to limp into the room.

The bags under her eyes had turned into steamer trunks, and her hair was flat on her head, indicating she'd showered then gone to bed without rolling it. Ronald took one look at her and yelped. Then he jumped up, rambling about wigs and eye masks, and ran out the back door.

"What the heck is he all in a tizz for?" Gertie asked as she sank into a chair. "Like I'm the one who looks weird. Who wears a tux for coffee at their neighbor's house?"

"Someone who didn't injure themselves on a runaway camel?" Ida Belle suggested. "Or maybe a profound but fashionably misplaced respect for Fortune and her coffee."

"Oh, he hates my coffee," I said. "So how are you two feeling?"

Ida Belle, who looked as she had every day since I'd known her, nodded. "Feeling great. Had a good night's sleep. This morning, I got my laundry done, washed the SUV, and cleaned out my deep freezer."

"I got out of bed," Gertie said.

"Don't worry," I said. "That's pretty much all I've managed this morning aside from feeding the cat, and that was self-defense. Heck, I didn't get up until a half hour ago."

Ida Belle and Gertie glanced at each other with that unspoken communication thing they had, then gave me concerned looks.

"What?" I asked. "We're home. I'm fine. Harrison and Mannie are fine. Carter is a little banged up, but he's safe and will be home soon. Everything is grand."

"We've just been worried about how much strain all of this put on you," Gertie said.

"Guys, I did this exact thing for years, and a lot of missions were way riskier than this one."

"But none of them were personal." Ida Belle said the one thing I'd been thinking the whole time but never voiced.

"It's okay to be off after what you went through," she continued. "The fact is you had to clamp down your feelings in order to make this happen. But now that it's over, if you didn't experience a rush of being overwhelmed, I'd be shocked."

She was absolutely right. The moment the adrenaline had started to exit my system, all the emotions I'd choked back had come rushing in like a tidal wave. But that wasn't the sort of thing I liked to talk about. It wasn't even the sort of thing I liked to dwell on myself.

"I'll be fine," I said. "I slept really well and I'm barely sore anymore. That lingering bit of worry I have will be gone completely as soon as Carter is back in Sinful—where he's agreed to stay. No more hero crap for either of us."

"You're both heroes here," Gertie pointed out. "And you both do your share of putting yourself on the line."

"No one is perfect. But the worst I've ever felt here is frustrated when I couldn't figure things out. I have never felt like I was in over my head. Compared to what I used to do, Sinful is wading in the shallows."

"That's where the alligators wait to snag a meal," Ida Belle said.

I laughed. "Okay, so there's been some animal encounters that were iffy, but Gertie's purse has been a bigger threat than the bad guys I've gone toe to toe with."

Ida Belle nodded. "Valid."

"What do I have to do to make you guys stop worrying about what I'm carrying?" Gertie asked.

"Carry a wallet," I said.

"In your hand," Ida Belle added. "No pockets. Pockets are problematic."

"For that matter, so is her bra," I pointed out.

"If I go without a bra, I'd knock myself out running," Gertie said. "And I always end up running. Besides, without a bra, I can stuff two sticks of dynamite under my boobs and hold them in place, even jumping up and down. Ask me how I know."

"I will *not*."

I grinned. Ida Belle's dismay was hilarious. Also understandable.

"Anyway," Ida Belle said, "I dragged this one over here to see what was on the agenda for today. I know we have to decompress, but I'm having trouble just sitting around."

"The only time you sat after waking up was on the john," Gertie said.

"Not true," Ida Belle said. "I drove over here and I'm sitting now."

"Blanchet is probably going to be here a while longer since Carter's injured, right?" Gertie asked. "If so, then we need to find him another place to stay."

Blanchet had been staying in Carter's house, but Gertie was right. Carter wouldn't want company after what he'd been through.

"It's all taken care of," Ida Belle said. "Since Walter spends most of his time at my house, he got Blanchet moved to his."

Gertie looked at me. "Well?"

"I hate to disappoint you with my lack of chores," I said, "but the only thing on my agenda today is visiting the Heberts."

Gertie sighed. "I'm going to have to shower again and do my hair...maybe put on real clothes even."

Ronald burst in the back door, waving a wig in one hand and a hat in the other, and Gertie perked up.

"That hat matches my robe," she said.

Ida Belle shook her head. "Absolutely not."

I grinned. It was good to be home.

———

I WAS HAPPY TO SEE MANNIE AT THE WAREHOUSE WHERE BIG and Little resided. Given the way he seemed to materialize out of thin air, I was almost expecting him to be at the airport to pick us up, looking as though he'd never left the country. He gave us a huge grin when he opened the door.

"The Heberts are so excited that you're visiting them today," he said as we headed upstairs. "I told them you might need decompression time, but I guess I should have known better."

"I owe them a huge debt, and a display of gratitude that big shouldn't wait any longer than it has to," I said.

He nodded. "Your sense of honor and respect is one of the many reasons they're happy to help. In the years I've worked for them, I've never heard them refer to anyone as a friend until you."

I stopped walking and stared. "Seriously?"

"They're very cautious with their time and money, but even more so with their personal lives. You've infiltrated their everyday quicker and more effectively than Special Forces."

I laughed. "Well, yeah, but I was CIA."

He grinned again and we continued down the hall, but instead of stopping at Big's office as we always did, Mannie walked past that door and headed farther toward the west end of the building. I glanced over at Ida Belle and Gertie, who looked as confused as I was, but there was never any telling what the Heberts had been up to.

"Did Big change his office?" I asked.

"No," Mannie said.

Gertie let out an audible sigh at his completely unhelpful response, and he smiled at her obvious frustration. Then we reached a set of double doors at the end of the hall and

Mannie motioned to me to open them. Realizing that something was definitely up, I grabbed the door handle and shoved the doors open, not even hazarding a guess as to what was on the other side.

And then I almost fell out in the hall when I saw Carter standing there.

I heard Gertie gasp as I launched myself at Carter, making sure I reeled myself in before actually tackling him. Even though he was standing with a huge smile on his face, I knew he was injured. I felt him involuntarily flinch when he pulled me in close to him, and I buried my face in his neck, taking a moment to lose myself in that scent that was undeniably him.

When we finally released each other, I glanced around the room and saw big grins on everyone's faces, some tears from Gertie, and even Little was sniffling. I'd always suspected he was a softy under those custom-made suits and impeccable manners.

"How?" I asked.

Carter nodded his head toward Big. "Ask your friend. I just told the Marines I was done talking and said 'heck yes' to the offer of a ride home."

Big gave us both a huge smile. "Private jets make everything so much easier."

"You own a jet?" I asked.

"No. I don't have the need as I'm not a traveler, but I have a friend."

"Must be some friend," I said.

He laughed. "The best kind. Ridiculously wealthy and he owes me."

I stepped over and gave him a kiss on the cheek, which I could tell delighted him. "I owe you too. For everything. I can't even begin to tell you how much I appreciate everything you did. Carter wouldn't be here if it wasn't for you, Little, and Mannie."

He clutched my hands and nodded. "Anything for you. Always."

I felt my eyes mist up and I released Big's hand and gave Little a cheek kiss as well. He seemed a bit surprised but also pleased. Mannie, I just gave a big hug, and he laughed.

When I stepped back, he grinned. "You are the most impressive operative I have ever worked with, and that's saying a lot. I knew you had to be special—your reputation preceded you and I've seen you in action here—but what you managed over there, you and Harrison, was incredible. I wish I could have been on the ground to see it."

I flushed at the compliment. "It was a little iffy there at the end."

"Until your father appeared," Big said. "Mannie filled us in. Very interesting, but I didn't find myself surprised that he was still alive and moving among the criminal element overseas. I can see where you got your focus and dedication. Fortunately for all of us, you've directed yours to benefit Sinful and its residents."

Carter wrapped his arms around me from behind and kissed the side of my face. "You're definitely benefiting me. You literally saved my life. All of you. Although I have to admit that I was surprised Gertie made it a whole trip without being arrested."

"It wasn't from lack of trying," Ida Belle said.

Gertie waved a hand in dismissal. "That was a fluke. It's not my fault that rented camel decided to go on a bender."

Carter smiled and shook his head. "Words you never want to hear in the same sentence—'rented camel' and 'bender.' You'll have to tell me all about it later—after I've seen my mother and Walter and gotten at least twenty-four hours of sleep."

Big perked up. "There's actually video."

I grinned. Of course there was.

————

Happy reunions occupied the entire afternoon, until Carter started yawning and clutching his shoulder. I knew pain and fatigue were setting in hard and fast. I signaled to Ida Belle, who rounded up everyone and got Carter's house cleared, then I set him up with a painkiller, water, closed blinds, and fluffed pillows, and sent him to bed. Tiny was still at Emmaline's and I'd turned off the ringer on his phone, so he could sleep as long as he needed to with zero worries. He was snoring before I left his bedroom.

When I stepped outside, I saw Emmaline waiting next to my Jeep. She had that worried look that only mothers wear. It wasn't as severe as the one she'd had before Carter was safely home, but it still went beyond her normal fare.

"How badly is he injured?" she asked as I approached. "I tried to get it out of him, but he just deflects. I know they... they tortured him. That's what they always do, right?"

I nodded. "We haven't had a chance to talk about what happened in detail, and to be honest, I'm not sure he ever will. But I've seen his injuries and how they affect movement often enough to guess what's going on. I think he's got some bruised ribs at minimum, more likely a few are broken, and a dislocated shoulder. His face looks rough, mostly because his nose is broken, and faces tend to do a full-on color display when damaged."

Emmaline's hand flew over her mouth. "Oh my God. My poor baby."

I reached for her hand and squeezed it. "But you can be certain that he had a full medical workup by military doctors, and I'll get him to check in with Cassidy for another review as soon as he's had a round of sleep."

Emmaline's shoulders slumped with relief. "You will? Of course you will. I should have known you'd be on it."

She wrapped her arms around me, clutching me tightly. "I can't tell you how much I love and appreciate you, Fortune. You're everything I ever wanted for my son and a million times more."

She released me and swiped at the tears on her cheek with one hand. "You're like a daughter to me. You know that, right? I always wanted more kids, but it wasn't meant to be. If I could have had a daughter, I would have wanted her to be just like you."

For what seemed like the fiftieth time that day, I felt my eyes mist. "And I'm grateful for you. I lost my mother entirely too young. I love knowing that I have you now."

She laughed. "I think you have a lot of mothers these days."

"Oh no. Ida Belle and Gertie are those crazy old aunts. Neither really suits for the motherly type, but they're loyal to a fault."

She nodded. "I think more people could do with some crazy old aunts in their lives. I'm going to head home and give Tiny a treat and have another long, relieved cry. I'm leaving Carter to you. The torch passed."

I felt my heart swell at her words and watched until her car turned the corner before finally climbing into my Jeep and heading for home. I had a long evening of doing nothing stretching in front of me, and while normal people would be happy about that, I was already feeling itchy. Relaxing was something I liked to schedule so that I knew it was coming. I had never been good at relaxing on the fly.

Fortunately, I had friends who knew me well. Ida Belle, Gertie, and Ronald were already in my hot tub and had a glass ready to pour me champagne. We stayed there until finally, it was past dinnertime and we all needed to get something to eat to offset the alcohol.

"We're going to have to hydrate and moisturize for the next hundred years to combat this," Ronald declared before he headed off.

Ida Belle and Gertie had left minutes before, so I closed up the tub and went inside to throw some more water on my body, this time in the form of a shower. By the time I'd dressed, grabbed a sandwich and a bottle of water from the fridge, and sunk into my recliner, I was so relaxed that I didn't even want to lift my arm to eat.

When I finished the sandwich, I put on an old movie, reclined my chair back and waited for the drift that I knew was coming. The sound of my front door opening sent me right into fully awake. I vaulted from the chair, grabbed my pistol from the side table, and landed with it pointed center mass at the door.

Carter stepped inside with his hands up and wearing a huge grin.

"It never gets old," he said. "You should oil those hinges."

"Then I wouldn't be prepared to kill intruders. And why aren't you sleeping?"

He gathered me in his arms. "I missed you too much to sleep. Besides, when I do get around to sleeping some more, I was hoping it wouldn't be alone."

"Fine by me. Are you hungry?"

He gave me a sexy grin. "Yes, but not for food."

"You're injured."

"No man is ever that injured."

CHAPTER SIX

I was in that state of semiconsciousness where you have bizarre dreams and feel as if you just did an hour of military PT when my cell phone rang, sending me straight from bizarre into reality. Well, it was Sinful, so more likely from bizarre right back into bizarre.

I glanced at the display and frowned when I saw Blanchet's name. If he was calling me at 7:00 a.m. the day after I arrived home, then there was trouble that he needed help with. Sinful sort of trouble. I'd talked to him the day before and he'd sounded a little harried, but I hadn't seen him yet. I assumed he was busy with the usual Sinful nonsense that people around here got up to.

I hopped out of bed as I answered and headed for the kitchen to prevent waking up Carter and to get coffee started.

"What's up, Andy?"

"I've got an odd situation."

"You're in Sinful. You're going to have to be more specific."

He chuckled. "I didn't wake you up, did I?"

"I was already well on my way. I just headed for the kitchen so I wouldn't wake Carter up talking."

"Too late." His voice sounded behind me.

"Crap," Blanchet said. "I was trying to avoid bothering him with anything the instant he got back."

"Might as well put him on speaker," Carter said and slid into a chair, giving the empty coffeepot a wistful glance.

"Working on it," I said as I set the coffee to brew. Then I put the phone on the table. "Blanchet, you're on speaker. Go ahead and explain your odd situation."

"Well, it starts with your friend Celia."

Carter shook his head. "So you're leading with the odd part."

"Actually, no. She does take the award for overly dramatic pain in my—you know—but she's not the worst thing. However, the day's still young. Nora's cat might discover switchblades or dynamite."

Carter grimaced.

"So what's up Celia's butt this morning?" I asked. "Besides her big panties."

"Did you happen to notice that bass boat display on the highway?"

"Hard to miss a bass boat perched thirty feet up in the air."

"Well, apparently, the dealership decided to up their advertising game and put a dummy fishing in the boat."

"Again, this is Sinful. Specifics, please. Which dummy is sitting in the boat?"

Carter snorted and went to pour the coffee.

"Good God, none of them that I'm aware of. I meant a mannequin."

"Okay," I said. "Not seeing the problem yet."

"They went for a play on Lent—you know, eating fish and all? Even put up a sign implying that buying a new boat would get them right with God and solve their Friday night dinner problems."

"Given all the devout Catholics around here—during Lent, anyway—it sounds like smart advertising. What's Celia's beef? Did they dress the mannequin like her?"

"No. A nun. Holding a beer."

Carter spit out his coffee.

I had to laugh. The thought of a beer-drinking nun pimping boats as a Lent-approved purchase had a high level of hilarity and more than a little marketing genius. But now I understood why Celia had sucked her panties up to her vocal cords.

"What does she expect you to do about it?" I asked.

"She said that it's blasphemy and that some law from around the time Moses was leading his people out of Egypt forbids anyone from profiting from blasphemy during Lent. Is that true?"

"Probably. But she'd have to prove they're making a profit on the sales, and my understanding is they'll be lucky to break even."

"A loophole! I can work with that. I'll sic her on the boat shop. By the time she gets a subpoena for their financials, Christ will have returned. Thanks."

Carter tossed the dishrag he'd been using to mop up coffee into the sink and sat down next to me. "Sounds like you and Blanchet got along. How did he do?"

"Fantastic. We busted a major human trafficking and drug ring that had been living deep in the bayous and rescued the woman he loved, who disappeared twenty years ago. Gertie got to parachute and dump pink glitter on the bad guys, Ida Belle got to be getaway airboat driver, and I got to shoot a corrupt cop and ensure the ADA will never get that promotion he's been bucking for."

"You know, anyone but me would think they were being punked."

"That was just the highlights."

"You'll have to fill me in on all of it later." He leaned back in his chair, started to lift both arms over his head, then winced and lowered them again. "It's good to be home. Celia doesn't seem nearly as problematic as she did before I left."

"That's because she's still Blanchet's problem. Until your doctor releases you, anyway. And shouldn't you have that arm in a sling? I know it's bothering you."

"The sling bothers me more, and nothing is going to stop me from getting some pictures of that display before the boat store gets pressured into taking it down. You going?"

"Heck yeah."

By the time we got to the highway where the boat display was, a small crowd had already gathered, representing two factions—the people there for pictures and a laugh, and the Catholics, who were there to be outraged with Celia and ruin the fun. I had to admit, the nun fishing was definitely an attention-getter, although she was a little slumped at the moment.

"Wind must have gotten it," I said as we climbed out of Carter's truck. "Someone needs to go up there and straighten it back up. Better pictures that way."

The slumped figure wore a full habit, but the veil had fallen forward, covering the face. One arm was propped on the side of the boat, and a hand, barely protruding from the long black garment, clutched a beer can.

"You think she's going commando?" a man yelled.

"Gonna need a baptism to clean the fish smell out of those robes," a woman said.

"That little sprinkle of holy water won't cut it," a man replied. "Better check with the Baptists and see if we can borrow that wading pool of theirs."

Everyone started howling with laughter and Celia spotted

us and stomped over. "I demand that you do something about this blasphemy!"

Carter shook his head. "No can do. My doctors haven't released me. And I know you, of all people, wouldn't want me to break the law by working without a medical release. That might be a problem for the city's liability insurance."

Celia sputtered a bit, clearly perplexed by the dilemma Carter had presented. As she was trying to formulate a thought, Wade Willis, the owner of the boat store, hurried up.

"I swear, we had nothing to do with this," he said to Carter. "The person, I mean. And the sign."

Celia glared at him. "Who else would it have been? That sign is clearly mocking Lent, and the nun is beyond the pale. I'm surprised God didn't send lightning right through your store."

Wade cast a nervous glance up at the boat. "I don't know who did it, but I promise you, it wasn't anyone I employ. We would never—well, to be honest, we might have if we'd thought of it, but we didn't."

I frowned. Wade looked irritated and confused, which meant he wasn't lying, and that made the entire thing more interesting. Granted, his memory had been on the decline lately, but surely he wouldn't forget something of this magnitude. Forgetting to place an order was one thing and something he did on the regular. Forgetting you'd put a nun in a boat to take advantage of Lent sales was a huge leap. But it also sent me down another train of thought—the hit-by-a-train kind. I stepped closer to the display and pulled out my phone and took a picture, then I expanded it to get a closer look at the hand.

"Crap," I said to Carter. "That's not a mannequin. It's a person. And I'm pretty sure he's dead."

———

OF COURSE, I TEXTED IDA BELLE AND GERTIE AS SOON AS I made my deadly declaration to Carter. He called Blanchet and then we went to work on the problem of getting into the boat for a closer look at the nun. Carter located a road crew nearby and they agreed to lend a front-end loader to aid in the pursuit. The loader bucket and an extension ladder from a contractor who'd stopped to see what the fuss was about would be enough to get me into the boat. Between his shoulder and the ribs, Carter needed to stay grounded.

Blanchet, Ida Belle, and Gertie arrived as the contractor and loader operator were coordinating my access, and I was surprised to see Gertie's parrot, Francis, perched on her shoulder. As they approached, I spotted a pink sequined halter around the bird with a leash that connected to a matching bracelet on Gertie's wrist. The pink clashed with Gertie's orange track suit and Francis's feathers, but at least Ronald wasn't here to see the fashion faux paus. Otherwise, we might have two dead bodies.

"The halter is stuck," Gertie explained before I could ask. "I got one with a childproof clasp, and now I can't get it off."

Ida Belle stared at her, one eyebrow raised, and I tried my best not to smile.

"Well, this is an interesting way to start the morning," Ida Belle said, looking up at the boat and nun. "But it's still not the oddest thing I've seen before 8:00 a.m."

"You picked up Gertie before 8:00 a.m.," Carter pointed out.

Gertie lifted her hand, probably to give him the bird, but it set off the actual bird on her shoulder. Francis flapped at the sudden movement and the previously stuck halter slid right off him. He launched upward, a bit surprised at his sudden freedom, then he spotted the nun in the boat and took off for it. Given that Francis had spent years living with nuns, that wasn't surprising, at least not to those of us who knew, but the rest of the crowd sucked in a collective breath so hard, I'm surprised they didn't create a sinkhole.

Francis perched right on the nun's head and said, "The power of Christ compels me."

One of the women in the crowd passed out and Ida Belle sighed. "You've been watching horror movies with that bird, haven't you?"

"Blasphemy!" Celia yelled, shaking her hand at the boat. "You're all going to hell for this, including that bird."

"I'll race you," Gertie said.

"She'll only run if banana pudding is involved," I pointed out.

The contractor cast a nervous glance up at Francis and motioned to me that the makeshift ladder situation was ready to go. I headed up the ladder and carefully stepped into the boat. Francis hopped from the nun's head to the bench and shifted from his exorcism performance to *The Godfather*.

"He sleeps with the fishes," Francis said.

I checked the pulse of the obviously human hand and discovered the bird had called it correctly. I looked down, shaking my head.

Blanchet cursed.

Celia put her hands on her hips and glared at Wade. "I *told* you God would not be mocked. This blood is on your hands."

"Blood is a big expense," Francis said. "I'm a businessman."

Wade's eyes widened and he looked over at Blanchet, clearly panicked. "I swear, I don't know anything about that nun, and I definitely don't know anything about a dead guy. Between my bad knees and back, I can barely lift fifty pounds of rope anymore. How the heck would I even get a man that size up there?"

It was a good question. It could have been done easily enough with a crane—which I'm sure was how the boat was erected—but cranes weren't exactly sitting around every corner, and it would have taken a skilled operator to make it happen without dislodging the boat. It also would have taken some time to achieve, and someone would have seen it happening. Even in the middle of the night, there was still occasional traffic on the highway, mostly from the oil crew personnel, who didn't keep regular hours.

Granted, it was always possible someone *had* seen something, and we just didn't know about it. Which meant Blanchet's second job would be tracking down a witness. His first would be identifying the nun and figuring out cause of death.

I decided I could probably help with the identifying part, so I moved to wrap up two problems at once. One with a literal wrap. I popped the veil off the dead man and dropped it over Francis, then tied it at the bottom. He flapped around for a couple seconds while I snapped a shot of the man's face, then he went still. I texted the picture to Carter, Ida Belle, and Gertie, then I stared at the man, frowning. He looked familiar, but I didn't think we'd ever officially met.

"Gage Babin."

All three of them spoke at once.

A hush swept through the crowd, and the men wearing hats took them off. The Catholics all made the sign of the cross. The Baptists and the unhatted atheists just shuffled uncomfortably since they didn't have a religious or polite society rule to comply with.

Except Celia. She uttered one word. *Heathen*.

Now that I had his name, I remembered where I'd seen

him—the Swamp Bar. He was there at a table of men playing cards, laughing entirely too loud and looking entirely too long at the servers' butts. Whiskey had told him to take it down a notch or he was going to have him tossed in the bayou and let the gators sort him out.

Since I'd ascertained that the man was beyond medical aid, I figured I best get out of the boat before I contaminated what might turn out to be a crime scene. In Sinful, it was always best to assume homicide rather than natural causes. And even though I knew he had plenty of air, Francis was stirring again, and I was certain he wanted out of that veil.

I climbed back down the ladder into the bucket, one hand clutching the veiled bird. The contractor grabbed the ladder as the loader operator lowered us back down. I thanked them both, then stepped out of the bucket. They both made minimal eye contact and hurried to be on their way. The dead guy had kinda taken the fun out of it.

Celia gave Blanchet a triumphant look and drew herself up straight. "I guess you'll be doing something about it now, won't you?"

"You realize all that judgment is directed at a dead man," Gertie said. "Maybe those ashes need reapplying. Or you need a biblical refresher. Despite what you might believe, you're not God."

"The only thing that scares me is Keyser Soze." Francis's voice sounded from inside the veil.

Celia's face turned red, and I could see her straining to come up with a viable argument, but apparently, she no longer had one. She glared at all of us, whirled around, and stomped back to her car. Everyone else was close behind. Corpses tended to clear a room. Or the side of the road as the case was here.

Gertie took the veil from me and headed for the SUV. "Let's get that halter back on you and let you perch on a seat."

"If that bird craps in my vehicle, you owe me a detail," Ida Belle said.

Gertie flicked her hand. "I'll drape the veil over the seat."

"Good thing Celia left before that declaration," I said.

Blanchet pulled out his phone and walked off, probably trying to figure out how to get a forensics team up in the boat. Carter was on his phone, and I could hear Deputy Breaux's raised voice on the other end. Carter had already instructed him to break every speed limit known to man getting over to Gage's house to inform his wife of the situation. I hoped his wife wasn't one of those people who lived with her phone in her hand, because I was pretty sure a vehicle hadn't been made that could outrun Sinful gossip, even if Ida Belle was driving it.

As Carter continued to issue instructions, I headed over to a distraught Wade, who was sitting on the side of the highway, clutching his head in his hands.

"I don't understand," he said as I approached. "Gage was only forty. He couldn't have pickled his liver already. There's people walking around this town who've been drinking professionally for far longer than that."

"Might not have been the drinking," I said. "The bigger question is why is someone playing *Weekend at Bernie's* with him on your display?"

Wade shook his head. "Oh, he probably climbed up there himself."

"Why in the world would he do that?"

"Because Gage was a big prankster," Wade said. "Heck, he's pulled a fast one on most everyone in town at some point or another. Been that way since he was a kid."

I looked over at Ida Belle and Gertie, who'd just walked up. They both nodded.

"That would be an efficient solution to the 'how did a dead guy get in the boat?' question," I said. "Except there was no way for him to climb up, remember? And did any of you spot his vehicle nearby?"

"I'm sure he had help," Ida Belle said. "He had drinking buddies who wouldn't hesitate to help him get one over, especially if they thought it would stir people like Celia up."

"Remember that Easter when him and Hooch set all those rabbits loose in the Catholic church?" Gertie said. "And then they started having sexy time, right there in the sanctuary. Some of the older women passed out and Father Michael, who was already three sheets to the wind before service started, tried to give one of the rabbits Communion wine."

Ida Belle shook her head. "I hope the man upstairs doesn't take issue with his final prank. He was a Catholic, after all. That's not a good last look."

Wade sighed. "I'm never going to sell that boat."

"Why not?" I asked. "People die in boats around here all the time."

"Not dressed like a nun drinking a beer and mocking Lent," Wade said.

"Buck up," Ida Belle told him. "Only 40 percent of the population is Catholic. Way less than that is devout."

"And even the devout ones will go for a discount and just get Father Michael to bless the boat," Gertie said.

"Or exorcise it," Ida Belle said. "Whatever's needed."

Wade looked a little hesitant at the word *exorcise* but otherwise perked up. "I suppose you're right."

Carter and Blanchet stepped over and Carter made the introductions.

"Mr. Willis," Blanchet said, "I'm going to need some information on this display of yours."

Wade's eyes widened. "I'm not in any trouble, am I?"

"Not that I'm aware of," Blanchet said. "Just some basic questions for the file, but you don't have to hang around here. It's going to be a while before I can put together a crew that can handle this. If I could get your phone number, I'll be in touch."

Wade struggled to his feet and pulled a business card out of his wallet. "Am I going to get my boat back?"

Blanchet raised one eyebrow. "You want it back with the body or without?"

Wade paled a bit. "Good Lord! Without, of course."

"Then it's probably not going to be today."

Blanchet stuck the card in his jeans pocket and gave Wade a nod, stepping away, already making another call. Wade took Blanchet's turned back as an opportunity to get the heck out of there, which left only the five of us standing on the side of the road and the dead guy in the boat.

Blanchet finished his phone call and headed back over. "They're sending a forensics team, and the utility company is kindly providing us with a lift to retrieve the body. His death might not be suspicious but it's odd enough that I want everything documented. Was this guy a bad drinker?"

"I'd say professional," Gertie said. "He's not that old, but it's possible his kidneys packed up and left his body."

I frowned. "I don't think drinking killed him."

Carter groaned.

"What?" Blanchet asked, then his eyes widened. "Oh no. It's not that sixth sense of yours again, is it?"

"That and some other things. He'd been sick to his stomach."

"Which is common with drunks," Blanchet said.

"But he was still clutching the beer can. He should have dropped it when he died, but it's like his muscles were locked into place until rigor set in."

"Like a seizure?" Gertie asked.

Blanchet cursed. "You think he was poisoned."

"Maybe."

"How long do you think he's been up there like that?"

I shrugged. "Two or three hours maybe."

Blanchet looked at Carter. "You sure you can't get a doctor's release and take over?"

"And let you miss all the fun?" Carter shook his head. "I'll help any way I can, but it can't be on the record, and our friend Celia can't get even a whiff of it, or my run for sheriff will be over before it begins."

"That's okay," Gertie said. "We're always available for consultation and it won't interfere with our careers at all. Making Celia mad is just a bonus."

Carter clapped Blanchet on the back and smiled. "It's all yours."

CHAPTER SEVEN

I HAD JUST PUT A BATCH OF SWEET TEA IN THE refrigerator when I heard Ida Belle and Gertie call out from my front door. I yelled my kitchen location and a couple seconds later, they came in. Carter and I had left the highway right after I'd made my declaration about a suspicious death, not wanting the forensics team to catch sight of him at what might end up being a crime scene. Obviously, people had seen him there earlier and would say so, but then, a good percentage of Sinful had been there. And since there was nothing illegal about being an onlooker, and Carter had never acted in a professional capacity, he was in the clear as far as the job was concerned.

Ida Belle and Gertie had offered to stay behind and help move along any more lookie-loos until Deputy Breaux got there to help Blanchet secure the scene. They were also going to fill him in on all the important things he needed to know about Gage Babin, in case my sixth sense was still on point. Gertie didn't want Francis hanging out in the car for that long, so I'd taken the bird home for her, put him back in his cage—sans the sketchy halter—and given him a couple grapes to wind down his morning. He was singing '80s hair band songs when I left and bobbing his head to the rhythm.

After we'd gotten the bird situated, Carter had dropped me off at my house, intending to head home for a shower and hopefully, more sleep. He'd been restless the night before and although he'd attempted to be quiet, I knew he'd been up several times, pacing or standing in front of the window, staring outside. Between the pain of the injuries—which always seemed to multiply at night— and everything he was still processing, I knew from experience that he hadn't gotten enough rest. And even though it annoyed him to take it easy, that's exactly what he needed to do. Otherwise, everything would just take longer to heal, which was something else I knew from experience.

"I just put some tea in the fridge, but I can serve it up with some ice."

They both sank into chairs, looking a little tired themselves. Gertie shook her head. "It's still early. I wouldn't mind a round of coffee."

"Agreed," Ida Belle said.

I glanced at my watch as I put the coffee on, somewhat surprised to see it was only 9:00 a.m. Carter and I had rushed out the door right after the phone call and I'd never actually poured myself a cup, which meant I'd officially gone the better part of the morning without it. Well, that was something I was prepared to fix.

I procured a plate of cookies—courtesy of Ally—and plopped them on the table before sitting. Gertie grabbed one immediately and started nibbling on the end.

"Did the forensics team show up?" I asked.

Ida Belle nodded. "They started documenting the scene, but the lift was going to be a little bit, so they couldn't work the body unless they wanted to figure out a way to climb up there. No one burst forward volunteering for that one."

"Lazy," Gertie said. "I wouldn't have any problem doing it if it was my job."

"You wouldn't have any problem doing it if it *wasn't* your job," Ida Belle said. "Let's pray the rest of the world doesn't adopt your limits on what they will and will not do. It would probably bring on the apocalypse."

Gertie shrugged. "We've all got to go somehow. An apocalypse is a lot more exciting than dying in a recliner at home, like most of Sinful does. Gage may have been a fool, but at least he went out with pizzazz."

"If that's what it takes to die with pizzazz, I'll just go on and bore you all with my recliner," Ida Belle said.

"You could make it more personal and die in your SUV," I suggested.

She stared at me as if I'd lost my mind. "I just had my carpets redone. Besides, dead people tend to lower the value."

"Neither of which matters if you're the one who's dead," Gertie pointed out.

"It matters if I plan on haunting my SUV. It needs to bring a high price so the buyer is incentivized to upkeep it properly."

I had to laugh. Even Gertie didn't have an argument for that one.

"So what's the story on Gage Babin?" I asked.

Ida Belle cocked her head. "You really think he was murdered?"

I shrugged. "It feels wrong. I can't explain it."

"Good enough for me. Gage Babin—where do I start?"

"At the beginning?" I suggested. "Sinful resident? I know he's married but not to whom. Kids? Employed? I know he's a drinker and likes practical jokes, but that's about it."

"He was born and raised in Sinful," Ida Belle said. "One

brother, Graham. His mother Miriam is in a nursing home up the highway. Been there about a year now. Heart problems. Father ran off when the boys were teens. Probably the only positive thing he ever did for them."

Gertie nodded. "He was an abusive drunk. Miriam should have sent him packing the first time he laid hands on her, but you know too often how that goes."

"Different times, too," Ida Belle said. "And Miriam didn't have any skills to speak of. She worked cleaning motels up the highway when he first split, then over time got some individual homes and a couple of commercial gigs. Did well enough to support them, as the house was paid for. It was her grandparents' place and they'd left it to her. Only smart thing she did where that man was concerned was never add him to the deed."

"He never came to see the boys?" I asked.

They both shook their heads.

"Miriam told me he never made contact with any of them again," Gertie said. "She said she tried to run him down for a while to get him on the books for child support but never could get anywhere. His family was uncooperative but my understanding is they weren't any better than him, which I suppose stands to reason as they produced him."

Ida Belle nodded. "Miriam said one of the aunts finally told her he'd run off with his cousin's wife and they weren't welcome anymore, so no one could help her."

"I guess that would do it," I agreed. "Since Carter called Deputy Breaux to notify, I know Gage was married."

"Yes," Gertie said. "To a local girl, Jenny Reed. Two years younger than Gage. She lived next door to the Babins with her mother Selma—a miserable, hateful old bat who never saw a smile she didn't try to erase."

"She erased her husband's all the way to Canada," Ida Belle

added. "That's where he was from originally and where he fled to after being married to Selma for a couple years."

"She sounds like a real treat," I said. "I'm surprised he made it that long with a whole other country to hide in."

"Selma got pregnant right away," Gertie said. "I always figured it was on purpose. She knew she was no catch and probably figured a child was the way to keep him tied to her. He cared about Jenny, but not enough to deal with Selma. She could suck the joy out of an angel."

I shook my head. "So he bounced and left his child to deal with the monster. Great guy."

"Karma caught up to him," Gertie said. "Got beheaded in a traffic accident while he was ditching his second wife and kid. Selma had a small inheritance they'd been living on, and she was able to get some benefits for Jenny after that—dead father and all."

"Says something about a man when a dead father is more useful than a live one," Ida Belle said.

"And nothing good," Gertie said. "But the Babin boys were in the same boat. Anyway, Jenny was starved for affection—not attention, mind you, because her mother gave her plenty of that, just all negative. These days, they'd call it emotional abuse. She found sympathetic ears with the Babin boys, given their own situation, and Miriam was the mother figure she needed."

"So she took up with Gage and married him," I said. "Please tell me she at least finished high school."

"Actually, she didn't marry Gage back then," Gertie said. "Far as I know, there was never anything romantic between any of them in high school. In fact, the rumor was always that his brother Graham was the one with a thing for Jenny."

Ida Bell nodded. "But the day after graduation, she lit out of here for New Orleans like she was on fire. She'd been working part time cleaning with Miriam and got a house-keeping job with a hotel in the French Quarter. That's where she met her first husband, Brent Copeland."

"Really?" This had taken an interesting turn. "So what happened with them?"

"No one can say for certain," Ida Belle said. "But we all have our guesses. The Copelands owned several hotels in NOLA, and Brent was their only child and spoiled rotten. He was charming, handsome, rich, and a complete butthole, according to the social scene gossip from back then."

"There were also rumors that Jenny was pregnant when they married," Gertie said, "but a baby never materialized."

"Probably jealousy," Ida Belle said. "A young, pretty girl from a small bayou town who worked in housekeeping swooped in and married one of the most eligible bachelors in the city. She went from wiping down toilets to having her own housekeepers and driving a Mercedes."

I frowned. "Most eligible? But you said he was a butthole."

"A lot of money can gloss up the whole butthole thing," Gertie said. "At least when it comes to NOLA society."

"I'm glad I always made my own money," I said.

Ida Belle raised her coffee cup in salute.

"So how did Jenny go from playing hotel heiress to marrying Sinful's Will Ferrell?" I asked.

"Gossip says Brent was running around on her," Gertie said. "And he probably was, but those rumors had been floating for years and she hadn't done anything about it. Not until her mother died. Then she packed her things, came back to Sinful, and said she was here to stay. Being an only child, I'm sure she thought she'd be inheriting everything."

"And she didn't?"

"Not unless you count debt as inheritance," Gertie said.

"Selma had never been much for working, and truth be told, no one who'd spent more than thirty seconds around her would have hired her, so her bit of inheritance was long gone, and she'd done one of those reverse mortgages that came due when she passed. By the time the fees and the bank were paid, there wasn't enough left from the sale of the house for Jenny to rent a motel room."

"So she went back to work cleaning with Miriam," Ida Belle continued, "who let her move in until she got her bearings. Gage and Graham were both living and working in NOLA when all that went down—Gage in sales and Graham as an accountant—but they'd come home every weekend to check on Miriam."

Gertie snorted. "Gage came home for free meals and to get his laundry done. Twenty-eight years old by then and still wasn't independent. Graham should have been out making friends his own age, but I think he used visiting his mother as his excuse for not socializing, something he's never been good at. Miriam should have cut the umbilical cord on both her boys years before."

"You ask me, she likes things just as they are," Ida Belle said. "One dotes on her and the other needs her."

"You're probably right," Gertie said. "They are definitely both mama's boys, but Graham is the mature one. At least he can 'adult' even though he was what my mother would have called 'delicate.'"

"Was he weak or did he break easily?" I asked.

Gertie laughed. "He liked classical music, literature, and art and never once did he attend a football game even though Gage was the star quarterback. He taught himself French and used to spend every Sunday after church knitting with Miriam. Still does, as far as I know, even though she's in the home now."

"I can see why all that culture might confuse most Sinful residents," I said.

Ida Belle nodded. "But you add that culture to never being linked to a woman—not even once—and 'delicate' takes on a different meaning to a lot of folk."

"Ah," I said, cluing in. "He's gay."

"Couldn't say," Ida Belle said. "He's never been linked to a man either."

"But that would be easy enough to hide living in NOLA, right?" I asked.

"It would," Ida Belle agreed. "But he moved back this way around the same time Gage did. Different reasons, of course. Rumor was Gage had a deal go wrong and got the axe, so he came running home with his tail tucked for Miriam to puff him back up again."

I nodded. "And Graham?"

"One of the original partners at a CPA firm in Mudbug was finally bowing out and they offered Graham a senior position with an ownership interest that increased every year he was there. It was a good opportunity to secure his future, so he jumped right on it."

"Good Lord, Miriam's house got crowded fast," I said.

"Oh, Graham didn't move back home," Gertie said. "He's always been smart with money. He bought a house in Mudbug and still lives there now. Gage moved back in with Miriam, made his play for Jenny, and they've been there ever since."

"They're still living in that same house?"

Ida Belle nodded. "Miriam didn't require enough of Gage, in my opinion, but she wasn't blind to her son's faults. My understanding is before she made the move to the nursing home, the house was put into a trust in both the sons' names with Graham as the trustee. Gage and Jenny can live there as long as they're married, and Gage has to pay all the house expenses and for the upkeep. If he defaults on taxes or fails to maintain the property in livable condition, or he and Jenny divorce, then Graham can sell the house, split the money, and be done with all of it."

"Miriam's kept that house deed close to the vest," I said. "First her husband, now her sons."

"Graham is probably praying Gage misses a bill or lets the roof leak," Gertie said. "Who wants to be responsible for a grown man their entire adult life?"

"Miriam, apparently," Ida Belle said. "All she's managed to do was shift her misplaced responsibility onto Graham, which isn't exactly fair, but I'm hopeful that it was more about taking care of Jenny than Gage."

"Hence the divorce clause," I said and nodded, forming a picture of the key players in my mind. "What happened to the ex-husband, Brent?"

They looked at each other and shrugged.

"That was a long time ago, and they're not exactly our people," Gertie said. "I never heard about any dust-up during the divorce, but I'm sure there was a prenuptial. Jenny certainly didn't come into a passel of money, or we would have heard about it."

"Those old-money families know how to structure things for control and to protect generational wealth," Ida Belle said. "The kids and grandkids have plenty of access to cash, but they don't own things."

"Things that appreciate and need paying out in a divorce," I said. "Got it. Did he remarry?"

"No idea," Gertie said. "His family isn't prominent enough to be major news, so we don't hear anything about them out this way."

"You should ask Ronald," Ida Belle said. "I bet he'd know the gossip if there is any."

"There's always gossip," Gertie said. "The trick is figuring out how much truth lies in it."

"Kids?" I asked.

They both shook their heads.

"Miriam told me they'd tried for years," Gertie said. "Apparently, Gage had always wanted a big family, but it never happened. They even checked into fertility treatments, but they didn't have the money for them. Miriam was always disappointed that she never got to become a grandmother, because it doesn't look like Graham is ever going to make a move in that direction either."

"Even if he did," Ida Belle said, "we don't know that Miriam would still be here by the time any grandchildren arrived. Her condition has to be pretty bad for her to need full-time care."

I nodded. "Did Gage have any enemies?"

"He was a used car salesman, so probably," Ida Belle said. "But I don't know that someone would go so far as to murder him over buying a lemon or agreeing to an interest rate that was too high."

"It would be a pretty elaborate setup for a disgruntled used car buyer," I agreed.

"Maybe it wasn't murder," Gertie said. "I'm not trying to malign your instincts, which have always been spot-on, but is it possible that with everything that's gone on recently, maybe you're picking up on something that isn't there?"

I considered this. My first inclination had been to issue an automatic no, but it deserved a harder look. As a CIA operative, I'd been trained to do my job without any personal thoughts, experiences, prejudices, wants, or desire interfering with the facts. And I'd been excellent at remaining completely and totally neutral. But maybe I had been a civilian long enough that my own feelings had led me to make a leap to the darker side of human nature that I wouldn't have if I hadn't just rescued Carter from torture and certain death.

"Even if we go with a prank and natural causes, he had to have help," I said. "Any idea who that might be? You mentioned Hooch earlier, and from what little I knew of the guy, this would have been right up his alley, but since he's dead himself, I don't think he would have been much use."

Ida Belle nodded. "There are some guys from back in high school that he still ran with—or a more accurate description is got drunk at the Swamp Bar with. With some help, he could have managed getting up there with an extension ladder on the top of a pickup truck."

"What are the chances his help comes forward when he finds out Gage is dead?"

"Slim to none," Ida Belle said. "But there would be marks on the top of the cab."

"Half of Sinful hauls things around on the top of their trucks," Gertie said. "They don't all worship their vehicles like you do. I saw Timmy Benoit drive right down Main Street the other day with a push mower on top of his truck."

Ida Belle winced. "Timmy Benoit had to have help lifting a case of water at the General Store the other day. And why would he have it on top of the cab when it would easily fit in the bed?"

"He had a bunch of goats in the bed. Maybe Fortune got it wrong for once. Maybe she's still in CIA mode and everyone's a bad guy."

Ida Belle frowned. "It's not like you to want a death to be natural causes instead of a homicide."

"You're right," Gertie agreed. "Maybe I need a vacation too."

"The last time we went on vacation, you were arrested for murder," Ida Belle reminded her.

Gertie threw her hands in the air. "Well, I would suggest a staycation, but this is Sinful. I don't think I'd be any better off."

I considered everything that I knew about this situation, about myself, and about general Sinful weirdness. But after several seconds of mulling it over, I finally sighed.

"I'm still able to separate myself from a case or mission. But maybe Gertie's right, and given recent events, my sensor could be off. It would be a first, but it was bound to happen at some point. It's not getting the workout it did with the CIA, although I *have* used it more here than I ever thought I would."

"If you're even insinuating you might be losing your touch, I'm going to have to disagree," Ida Belle said. "I think you're as perceptive as ever. If you think something's off with this whole mess, then I'm going to bet there is."

"Doesn't matter anyway," Gertie grumbled. "It will be all 'police matter' and stuff, and we don't have a client to throw into the mix."

"Maybe not," I said, "but remember, Blanchet is temporary sheriff, and he's not gunning for a permanent slot, so he doesn't care what voters think. And he knows what we're capable of."

Gertie's eyes widened and she clapped. "That's right! We're in there like swimwear!"

Ida Belle cringed. "What are you wearing to swim?"

CHAPTER EIGHT

WE TOSSED AROUND THE SOCIAL GRACES OF BRINGING JENNY a casserole that day versus waiting for an official announcement. Gertie was loaded with casseroles and voted to head out as soon as we'd finished breakfast. Ida Belle had wondered if it was too soon. I'd swayed her vote by pointing out that speaking to Jenny at the height of the emotional surge would be the best time to for her to give things away that she might not otherwise.

So we compromised and opted for a long, leisurely breakfast, a couple hours of television, and then a visit to Jenny early afternoon, leaving her morning alone. Gertie had opted for a beef pot pie over chicken casserole, because she'd always liked Jenny and knew Jenny loved red meat, and we'd even picked up a box of cookies from Ally's bakery before heading out.

I hadn't heard a peep from Blanchet yet, but I figured he would be tied up for a while. It was going to take some effort just to get the scene documented then get the body down from there. After that, the ME had to do his thing. It might be days before we knew anything.

I also hadn't heard from Carter, so I hoped that meant he

was getting some much-needed sleep. I wasn't about to admit it to anyone, but I was worried about him. He was in more pain than he was admitting—not that it surprised me—but sometimes I'd catch him staring off, kind of vacant, and I wondered where his mind was going. I knew he'd dealt with a lot of stuff after leaving the Marines. So much so that he took a year off from life just to figure out how he wanted the rest of it to play out, so now I worried that everything that had happened had sent him back to that dark place that he'd worked himself out of a long time ago.

But that would remain my secret worry, because telling someone else was betraying him, and that was the one thing I knew I could never do.

Jenny lived a couple blocks away, and when she opened the door, I realized I had seen her many times around town, conducting normal, everyday business. But I was certain we'd never spoken or been introduced. Which wasn't all that big a surprise. I wasn't exactly Ms. Congeniality and people with things to hide—which was pretty much everyone—tended to shy away from pushing a friendship with a CIA operative.

Late thirties, five foot six, a hundred forty pounds, good muscle tone from all the cleaning, dark circles under her eyes. Threat level zero. This woman was a caretaker, not a fighter.

Even though she'd obviously been crying, she was still a pretty woman. Age hadn't taken over her body and face as it did most people. When she'd first opened the door, I'd been a tiny bit taken aback because I would have never known she was closing in on forty if Ida Belle and Gertie hadn't just told me her life story.

"We're so sorry, Jenny," Gertie said, and thrust the pot pie at me so that she could give Jenny a hug. "It's beef. Your favorite."

Jenny clutched her and sobbed a bit before stepping back

and motioning for us to come in. We followed her back to the kitchen, where she grabbed a tissue and dabbed at her face as we sat at the kitchen table. Then she began to hurry around us, moving potted plants off the table and onto the floor near the sliding doors. I spotted a stack of lumber in the rear of the yard and a partially torn-up deck just outside the sliders.

"Please excuse the mess," she said. "Gage got it in his head that we needed a hot tub. He wanted an in-ground one and Graham told him no way it would work in our soil here. He said to pour a concrete pad off to the side, but Gage never listened to anyone, especially Graham. He started tearing it apart a couple days ago, and it's already a nightmare. The size of the posts is all wrong and some are rotted, so they have to be dug up and replaced with bigger ones. I pulled all my plants inside to protect them—and I'm babbling."

She blew out a breath and dropped into a chair, clearly overwhelmed.

"Don't worry about it," Gertie said. "Your fern is lovely."

"Thank you for coming," she said gratefully. "I've been wandering around the house for the last hour, thinking I should be doing something but not having any idea what that could be. I figured people would line up at the front door—the Sinful way, you know—but the minutes kept ticking by and no one appeared. I had a million calls and texts, of course, but most were from people looking for the story, not really interested in how they could help."

"We debated it ourselves," Ida Belle said. "Whether it was crass or not to come so soon."

"God no!" Jenny said. "You've saved me from my own thoughts, and I really needed saving. I haven't been this overwhelmed since I was a teenager. At least now I have something to do. I can pour you up some sweet tea. I made a batch earlier, figuring on company, but it's just been sitting there chilling."

She glanced at me, and I extended my hand. "We've never officially met, but I'm Fortune. I'm so sorry for your loss."

Jenny clutched my hand and nodded. "I feel like I know you just by reputation. You've done a lot of good things for this town since you've been here. I was just reading an article the other day about all those women and children that you helped save. It was so outlandish I would have thought it made up if I didn't know it to be true."

"It was definitely one of the odder things I've encountered."

She gave me a small smile. "And then you've got my husband, dead in a boat, dressed as a nun, to throw you right back into normal Sinful."

"*Normal* and *Sinful* are two words that don't really belong in the same sentence."

She nodded. "I heard you were the one who climbed up there to check on him. Thank you for that. All those other people, just standing around while he was up there dying..."

Her voice cracked as she delivered the last few words, and my heart went out to her. The things she was imagining were worse than reality, which meant I could help. At least in one small way.

"They weren't being neglectful," I said. "Everyone thought it was a mannequin. It never occurred to anyone that it could be a person. And even if they'd known, they couldn't have helped him. He'd been gone for hours before anyone saw him up there."

Her hand flew up to her chest. "You're sure?"

"Absolutely positive. I have some experience with, uh...that sort of thing."

Jenny looked over at Ida Belle and Gertie, who nodded,

and her shoulders relaxed a bit. "That makes me feel a bit better. I just kept thinking if someone had *done* something, you know?"

"I'm so sorry, honey," Gertie said. "We didn't realize that you didn't know the whole story."

She shook her head. "Poor Deputy Breaux looked like he was going to pass out when he told me. He got me out of bed, so I was having a bit of trouble processing everything, but he didn't offer much in the way of information. Not that I'm blaming him, mind you. That's got to be one of the worst job responsibilities I can think of."

I could think of far worse. Heck, I'd done far worse, but knowing that wouldn't help Jenny.

"Thank you so much for checking," she said. "Even if there was nothing to be done, you made sure."

I nodded. "I don't suppose you have any idea who helped him with the prank, do you?"

Jenny frowned. "What do you mean? I assumed he was alone."

I shook my head. "I had to use an extension ladder in the bucket of a front-end loader to get up there. And neither were sitting around."

Jenny peered outside, then gave me an aggrieved look. "He has an extension ladder, but it's not next to his tool shed like it used to be. He was at the Swamp Bar last night, so I assume one of his drinking buddies helped him. They were always egging him on, seeing what they could get him to do, and he was always happy to oblige."

"Anyone among those buddies stand out?" I asked. "The police are going to want to talk to whoever it was."

"No one in particular. They were Gage's friends and not exactly the people I'd want over for Sunday dinner. Whiskey probably knows them better than I do."

I nodded. I figured the Swamp Bar would be at the top of Blanchet's list to check on while trying to establish a timeline of the events.

"You hadn't noticed that he didn't come home?" I asked.

She dropped her gaze to the table and shook her head. "I didn't like all the drinking. He usually passed out on the couch when he stumbled in."

She fidgeted in her chair. "What happens... I mean, what do I do now? With my mother, there wasn't all this uncertainty, at least not about the funeral. She'd already stated she wanted to be cremated and didn't want a service, which was good because there wasn't money to pay for all that, and I can't imagine many would have turned out for it anyway given how she treated people."

"There's nothing to be gained dwelling on the past," Ida Belle said. "Your mother and Gage both lived their lives the way they wanted, which is all any of us can hope for. But there's always consequences to actions. Those don't fall on you."

Gertie nodded. "And don't you go worrying about that stuff just yet. You've got some time, and besides, you know Graham will be here to help. I'm surprised he isn't here now."

"He called right after Deputy Breaux left. One of his biggest clients is in a legal battle with the IRS and he's in NOLA in court. He tried to get a postponement, but his attorney said the IRS would never agree and none of the partners at the CPA firm knew the client's books like Graham did. I told him to stay and take care of his job. No use for his client to lose a battle with the IRS just for Graham to sit here not being able to do anything either."

"I'm sure he'll be here as soon as he can," Gertie said. "How was he taking it?"

"Deputy Breaux called him on his way over here, but

honestly, I don't think he believed it until he talked to me. I can't say that I blame him. After Deputy Breaux left, I kept thinking that maybe I'd imagined the whole thing, but then I checked my phone, and the number of calls and texts made it all real."

Gertie nodded. "It's a lot to take in, especially when it's a surprise. If you and Graham need any help making arrangements, you give us a call. Ida Belle and I know what to do. In the meantime, is there anything we can help with here? We could eat off your floors, so clearly housekeeping doesn't need tending to."

"I've mopped them twice already this morning. Once because it's mopping day and then again because I couldn't sit still. I leave Tuesdays open to take care of all my own personal stuff—groceries, doctors, cleaning. I like to keep a neat home, just like Miriam always did. Oh my God, Miriam."

Jenny's eyes filled with tears again. "Graham said we'd go together to tell her, but how are we supposed to do that?"

"How bad off is she?" Gertie asked.

"Pretty bad. Graham still goes to see her every Sunday, and I get out there myself at least once a week—it would normally be this afternoon—but sometimes she doesn't recognize me. It's really hard to take. I can't imagine how much more difficult it is for Graham."

"I didn't realize her mind was going," Gertie said.

Jenny nodded. "The heart problems were something I could manage. I just made sure she took the right meds at the right time and didn't overdo on anything. Not that it was easy, as she'd always been such a hard worker, but she understood she had to cut way back and never gave me any grief over it. But when her memory started to go, that was something we weren't equipped to handle. I couldn't reason with her sometimes and we were afraid she'd end up having another heart attack. She needed eyes on her 24/7 but Gage, Graham, and I all had to work."

"How badly has she regressed?" Ida Belle asked.

"It comes and goes, but like her heart, it's getting worse. Gage was with me last time I went and she brightened up when he first walked in the room, but then she asked who he was. It was like it was right there for a second and then slipped away."

"It's a hard thing to watch," Ida Belle said. "Maybe you should talk to her doctor before you talk to her. It might be that he recommends not telling her at all. Sometimes it's the kindest thing to do."

Jenny looked a little relieved at the suggestion. "Do you think? It seems so...dishonest."

Gertie shook her head. "Depends on how far her memory is gone. If she wouldn't remember what you told her and you had to tell her over and over again, then she'd grieve every time like it was the first time she'd heard it. Better to say he had to work or was ill, as she would be unlikely to remember that either."

"Oh no!" Jenny looked horrified. "That's awful. I hadn't even thought... I'll tell Graham we need to consult with the doctor on how to proceed."

"Graham is a good and practical man," Ida Belle said. "I'm sure he'll do what's best for his mother. He always has."

Jenny gave us all a grateful look. "I'm so glad you came. I can't tell you how much better I feel now. I mean—"

A knock at the front door interrupted her and I rose from my chair. "I'll get it."

Jenny had left the front door open when we'd come in and I spotted Blanchet through the screen. He gave me a nod as he stepped inside, not even remotely surprised to see me.

"How's she doing?" he asked, his voice low.

"As well as can be expected, I guess. But then, my only experience with this side of death has been since I arrived in Sinful. I'm not exactly an expert. Is everything wrapped up at the boat?"

"The body's down and on the way to the ME. The team documented the scene and secured the beer can he was drinking from. The boat's still up there, but Wade is welcome to take it down whenever he wants. Might take a while to sell, though. These small towns are filled with superstition."

"They're also filled with cheap. He'll find a buyer with the right discount. What about Gage's truck?"

"Found it stashed in some trees a little bit down from the boat. Had an extension ladder in the back. We'll run it for prints, but I don't expect we'll get much."

"I don't suppose anyone's fessed up to helping him."

"No. And I'm not really expecting them to, given how things turned out."

I nodded. "Come on back and I'll introduce you. We'll get out of here and let you do your police thing."

He grinned. "I'm pretty sure you were already here doing my 'police thing.'"

"Well, you can make it official."

———

WE DIDN'T HAVE ANYTHING ELSE ON THE SCHEDULE FOR THE rest of the day, so we all decided to head to our respective homes and take care of everyday life things that had gone untended while we were off on our rescue mission. Except Ida Belle, of course. Walter had seen to most of the house stuff, and she'd gotten up with the chickens and completed everything else. She claimed she needed to work on her boat motor because it had been running sluggish, so I took that to mean that it didn't actually launch out of the water like an airplane anymore. I made a mental note to bring my life jacket and goggles the next time I rode in it. Maybe ask Ronald where he got those pants with butt pads.

There was a box on my front porch when Ida Belle dropped me off, and I frowned at first, because I hadn't ordered anything. The delivery guy must have gotten the wrong place. But when I peered down at the label, sure enough, there was my name. I looked at the sender and immediately grabbed the package up and glanced around. It listed only an address. An address in Iran.

I headed straight for the kitchen and my box cutter, carefully cutting the edge. Inside the plain brown mailing box was another box, this one fancy and sapphire blue, made of that hard cardboard that expensive things came packed in. I opened the blue box and blinked at the black Arabian horse statue contained inside. It was exquisite, but I was certain I hadn't bought it.

There was a business card tucked in the corner of the box and I pulled it out, then laughed.

Nine Lives Antiques

The only other information on the card was a phone number. I pulled the statue from the box and took it and the card to my office. Then I placed the statue on a bookshelf where I could see it from my desk...a constant reminder of our great escape, as the horse I'd ridden away from the compound had looked almost exactly like this one. The card I tucked away in my safe. I knew the number had been provided in case of an extreme emergency, and my father knew I wouldn't risk contacting him for any other reason. But it made my chest clench just a little to know it was there.

To know he'd made the effort to send it.

Maybe Morrow had been more right than wrong when he'd

suggested that my father had left me behind for my own good. But I would never fool myself into thinking that was the only reason. Even now, he was clearly still working to take down the bad guys. I didn't even know if he was on anyone's payroll, but I also figured it didn't matter. He'd do it for free. That's just who he was.

I'd gotten more of my personality from him than I cared to admit, but at least I'd finally narrowed my focus to this community—to my newly created family. I'd admit that sometimes I missed the exhilaration of the big takedown, but it was also a very lonely job, hiding in the shadows and disappearing before anyone even knew you'd been there. At one time, I'd been happy being invisible, but things had changed. Sinful had changed me. And I was okay with that. More than okay, actually.

I was happy.

I felt a tiny jolt of surprise as I realized just how true that statement was. Emotions were things I tended not to dwell on. I was a person driven to action, not thought. Accomplishing things was what gave me energy. But somewhere along the line, I'd found the perfect blend of location, people, and work that I could happily live with the rest of my life. Not saying every day was going to be joyful. This was life, after all. But when the dark clouds cleared, there was always going to be that silver lining behind them.

I threw on some laundry and unloaded the dishwasher, but the rest of the house was cleaner than I'd left it, thanks to Ally. I imagined she'd spent her time here stress cleaning, as Jenny had this morning. And baking. I'd discovered four boxes of cookies in my freezer last night when I'd taken some chicken out to thaw. It made my chest clench again when I imagined how hard it had been on Ally, Emmaline, and Walter...being back here and having nothing to do but wait and pray.

I'd just finished rearranging the bookshelves in my office when I heard a knock on the door. It was Andy and he looked beat. We hadn't had a chance to really talk since I'd returned, so I waved him into the kitchen, figuring he needed something to drink and an ear to bend. He'd had a long day.

"Is it quitting time?" I asked, checking my phone. It was a little after 5:00 p.m.

"I'm pretty sure my mind quit a couple hours back. My body's just been going through the motions."

I pulled a beer out of the fridge and popped the top before sitting.

"How's Maya doing?" I asked.

Maya Delgado was Blanchet's long-lost love who had been found during our last case. She had been in a Mexican prison for the past ten years, but I'd pulled some strings and managed to get her released. Now she was living in Mudbug with her daughter, Lara, and granddaughter, Mariela—also victims of the traffickers—and they were trying to make up for lost time.

Blanchet broke into a huge smile as soon as I said her name. "She's doing great, especially considering everything she's been through. She and Lara are in DC right now, helping the FBI finish up their case."

"And Mariela?"

"She's staying with Lottie, who's delighted to spoil her to death."

"She deserves it."

Lottie was a senior who'd helped Maya with a place to live years ago when Maya had managed to escape. She'd been as thrilled as Blanchet when she'd found out Maya was still alive.

"Definitely," he said.

"Rough one today," I said.

He sighed. "What a mess. Pulling forensics off a crime scene on the side of the highway is bad enough, but I swear, that man's truck was even worse than the road. I'm convinced he's never thrown a single thing away in his life. And I'm including actual trash in that statement."

"He'd made quite the mess in his backyard as well. I guess no one has admitted to being out there with him."

Blanchet snorted. "Given the type of people he ran with, I don't see it happening."

"What about his cell phone? If they didn't leave the bar together, maybe someone called or texted. Jenny might know the password."

"His phone was in his pants pocket. I even took a stab at the password before I went to see Jenny and got it right—1, 2, 3, 4—what an idiot. But there were no calls, and all the texts had been deleted."

I frowned. "That doesn't sound like something a man who keeps a trash collection in his truck would do."

"No. It doesn't. It's darn suspicious. I got a subpoena for the phone records, but you know how long that will take."

"He and Jenny didn't share an account?"

"No. Since they both used their phones for work as well as personal, they kept them separate."

"What did the ME have to say?"

"You mean aside from 'take a number'?"

"Didn't you figure that would be the case? I mean, the circumstances are unusual but they don't blatantly point to homicide."

"Yeah, but I'm with you on this one. It doesn't feel right." He rose from the table. "But I guess we're both going to have to wait and see."

CHAPTER NINE

I AWAKENED THE NEXT MORNING, GRATEFUL AND frustrated. Grateful that Carter was back home and frustrated that he still wasn't engaged with life. Every day, he seemed to be slipping more into his thoughts and less into the present. He'd come by the night before and we'd hung out for a couple hours and watched a movie, but then he'd gone home, citing Tiny being back home with him and needing food and a bathroom break. Both were things he often did before spending the night with me, but I knew better than to point that out. Whatever he was trying to work out, he'd talk when he was ready.

Which might be never.

With no word from the ME and no insurance cases on my agenda, I had a woefully large amount of free time, so I figured I'd eat breakfast, then head downtown to make up for some lost 'people' time since I hadn't had an opportunity to get much in since I'd returned. I'd swing by the General Store and the bakery, then I'd head out to Emmaline's and spend some time reassuring her that Carter was going to be fine. I was pretty sure she'd take all of that I could dole out, even though I'd be hedging a bit on my own certainty on that one.

There was a line in the bakery, so I decided to hit the General Store first. Only a couple cars were parked in front of it, so I figured I'd have a better chance at shooting the breeze with Walter, and I needed to pick up a few things for my pantry as well. Walter was sitting behind the counter when I walked in. He looked up when the bell above the door rang and his face broke into a huge smile.

"I hear you're already back in the Sinful mystery saddle," he said as I approached.

He brought a stool around for me and I took a seat. "Not sure it's any big mystery. Everyone says Gage was known for his practical jokes and wasn't exactly healthy, so this one might just be the case of the joker overextending himself."

Walter nodded. "But it's been all the buzz in the store."

"What are people saying?"

"Most people think it was funny, except for the part where he died. A few of the hard-core Catholics are siding with Celia with the blasphemy claim and have decided that God himself took care of the situation."

"Seems a little harsh, even for devout Catholics. He *was* one of theirs."

"I'm pretty sure it's pettiness and pure meanness rather than religion that's got them thinking that way."

"You sure Gage didn't have enemies? Practical jokes are usually at someone else's expense."

"That's true, but I swear I can't think of any. Sure, people found him to be a 'bit much,' but you don't go celebrating a man's death because he's an extreme extrovert with a questionable sense of humor, much less seeing that it occurs."

"I guess not. Oh well, none of it matters unless the ME comes back with something besides natural causes."

Walter narrowed his eyes at me. "Is that what you're thinking is going to happen?"

I shrugged. "Who knows? It's Sinful, right?"

He knew I was skirting the question, but he let it slide.

"How is Carter doing?" he asked. "Really doing? Not just what he's saying."

"He's going to be fine as soon as his injuries heal up," I said, hedging yet another answer. But then, I only had my own suspicions that Carter was struggling with something. And even if I knew for sure, it wasn't my place to share his personal business with anyone, not even Walter. Not even Emmaline, and I was certain she was going to ask the same question.

Walter raised one eyebrow, his polite way of calling me on my answer.

I shook my head. "He hasn't talked to me about any of it, I swear."

"But you'd know if something was wrong. Something that bandages and aspirin aren't going to fix."

"Maybe. But it's too soon to tell. He's exhausted, injured, and disappointed in the whole thing. And there's the chance of a DOD investigation, which will be on his mind as well."

Finally, Walter nodded. "I suppose you're right. Do you think he's going to be in any trouble over this?"

"I can't see how. The military gets enough bad press without attempting to punish a hostage victim."

"What about you, Harrison, and Mannie?"

"We were never there, remember? And even if someone proved that we were in Dubai, so what? The worst crime we committed was traveling under a fake passport, and given both our histories with the CIA, that's a reasonable action to take, if not entirely legal. Besides, I've got the best attorney in the country, and if Colonel Kitts wants to press the issues, I have zero problem pointing my finger back at him—loudly and publicly."

Walter nodded, his eyes misting up a little. "You're a good woman, Fortune. I couldn't have picked a better partner for my nephew if I'd ordered you up out of my catalog."

I inclined my head. "What department would I be under?"

He chuckled. "I don't know—maybe fuel and lighters and fast engines."

"Fuel and lighters sounds more like Gertie. Engines is Ida Belle's department."

"Ha! That woman probably spends more of her time on the sandpaper aisle, but if you tell her I said so, I'll call you a liar."

I laughed. "It will be our secret."

I headed out and across the street to the bakery. The crowd had cleared a bit, with only a couple of tables occupied and no one at the counter. Ally gave me a huge smile when I walked in and waved me to a seat.

"Perfect timing," she said. "I'm on break. You want some sweet tea?"

"Just water for me."

She grabbed a couple of bottled waters, a cinnamon roll, and two forks and headed my way. "It's the last one. If we don't eat it, I'll have to throw it out."

"It's a good thing you sell out of most things every day. Otherwise, you'd be asking Ronald about his stretchy pants."

She laughed. "At least shopping with him I actually get to go to a store. With you, I don't get further than Amazon. So what's the scoop on Gage Babin?"

"I guess everyone's been talking about it?"

"Nonstop. Aunt Celia came in ready to have kittens. Like God was going to opt out of Easter in Sinful because the man died in a nun's habit. She said she was marching over to Marie's house and going to demand she press charges against Wade for blasphemy."

"But Wade didn't put Gage up there. Technically, Wade is also a victim. He's going to have to pay for a cleaning and sell that boat at a discount."

"You know Celia."

"All too well, unfortunately. Poor Marie. Celia just might be the worst thing about being mayor."

"Definitely."

"Thanks again for watching Merlin while I was away, and cleaning my house, and leaving me enough cookies to last until summer."

She rolled her eyes. "Please. They'll be gone by next weekend."

"Maybe. Have you had plenty of reunion time with Mannie?"

Ally blushed, which answered my question.

"He showed up at my house around midnight the night before you guys got back. All he told me was that everyone was safe and Carter was a little banged up but would be fine. Don't get me wrong, even if it was okay for me to know what happened, I don't think I'd want to. It's enough to know the three of you risked your lives. If I had details, it might give me a heart attack."

I nodded. "I *will* tell you that none of it could have happened without Mannie's connections and the Heberts' money. Even I don't know the details from his end of things. We all agreed that the less we knew of each other's roles, the better."

She laughed. "Mannie said you can't be compelled to tell things you don't know."

"Words to live by when you're in our line of work. Or our line of work adjacent. He's a good man, Ally. I can't say I would have ever put the two of you together, but then, I'm not exactly known for my Hallmark romance thinking. But it works."

She smiled and it lit up her entire face. "It does work. And trust me, I was just as surprised as you. Now, you and Carter, on the other hand—it's like you were a matched set from the beginning. He had plenty of women make a run at him before you arrived, but he never even raised an eyebrow until you. He needed an equal. Nothing else was going to do."

"Matchups are interesting things, right? We went and saw Jenny yesterday."

Ally gave me a sad nod. "Such a nice woman. Always so polite and soft-spoken. She and Gage were two I would have never put together, but then, when you know about their childhoods, it makes more sense. Sometimes there's comfort in what you know. How is she doing?"

"Upset. Stressed. She's worried about Miriam, but Ida Belle and Gertie convinced her to get Graham to talk to Miriam's doctors before telling her anything. Apparently her mind is starting to go."

"That's so sad, but it's smart advice. I know toward the end with my mom, I told more half-truths and lies by omission in a matter of months than I probably had my entire life. I felt guilty about it, but I knew her doctor was right. Her knowing things wouldn't have improved her quality of life. Quite the opposite, in fact, but I still hated when she'd ask me how one of her friends who'd already passed was doing."

"How well did you know Jenny and Gage?"

"I didn't know either well. Different generation, and Jenny was a homebody when she wasn't working. Gage was more likely to be in the Swamp Bar than at the café or church. Jenny usually comes to mass, but she sits in the back and leaves as soon as the doors are open."

She gave me a curious look. "Why are you asking about them? You don't think something's wrong with how he died, do you?"

"I'm suspicious of the sunrise."

She laughed. "True."

"Anyway, it's probably nothing. It sounds like he was well on his way to pickling his liver and for all we know, those heart problems of his mother's are of the hereditary type. It took a good amount of effort for someone drunk and that out of shape to climb up in the boat."

Ally's assistant Lillie Mae called to her from the kitchen door and she jumped up.

"I better get back in there, but let me grab a box of vanilla croissants I set aside for Carter."

I collected the croissants and left. It was getting on toward noon and I was a little surprised that I still hadn't heard from Carter. I figured I'd swing by Emmaline's and if he hadn't surfaced by the time I was done there, then I'd head over to his place. I'd had a key for a long time now and could traverse a floor of bubble wrap without making a sound, so if he was resting, I'd just let myself back out and go on home.

But when I reached my Jeep, all hell broke loose.

When I'd exited the bakery, I'd spotted Ida Belle's SUV parked a bit down from my Jeep and had assumed she'd come into town to see Walter. And it wasn't surprising that Rambo, her bloodhound puppy, was with her. But what I didn't expect was to see him chasing Celia out of the General Store. Ida Belle flew out the door after him yelling for him to stop, I'm certain more worried that he'd run into traffic than he'd somehow injure Celia.

I was a little surprised when he continued apace because he usually responded well to commands. But instead, he dashed after Celia, with zero indication that Ida Belle was issuing orders from behind. The entire situation was ridiculous, of course, because all that was required to rectify the situation was for her to stop running. Rambo wasn't going to hurt her, but my experiences with her so far had indicated a somewhat unwarranted fear of dogs. She'd do better to exchange it for a fear of running, as that choice hadn't turned out well for her most of the time.

In her quest to escape what she was currently calling the "Hound of Hell," she ran right for the street. Fortunately, this was Sinful and not NOLA, but there were still three vehicles, a four-wheeler, and Sheriff Lee on his horse traversing Main Street at the time, but her screaming was loud enough to startle the practically deaf horse and send him bolting into the florist's shop. Seconds later, he came running back out, a bouquet in his mouth and the florist chasing him, and took off down Main Street, Sheriff Lee holding on for dear life.

She continued her reign of terror by pivoting away from the scared horse and ran straight into traffic where she promptly hit the back of a car bumper. I saw the driver's eyes widen as he stared in his rearview mirror, then I can only assume he had spotted Celia, because he floored it and took off so fast that she lost her balance and went stumbling into oncoming traffic.

A truck pulling a boat was in the oncoming lane, and he swerved and slammed on his brakes. The trailer must not have been attached to the truck hitch properly, because it popped off the hitch, and in a move that only escaped boat trailers can manage, swung out to the left, flew by the truck, and barreled straight for the Catholic church.

Celia whirled around, changing course back to the other lane as the boat and trailer swept by, but she didn't manage to stay upright this time. She slid into the lane of oncoming traffic like a professional baseball player who'd just hit a home run. Well, except for the part where she didn't quite slide so much as she bounced a couple times, then collapsed.

Right into the path of the four-wheeler guy.

The four-wheeler driver yanked his handlebars to avoid her, but it was too late. One front wheel rolled over her shoulders and the other over her rear. Given that her rear was a steeper climb than her shoulders, the four-wheeler pitched off to the right and crashed into a light pole, where a family of four, each holding a milkshake, had been waiting to cross the road. As the family scrambled, the milkshakes went up in the air and the four-wheeler and its driver got a fresh coat of pink.

"Looks like strawberry," Walter said as he stepped up beside me. "I prefer vanilla."

I nodded and watched as Rambo made a dash through the milkshake spill long enough to get in a few licks, then continued his pursuit of Celia, who was up and running again. Ida Belle was still scrambling after the puppy, who showed no sign of relinquishing the chase.

"Do we need to help her?" I asked. "And by her, I mean Ida Belle, not Celia."

Walter snorted. "I'm pretty sure there's no helping either of them, but for different reasons."

A huge racket disrupted our contemplation, and we looked over to see the source. The wayward boat had crashed into the Easter display at the Catholic church. The cross, which had been standing in the front, surrounded by Easter lilies, was uprooted and now leaned against the front entry, effectively blocking anyone from entering that way. The white cloth that had been draped over it was now wrapped around the center console of the boat like a scarf and blowing in the wind. Easter lilies dotted the boat and the surrounding grounds.

"The Catholics are going to accuse boats of starting a religious war before the month is over," I said.

Walter snorted. "Boats aren't religious."

"Fishing is. At least in Sinful."

We heard Celia let out another cry and turned in time to see her climb into the back of a pickup truck that had just pulled into town, hauling hay. And sheep. The startled driver slammed on his brakes, she pitched forward, and we lost sight of her. But the bleating sheep left no uncertainty of where she'd landed. Rambo put his paws on the bumper of the truck and set up a mournful howl. Then he spotted something on the ground nearby and grabbed the small package and took off running right toward Walter and me, Ida Belle still on his tail.

"He's got a package of hot dogs!" Ida Belle shouted as she ran by. "He'll choke on that plastic."

I decided that Main Street had seen enough excitement for one morning, and Blanchet didn't need more things to investigate. Ida Belle and Rambo had gotten in their cardio and Wade might just have a buyer for that cursed boat of his since the one that was currently trying to attend mass had received a hole in the side, courtesy of the cross. Seemed like a good time to wrap things up.

I sprinted for Rambo, who heard me coming and swerved, but even though he was a puppy, he was still a bloodhound, and they weren't exactly known for speed. I snagged him with one hand and curled him up to my stomach as I slid to a stop. I heard clapping and cheering around me as I removed the package of hot dogs from the wriggling puppy's mouth.

"Good job," I whispered to him as Ida Belle came hurrying up.

"Celia, you idiot!" she yelled at the truck, where Celia was now upright and peering over the bed, a sheep's head on each side of her own.

"Probably the first time she's ever looked 'sheepish,'" I said, and Walter chuckled.

"You had those hot dogs in your pocket, didn't you?" Ida Belle continued to yell.

"I ran out of hands," Celia yelled back. "It's not like I was going to steal them. I just put them there until I got to the cash register. That vicious dog of yours is the problem."

Everyone who hadn't fled the street started laughing.

"How the heck is that dog supposed to know you're not stealing?" Walter asked. "All store owners have been dealing with an increase in theft. He's just doing what he's supposed to. Next time ask for a basket. That's why I have the darn things."

He was still shaking his head when he walked back into the store.

The driver of the truck climbed out and pointed at Celia. "You need to get out of there. You're spooking my sheep and I need them to stand still for the shearing or it's going to look like a bloodbath."

"Blood of the lamb at Easter," I said. "Sinful's really turned up the dial on holidays this year."

Celia glared at me and then turned her look back at the truck driver. But she couldn't really argue his point as she'd single-handedly destroyed half of downtown. So she crawled out of the back of the truck and stomped off, her groceries apparently forgotten. It was just as well. Her entire back was covered in sheep poop and there was no way Walter would let her in his store like that.

Ida Belle gave me a nod. "Thanks for catching Rambo. Obviously, I need to start doing some sprints again. Should have thought about that before I got a puppy."

I laughed. "Probably should have never stopped, since you have a Gertie."

CHAPTER TEN

CARTER'S TRUCK WAS IN EMMALINE'S DRIVEWAY BY THE TIME I got there. Emmaline answered the door, her eyes a bit red and misty, and I immediately jumped to concern, but then she explained that she and Carter had been watching video of Celia and Rambo's adventures, and I relaxed.

"Good God, how does video get posted that quickly?" I asked.

"Videos. Plural," Carter said as I walked into the kitchen, happy to see he looked as though he'd gotten some rest. "Three different accounts, but no real names associated with them."

Emmaline laughed. "That's because none of them want to deal with the fallout if Celia finds out they're posting her embarrassing moments online."

Carter raised one eyebrow. "Do you know who those accounts belong to?"

"Of course," Emmaline said. "Those aren't the only ones posting crazy stuff that happens in Sinful, mind you, but those three happen to belong to Ally, Deputy Breaux, and Father Michael."

Carter spit out his iced tea and I had to join Emmaline laughing.

"So her niece, a cop, and her priest," I said. "No wonder they're anonymous."

Carter had winced a little when Emmaline had given Deputy Breaux's name, but then his lower lip started to tremble and finally he burst out laughing as well.

"I wish I would have been there," he said finally. "So tell us what we missed."

I recounted everything and by the time I was done, Emmaline had gone through a stack of tissues and Carter was clutching his injured ribs.

"Someone better warn Blanchet," Carter said. "All that mockery in one day and Celia will be down at the sheriff's department demanding he arrest Rambo."

Emmaline nodded. "She'll be convinced that Easter will be canceled."

My cell phone buzzed, and I glanced at the display. "Speak of the devil. It's Blanchet."

"I need a consultation," he said.

"Is this a secret, unofficial consultation?"

"That would be correct. And bring those nosy friends of yours, but leave Carter out of it."

"He heard what you said and is frowning at me now."

"Put me on speaker."

I switched the phone over.

"You can't get involved, Carter," Blanchet said.

"I get that part," Carter said, "but telling the three trouble-makers facts about an open investigation is just as problematic."

"Not for me. I'm retired. What are they going to do? Fire me?"

Carter shook his head but he knew Blanchet was right.

"I'll meet you at your house in fifteen," Blanchet said.

I slipped my phone back in my jeans and Emmaline gave me a worried look. "That doesn't sound good."

"It's probably nothing," I said. "He was going to try to run down whoever helped Gage with that prank today to help complete his file. There's no way the ME has filed a report yet."

Carter's shoulders relaxed a bit. "You're probably right. But you can bet that whoever it was has probably sewn his lips together. Still, it would help confirm time of death, and the file would look better if Blanchet had the facts on how it all transpired."

I rose from the table. "Then I better get to work. You coming by tonight? I thawed out steaks and bought twice-baked potatoes from Francine's. And Ally might have left me a freezer of cookies."

"You had me at steaks."

I texted Ida Belle and Gertie as soon as I climbed in my Jeep and headed out. We were already seated in the kitchen and had gone through some of the cookies before Blanchet arrived. He looked a bit worse for wear as he slid into a chair.

"Sorry I'm late," he said. "Celia showed up when I was leaving the sheriff's department."

"Let me guess," I said. "She wanted to file a complaint against Ida Belle's dog."

"Nailed it," he said.

Ida Belle rolled her eyes. "Of course she did. Did she tell you she had a package of hot dog weenies that she hadn't paid for shoved in her pocket?"

"She left that part out. But is that puppy really trained to catch thieves?"

"Of course not," Ida Belle said. "But Celia doesn't know that. If she wants to move forward with this, then Walter can press charges for theft, and then there's the boat guy, four-wheeler guy, the Catholic church, that family wearing their milkshakes, and those terrified sheep that can be heaped on her."

He blinked.

"It's easier if I just send you a link to the videos," I said. "So what do you need?"

"I'm trying to run down whoever helped Gage with that prank."

"I figured as much. No prints on the extension ladder?"

"Only Gage's."

"His helper could have been wearing gloves," Ida Belle said. "It's a smart move when dealing with a ladder, and most people around here keep a pair in their vehicle."

Blanchet nodded. "I'm sure you can guess that I'm having some trouble running this guy down with good old-fashioned legwork."

I nodded. "The locals are being less than forthcoming, right?"

"Yeah, I talked to Whiskey since everyone said Gage was a regular, but he said he was working the bar and didn't know if Gage was in there or not. Which sounded strange because he strikes me as the kind of guy who doesn't miss much."

"He doesn't," I agreed. "Did you explain that you're filling in for Carter and he handpicked you?"

"Yeah, and he said he didn't care if Jesus vouched for me, but I was thinking if you asked, it might be an entirely different story."

"I'll talk to him. No word from the ME, right?"

"I don't see that happening until tomorrow at the earliest."

I nodded as he rose from the table.

"Send me those video links," he said. "I'll forward it to

Celia and ask her if she'd like to call her lawyer before I bring her in for questioning."

He gave us a wave as he headed out.

Ida Belle waited until the door closed behind him and cocked her head to one side. "That was strange."

"What was?" Gertie asked.

"That he came over here to request something he could have asked for on the phone," I said.

"He looks worried," Ida Belle said. "You think he's on the same track as you with this?"

"About it being murder? I'm certain of it. Carter said he was a top-notch investigator, and we've seen him in action. If both our noses are out of joint on this, then there might be more to it than what it seems."

"So what's our next move?" Gertie asked. "No use sitting around when we could be information gathering."

"When we don't know that it's a crime, that's referred to as 'wasting time,'" Ida Belle said.

Gertie stared. "Do you have something better to do?"

"Good point. Rambo will be passed out the rest of the afternoon after all that running and the weenies Walter gave him. He's on poop duty for that one."

I said a quick prayer for Walter and nodded. "Sounds like a trip to the Swamp Bar is in order."

Gertie clapped her hands.

"It's not even happy hour yet," Ida Belle said. "There's literally no trouble you can get in there."

I raised my eyebrows.

"Never mind," Ida Belle grumbled. "But I'm not running again."

Despite the fact that it was a Wednesday and was early afternoon, the parking lot at the Swamp Bar was packed.

"What the heck is going on?" Ida Belle said.

Gertie gleefully pointed at the banner over at the dock.

Five Loaves and Two Fish—Fishing Rodeo
Fish Fry to Follow

"Looks like everyone is jumping on the Easter advertising bandwagon," Gertie said.

"I'm guessing Whiskey's route is going to work out better than Wade's, although technically, Wade didn't volunteer for the wagon ride. But I have to say, I'm a bit confused."

"About what?" Gertie asked.

"I thought Catholics gave up the thing they liked most for Lent," I said. "Wouldn't that be drinking for this lot?"

"They're *supposed* to give up the thing they like most," Ida Belle said. "You know, like Baptists aren't supposed to be drinking at all. Check out that crowd at the dock. I see at least five from our choir and two deacons."

Gertie nodded. "Most claim some form of food and give that up—like pastries or chicken-fried steak."

"The line at Ally's bakery is just as long as ever," I pointed out.

"Well, you can give up sugar cookies without giving up chocolate croissants," Gertie said.

"So you're saying there are as many loopholes in religion as there are in the law."

We went inside and I spotted Whiskey behind the bar, refilling snack bowls. He gave us a nod and a smile as we headed his way.

"I'm almost afraid to ask what brings you in," he said, "because it's never a cold beer."

I shrugged. "The same thing that always brings us in."

He raised one eyebrow. "Murder? I thought Gage died of natural causes."

"The ME hasn't issued an opinion yet," I said. "But I have my own thoughts on the matter."

He sighed. "I'll just bet you do. You know, I used to think if you and Carter didn't work out that I was going to ask you out before anyone else made that move, but honestly, you're a lot of work."

I grinned. "I take all of that as a compliment."

He laughed. "I'm sure you do. So what can I help you with?"

"Unless Gage can fly, he didn't get up in that boat without help. At the very least, someone had to remove the ladder and hide his truck."

Whiskey frowned. "Blanchet called me earlier asking if Gage was in last night and who he was hanging with."

"I heard. I also heard you didn't see anything. But unless you weren't here or were struck temporarily blind, we both know that's a lie. You could probably tell me every person who walked through that door last night and what they ordered."

"Maybe, but I don't want to get people in trouble for a prank. I didn't know it might be something more." He ran one hand over his head and cursed. "I still don't want to get anyone in trouble. None of the guys Gage pulled stunts with would have hurt him."

I shook my head. "You never really know."

Whiskey mumble-cursed, but I knew he couldn't disagree. Not with all the weird secrets that had surfaced since I'd arrived in town.

"Fine," he said finally. "He was throwing back beers with Dean Allard and old Red last night."

"Did they leave together?"

"I don't know."

I stared at him and he put his hands up.

"I swear. I had to go unclog a toilet and when I got back, Allard and Gage were gone. Red hung on 'til closing and caught a ride with one of the other fishermen."

"What time did you take on plumbing duties?"

"Around one thirty or a little before. I gave last call when I got back. That was about fifteen 'til."

"Guess I'll have to talk to Allard then. I don't suppose he's here now?"

"Said he was going to be, but I haven't seen him in the bar. Nickel is running the stuff outside. I've only stepped out there once, so could be he's out there."

"Before I run him down, is there anyone you can think of who was mad at Gage over a prank? Not everyone appreciates that kind of humor."

"Yeah. Me."

"You?"

"That fool lit up a whole packet of bottle rockets in the bar. Two people bailed through the windows and dove into the bayou when they caught on fire."

"Seems a reasonable response."

"The windows were closed. The glass guys charge me a premium *and* a trip charge for having to drive out here. That stunt also took out Mort Pitre's new cowboy hat and Minnie Johnson's spangly dress."

"So I should add Mort and Minnie to the list of people who might be holding a grudge."

"And everyone in the bar who saw Minnie after that dress turned to ashes. All she had on underneath was her birthday suit. Minnie's passed a lot of birthdays but never a birthday cake, if you know what I mean."

"I think my suspect list is getting a bit long."

"Well, unless you think I closed up the bar and headed out to assist someone I didn't even particularly like with a prank—something I'm not a fan of for the obvious reasons—then you can leave me off the list."

"Hmmmm, I don't know. Did he pay for those windows?"

"Darn right he did, and I banned him for a month." He sighed. "Maybe if I'd banned him for two, he'd still be alive."

"He sounds like someone who would have found trouble anyway, but I guess you're in the clear. Anyone else who might be looking for some revenge?"

He hesitated for a moment and frowned. "The regular kind, sure, but you're talking about killing someone. That's a whole different kettle of fish."

"But you had someone in mind."

"No. Maybe. Hell, a couple weeks ago, Gage rigged an airbag in Twinkie's recliner. Sent him straight through the ceiling and into his wife's craft room. Took out five dozen hand-painted ceramic Easter eggs that she'd sold on Etsy. His wife took away his Swamp Bar rights and cigars, and he's on painting duty until the entire order is redone."

"You have a regular named Twinkie?"

"Hey, the man likes his snacks along with his alcohol and smokes. Name's Birch Benoit."

Gertie shook her head. "In that case, I'd put my money on his wife Matilda. She's definitely running the show over there. And she's got a mean streak."

"How big is it?" I asked.

"Celia kicked her out of God's Wives for being mean-spirited," Ida Belle said.

"Good Lord. Then why does the man stay with her?"

"Probably scared to leave," Whiskey said.

I laughed. "Thanks for the info."

Whiskey nodded and leaned toward me. "Hey, I heard Carter's back. And there was some other talk about your recent...vacation. You all right?"

"Do I look all right?"

He grinned. "You look full of piss and vinegar, like always. How's Carter? I hear he came back a little worse for the wear."

"He'll be fine. But I think Blanchet's going to be covering for him a bit longer."

Whiskey gave me a single nod. "I won't stonewall him again. If you need anything, let me know. And be careful with this. The guys here all seem like a bunch of good ole boys, but if someone killed Gage and I don't even have a clue who it could be..."

"I get it."

We headed out for the dock to see if any of the people Whiskey had mentioned were around. We hadn't even made it ten paces when Ida Belle pointed out Red, sitting on an ice chest near the fish fryer.

He looked up as we approached and frowned for a second, then slowly broke into a smile and gave us a nod.

"Couldn't tell who you was at first," he said. "Damned eyesight is going as fast as my hair."

Since Red had more hair on his eyebrows than his head and had probably driven himself there, it was a somewhat alarming statement.

"Saw that new hound of yours at the General Store last week," he said to Ida Belle. "Walter was working on scent training. He's going to be something else."

Ida Belle nodded. "I'm thinking about training him as a cadaver dog."

Red's eyes widened. "Good Lord, why? Ain't nobody wanting to find a corpse, especially in the summer."

"I thought I might do some search-and-rescue volunteering," Ida Belle said. "You know, missing persons..."

"Ah. That's mighty nice of you. I'm guessin' folks would rather have a body to bury than just a bunch of unanswered questions to carry around." He looked over at me. "But it seems you already have a cadaver specialist. Heard you was the one who found Gage."

"No. I'm just the one who pointed out he wasn't a mannequin and climbed up there to confirm it."

He gave us a sober shake of his head. "That was a real shocker. Got a call yesterday morning from the guy who loaned you the ladder to climb up there. He didn't know Gage to speak of, but he knew we was friends and figured he'd let me know what happened. I still can't believe it. We was just in the bar throwing back beers. Hell, I keep expecting to see him stroll up with that grin of his, talking about some crazy stunt he wanted to pull."

"Whiskey said you were drinking with him the night before. Did he do any talking about that prank? Maybe tell you who was helping him? There wasn't any way up there without a ladder, so someone had to have removed it."

"Got no idea, and that's the God's honest truth. Me, Gage, and Dean Allard had some rounds, then Gage got a text a little before closing time and said he had to go. Dean stuck around for another round, then said he had to stop buying or he wouldn't be able to pay his child support. But Gage never once mentioned going to do a prank."

"Did he say who the text was from?"

"No. Dean ribbed him for letting his wife keep his...uh, well, 'stuff' in her purse, but I don't think it was Jenny."

"Why not?"

"Gage never seemed to care much what Jenny thought and he had this look about him...excited."

"Like he was meeting someone to set up a prank."

Red shrugged. "Can't say for sure. All I know is he never looked that happy when he was headed home."

Ida Belle elbowed me and inclined her head toward an embankment some ways down from the pier. I recognized the man fishing as Dean Allard. We thanked Red and headed off. Dean spotted us as we were approaching and scowled.

"What do you want?" he asked. "Can't a man get some peace and quiet?"

"If he stays home and lives alone he can," Ida Belle said. "People don't usually come to a holiday event at the Swamp Bar for either."

"Say your piece then and let me be."

"Tell us about Gage Babin," I said.

"What's there to tell? He died."

I watched him closely and saw a tiny twitch of his eye in his otherwise stony expression. But that could mean anything from 'I miss the guy' to 'glad I killed him.'

"Seems a pretty matter-of-fact statement to make about a buddy," I said, trying to goad him into a bigger response.

"Ain't got no buddies. Just a few people I drink with."

"Did you help him with pranks?"

He shook his head. "I'm not the whimsical type. Ask anyone."

I nodded, not necessarily believing him but certain he wasn't the person who'd texted Gage since Gage had received the text while all three men were sitting together.

"Any idea who did help him then?"

"Not a clue. Gage got a text and left the bar before I did. I don't know anything about that mess after. Went home and watched TV until I fell asleep in my recliner, like I always do. Didn't know about Gage until I got a text from one of the fishermen passing it on."

"You don't sound too broken up about it."

He shrugged. "My ex-wife says I'm not 'in touch with my emotions.' Guess she's right. Now, get on and let me fish. I paid my entry."

Ida Belle and I stepped away and I realized that at some point, Gertie had drifted off. I looked around but didn't spot her.

"What do you think?" Ida Belle asked as soon as we got out of earshot from Dean.

"I'm not sure. He's as crusty as ever but I get the impression he's hiding something. But at this point, that could be darn near anything, and absolutely nothing to do with Gage's death."

Ida Belle nodded. "His wife is right—he's definitely not an emotional sort."

"Except when he's whining about his child support."

Dean's grousing about the large support checks he had to write for his six kids probably accounted for half of his conversations.

"You've known him for a long time," I said. "What was your take?"

"Same as you. There's something he's not saying. And I got the impression he was angry, but then, that's his normal state."

I sighed. "I'm afraid this visit didn't really produce much, except pointing out something I hadn't thought about as far as timelines go."

"What's that?"

"Gage didn't leave the bar and go straight to that boat and climb up," I said. "There was no point in sitting there all night. The ME will be able to pin time of death, but I'm pretty sure it was a couple hours at least."

"That would make sense," Ida Belle agreed. "Climb up there just before sunrise. That way, no one sees him doing it, and when the sun comes up, he's up there waving at people on the highway."

"Except he died before he could wave. Or someone killed him." And I was strongly leaning that direction.

"So the question is, where was he between leaving the bar and climbing up into that boat?" Ida Belle said.

"My guess is whoever sent that text could tell us, but since he'd deleted them all, no chance of finding that out anytime soon."

Ida Belle frowned and looked around. "Where the heck is Gertie?"

"I don't know, but an unchaperoned Gertie at the Swamp Bar has never been a good thing."

A cheer went up at the dock and a crowd of people pressed together at the end of the pier. Ida Belle gave me an 'oh crap' look and we hurried that direction. We managed to squeeze through everyone and found Gertie and Nickel arguing at the end of the dock.

"When we were helping take care of your dad, you said I could borrow your boat any time," Gertie said. "And the winning fish is over on the other bank. I saw him first, and now there's three other boats headed that way, trying to catch *my* fish."

Nickel cast a desperate look over at us as we approached. "But that's my new boat, and I didn't mean you could borrow it now. I'm one of the hosts of the event. If I let you use my boat to fish, that's a conflict of interest."

Nickel looked pleased with himself for coming up with such a good excuse, but it was wasted. When Gertie was calling in a favor, she couldn't be deterred.

She looked around at the crowd. "Does anyone here have a problem with my borrowing Nickel's boat?"

"Heck no."

"Let the lady give it a whirl."

"I ain't scared of being beat by no woman."

They all responded at once and those who didn't call out shook their heads.

"See!" Gertie said, relishing her triumph.

Nickel sighed. "Fine. But you can only take it across the bayou. No joyriding and no going crazy. I just got the hull repaired and the whole thing repainted, and I haven't even had a chance to take her out myself yet."

Gertie waved a hand in dismissal. "Your boat will be fine."

"Not if she drives it like she does her own," Ida Belle whispered.

"Hasn't her boat been in the shop for a couple months?" I asked.

"Yes. But for consecutive damage. The woman has never come across a submerged item she didn't want to ram her boat into."

"Is there anything submerged on the other bank?"

"It's Sinful bayous. Atlantis could be down there."

I frowned as Gertie climbed into the boat. "I thought that boat belonged to Whiskey."

"It did. Walter said Whiskey wanted to buy a newer one so Nickel bought it from him."

A resigned Nickel untied his boat and gave it a shove away from the dock. A gleeful Gertie stood behind the center console and fired up the engine. She directed the boat toward the other bank and managed to anchor in between a couple other boats without incident. Nickel let out a breath of relief so loud I heard it even though I was standing a good twenty feet away. I couldn't blame him. His boat was nice and had just been refinished. And Gertie was, well...Gertie.

She grabbed a rod from the side of the boat and baited it, then cast it into the shallow waters near the bank. Line set, she moved to the fishing seat at the front of the boat, secured her rod in the chair's holster, and plopped down. To everyone's surprise, a couple minutes later, she hauled a huge fish into the boat. After wrestling it off the line, she held it up for everyone on the dock to see and a cheer went up.

"That's the winner, for sure," one of the fishermen grumbled.

Another one nodded. "Should have brought our boat."

"Or been due a favor from Nickel," the first one said.

"Look," the second fisherman pointed. "Stinky's got one on the line and from the way it's bending, it's a doozy."

The other guy checked his watch. "He's only got a couple minutes to get it in and back over here. The countdown is on."

Gertie had already gotten her fish secured in the ice chest and pulled up the anchor, and the crowd was urging her to get back across and get the fish on the scale before time ran out. She glanced over at Stinky—whose fish had just broken the surface and looked about as big as hers—and ran to stand behind the center console. As she fired up the engine, I prayed she'd take it easy on the boat and the dock as she made her hasty approach.

But I should have known better.

She followed boating etiquette and eased away from the other fishermen, but as soon as she'd gotten about twenty feet out, she shoved the throttle down. The boat leaped forward, sending her backward onto the driver's seat.

And that's when all hell broke loose.

CHAPTER ELEVEN

As soon as Gertie's butt hit the seat, it exploded and sent her straight up into the air. The boom startled us all so much that half of the crowd hit the dock and the other half pulled out a gun and tried to find a viable target. I settled on a half crouch; that way, I could still see what was going on, but the gunslingers wouldn't accidentally shoot me in their desperation to land the culprit.

Gertie was flailing around in the air, flapping her arms as though she might be able to fly away, but as quickly as she went up, she dropped into the bayou.

"What the heck?" Ida Belle exclaimed, and crouched beside me.

"Oh no! She didn't attach the kill switch!" a man yelled.

Good. God.

The boat barreled, driverless and at full speed, straight for the dock. There was zero way this was going to end well. Everyone scrambled to get off before the boat got there, but in the stampede, some people got shoved off in the water and a couple got trampled. I sprinted off the structure and whirled around as soon as I hit land, watching the boat fishtail in the water, changing direction every couple seconds.

Since no one could predict where the boat would connect with the bank, people were flat-out running for higher ground, and a bunch of old drunk fishermen running didn't remotely resemble a track-and-field event. There were casualties everywhere and I knew the local orthopedist was going to be fully booked come tomorrow morning.

The boat made a last-minute swerve and hit a grassy part of the embankment just to the right of the dock. Unfortunately, it was sloped just well enough that it didn't stop the boat at all. It simply launched it into the air where it crashed onto the top of a new BMW sedan.

I heard a scream of agony and thought maybe someone had gotten sideswiped by the boat, but it was just the BMW owner. The guy—who looked as if he might not even be of legal drinking age—ran over and threw himself on the hood of the smashed car and started weeping about how his father was going to kill him. I took that to mean the car belonged to his father and he probably wasn't supposed to be driving it, much less have it hanging out at the Swamp Bar.

"Gators!" One of the fishermen on the bank pointed, and I jerked around and spotted two of the stealthy creatures heading for the middle of the bayou and then submerging. Gertie was swimming for shore, but she was also being carried farther down the bayou by the current and fighting an uphill battle. The only positive was that a cushion off the seat had remained intact and she had something to float on.

"They've been hanging around ever since the fishing rodeo started," a fisherman next to Ida Belle said.

Everyone started yelling at Gertie to swim faster and at the fishermen with boats to help her out. Several of the gunslingers started firing into the water where the gators went under, but their skill level was all over the board. I heard a couple rounds hit metal and saw fishermen in two of the boats on the other bank leap over the far side into the bayou.

"Cease fire!" I yelled.

"We need to get those gators," one of the shooters said.

"You couldn't hit the side of a barn from ten feet away," Ida Belle said. "That resurrection thing only works on Jesus. You darn near shot your next-door neighbor."

"Leave the sharpshooting to the experts," I said. The men grumbled but lowered their weapons.

Ida Belle and I took aim at the gators, who'd now resurfaced and had locked in on Gertie. Nickel had borrowed a boat from the dock and both he and a boat from the other side of the bayou were headed her way, but even at top speed, they weren't going to get there before the gators did.

"There's a third one!" a woman yelled. "And he's closer."

I spotted the shadow behind Gertie and leveled my pistol for a shot, but Gertie was blocking my line of sight. He moved a little to the right but just when I'd locked in on him, Gertie waved one arm and yelled.

"Don't shoot! It's Godzilla!"

Ida Belle groaned. "She thinks that gator won't eat her."

"She's a floating steak as far as that gator is concerned," a man said.

I hated to agree with him, but no matter how many casseroles Gertie had fed the prehistoric beast, he wasn't tame. And a single swipe of those teeth would be the end. I took aim again but just as I tightened my finger on the trigger, he went under.

I cursed and watched as the other two gators approached. When they were about ten feet away, Godzilla emerged and launched at one of the other gators, his giant open jaw leaving no doubt as to his intention. The other gators, who were at least a foot smaller, immediately dropped underwater. A couple seconds later, Godzilla submerged again as well. As Nickel approached, I saw Godzilla resurface near Gertie and I swear he looked over at her before disappearing in the murky water once more.

Relief swept through me as Nickel pulled Gertie into the boat.

"I don't believe it," I said. "Godzilla warned those other gators off. He saved her life."

Ida Belle shook her head. "It's just not the natural order of things. And if you thought she was impossible about that gator before, she'll really be pushing for protection now. Maybe even knighthood."

"We're not British."

"If she thought it would save that gator, she might switch sides."

Nickel headed back to the dock with Gertie and we hurried over to help her out.

"What the heck happened?" she asked. "I was just driving back and then all of a sudden, there was an explosion and I was airborne."

Dean Allard stepped onto the dock. "I have a guess."

"Well, I'd love to hear it," Nickel said. "I just bought that boat from Whiskey and had it refinished."

Allard winced. "But Gage didn't know that, and my guess is he was looking for a way to get even with Whiskey for giving him that bar ban."

Nickel stared. "You're saying Gage rigged a bomb in my boat? I don't believe it. He took things too far, but he wouldn't kill someone."

"Not intentionally," Allard agreed, "and it wasn't a bomb. He rigged the seat with an airbag. He's done it before."

"Twinkie?" I asked.

Allard nodded. "That was a recliner, but it was the same principle. He probably came out here and did it that same night he...you know."

Nickel called Gage a few choice and well-deserved names and then stomped off toward his boat on the BMW, muttering something about it being a good thing Gage was already dead. I couldn't say I would have supported the level of retaliation this prank would have caused if the man hadn't already died, but I would have understood it.

"I don't suppose I can still have that fish weighed," Gertie said.

Ida Belle and I both stared.

"Well, I'm the one who got blown up and almost eaten by alligators," she said. "Seems only fair."

The fishermen looked around and mumbled among themselves. Finally one of them said, "We wouldn't have a problem with it, but ain't none of us climbing into Nickel's boat to get it. Fact is, he's strapped and madder than I've ever seen him."

Gertie sighed. "That's valid. Oh well, guess that will be the one that got away."

I clapped her on the back. "Everyone needs a good fish story."

We headed back to the parking lot and Whiskey spotted us and came over. "You all right?" he asked Gertie. "Nickel told me about the exploding seat."

"You think it was Gage?" I asked.

"Could be. Hell, probably."

I raised one eyebrow. "And you still can't think of anyone who might have wanted to kill him."

"I see your point. I guess he might have picked the wrong person and the wrong prank at the wrong time. God knows, he'd have been looking down the end of five fingers if I'd gone

133

up in that seat. Nickel's so mad he might go down to the ME's office and punch him anyway."

"Better there than at the funeral," Ida Belle said.

"Possibly, but it wouldn't be unheard of," Gertie said.

"Someone punched a corpse at a funeral?" I asked.

"Yes, but he deserved it," Gertie said.

I just nodded. She was probably right.

"Don't look now, but here comes Nickel," Ida Belle said.

"Are you all right, Ms. Gertie?" he asked as he approached, and I felt my heart tug. Nickel had a colorful past that included a stint in prison, and despite the fact that he'd just lost a serious amount of money, he'd come to check on Gertie. Granted, he'd checked on the boat first, but in Sinful allowances had to be made.

"I'm fine," Gertie said. "But I'm sorry about your boat."

"That's not on you," Nickel said, clearly frustrated. "I can't believe that fool rigged the seat. He could have gotten someone killed, but I guess that never entered his pea-sized brain. I know you're not supposed to talk ill of the dead—"

"I don't have a problem with it," Ida Belle said. "Not if it's the truth."

"Ha," Nickel huffed. "Yeah, I'm with you on that one."

"I'll help you with the repair costs," Gertie said.

Nickel shook his head. "The boat's insured. I'm not a fool like half those men over there...at least, not when it comes to certain things."

"But you'll have a deductible and there's always things you want done better than what insurance is going to cover. Let me pay it. I didn't rig that seat, but if I'd put on the lanyard for the kill switch like I was supposed to, it wouldn't have happened. Besides, your insurance is going to pass some of those costs on to you, especially after they see that BMW."

"I'm more worried about the kid's medical bills when his

father gets a look at his car. I'm certain the kid lifted the keys and he's parked in a No Parking zone. See? So that repair is going to be on his insurance's dime, not mine."

I looked over and sure enough, a big sign clearly indicated no parking and had a graphic that looked like a flying boat.

"Does this happen a lot?" I asked.

"More often than I'd like," Whiskey said. "Hence, the sign. My insurance company insisted. I wouldn't want to be in that kid's shoes when he gets home."

Nickel shook his head. "Shades of our youth. Remember in high school, when the four-wheeler was broken, and we 'borrowed' dad's tractor to take those two girls down to the Redfish Point?"

Whiskey chuckled. "We thought we were going to get lucky. Instead, we got the tractor stuck in between two huge pine trees and it took a crane and a bulldozer to get it out. Far as I know, we're still on restriction for that one."

I smiled. "What about the girls?"

"Never spoke to us again," Nickel said. "It started pouring down rain about the time the tractor got stuck and it was a good mile walk back home."

Whiskey shook his head. "One of them was wearing brand new white Keds. Lord, she was mad enough to spit when we set out on that trail."

"But the other was wearing a thin T-shirt and no bra," Nickel said, grinning. "So the night wasn't completely lost. At least, not when you're a teenage boy."

They grinned at each other and Ida Belle shook her head. "I think that's our call to leave. Gertie needs a shower and I need a shot of something."

Whiskey sobered and looked at me. "About that other thing... I'll give it some more thought. If I come up with anything, I'll let you know."

WE MADE THE TREK BACK INTO TOWN AND IDA BELLE dropped me off at my house before heading out with the still-dripping Gertie. I said silent prayers of thanks that we kept the SUV stocked with waterproof seat covers because otherwise, Gertie might have been walking home. Still, the smell of bayou mud and fish was going to require some time to dissipate.

I was pleased to see Carter's truck in my driveway when we got there and found him perched in my recliner. He was holding a beer and there was an old Western on television, but I could tell he wasn't really paying attention to it.

"You look like you could use one of these," he said, holding up his beer.

"You have no idea."

"Actually, I have a darn good idea."

I sighed. "You've already heard."

"Got sixteen calls in the last twenty minutes alone. As soon as one of those callers has a better cell phone connection, I'm sure the video will be up. Talk is the seat was rigged with an airbag and that Dean Allard said Gage did it."

I nodded. "That's his take."

"What do you think?"

I shrugged. "Completely plausible. Probably likely given the other stories I've heard. But it sheds a new light on who might have wanted Gage dead. There's pranks—like the beer-drinking nun thing—and then there's stuff that could get people seriously hurt or killed. That one crossed a bunch of lines."

"I also heard Godzilla warned off some other gators, but I figure everyone I talked to was half drunk."

"I know you're wanting me to tell you differently, but that's exactly what it looked like."

I gave him the blow-by-blow of the entire incident, and when I was done, he sighed. "We'll never get rid of that gator."

"No. At this point, he might be in Gertie's will." I gave him a once-over. "How are you feeling?"

He shrugged, but I noticed he also looked over at the TV, like all of a sudden, he was interested in whatever was on it that he hadn't been watching before.

"I'm okay," he said, his tone dismissive. "Just sore. You know how it is. Give me another week and I'll be fine enough to work at least."

I stared at him a couple seconds more before heading for the kitchen to grab a beer. He wasn't lying...exactly. Carter was young and in great shape. I had no doubt his physical injuries would heal up quickly and well. It was going to take longer than a week for those ribs, but by next week, he'd probably look mostly back to status quo.

But it was clear to me that mentally there was plenty unresolved. Granted, he had a lot to process. He'd been sent into a situation he was never supposed to be in, and the very people he dedicated years of his life to had abandoned him to his fate. He'd been tortured, although he had yet to talk about it, and I was certain he thought he was going to die over there, despite joking about me taking so long.

It was a lot.

I sighed as I popped the cap off a bottle of beer and took a big swig. I just wished he'd say something to me. I wasn't qualified to dole out therapy, but I was beyond qualified to hand over empathy in spades. I was one of the few people in his life whom he trusted who knew exactly how he felt, and I loved him. If he couldn't talk to me, I wasn't sure whom he'd be comfortable speaking with.

I headed back to the living room, pushing those thoughts out of my mind. I wasn't going to solve the problem tonight. Maybe I'd make a few phone calls—there were a couple of therapists with the CIA that I trusted. Perhaps one of them could give me some advice.

Carter was still in my recliner when I got back, so I plopped on the couch. "Are you watching this?" I asked.

"Not really. Did you have anything in mind?"

"Gertie's got me watching a mystery series set in the Shetland Islands."

He stared. "And you like it?"

I nodded. "The actors are all good and the location is isolated and the lead investigator has lived there forever. And the place has its share of characters. It's like Sinful with no trees, more sheep, and cool accents."

"Except you don't have to catch the bad guys. It sounds interesting enough, but I don't want you to start something over just for me."

"I've only gotten two episodes in, so it's no big deal."

He tossed me the remote and I located the show. I was about to turn it on when someone knocked on my door.

"You expecting anyone?" Carter asked.

"No. But that never matters. Not here."

I jumped up and opened the door, then waved a frustrated and exhausted Blanchet inside. He headed for the other end of the couch and plopped down. Carter straightened in the chair and gave him his full attention, obviously thinking the same thing I was—that this was no casual visit.

"Given all the press, the ME pushed up Gage's autopsy," he said. "He's ruling his death natural causes."

"He made a decision that quickly?" I asked.

"He said given the shape Gage was in and his drinking problem, that it was just a matter of time. Said heart problems ran in the family and Gage had been pushing his body to the limits since he was a teenager. His heart simply opted out of the lifestyle."

"Medical records?" Carter asked.

"Nope. His wife said the only time she's aware he saw a doctor was at the ER to have a fishhook removed from his hand. The ME's requesting the records, but I doubt they tell us anything."

"So the ME didn't think there was anything suspicious about the whole situation?" I asked.

"Not beyond the obvious. And I can't say that I blame him. Him up in that boat dressed as a nun wasn't even the most outlandish thing that's happened here the past two days. And he was well aware of Gage's past exploits, so he didn't see anything unusual with the circumstances surrounding his death."

Carter leaned forward in his chair. "But *you* don't think it was natural causes."

Blanchet stared at him for several seconds, then sighed. "No, dang it. I don't have that sixth sense like Fortune here, but if I'm being honest, everything about that situation feels off to me. I was just going to ignore it, assuming it was just me being out of my element, until Fortune said something."

He shook his head. "Maybe I'm wrong. Maybe we're both wrong. You were there, Carter. You know these people better than either of us. What do you think?"

Carter's brow wrinkled, and I could tell he was seriously considering Blanchet's question. Finally, he answered. "I don't think I'm firing on all cylinders yet, so I wouldn't rely on just my take on things, but when it's all laid out, I'd have to say I don't particularly like it."

Blanchet looked a tiny bit relieved. "So what the heck do I do about it?"

"You couldn't convince the ME to check for poison?" I asked.

"Nope. He said if I could bring him a motive for murder before the body is destroyed, then he'd consider running some panels. But without any clear indication that it was anything other than alcohol, extreme exertion, and a bad heart, there was no point in him spending his time and the parish's money on it, especially since the family isn't yelling about it."

I stared. "Destroyed?"

Blanchet nodded. "Jenny said he's going to be cremated."

"And she isn't asking for a harder look?"

"No. I talked to her myself...tried to convince her to appeal to the ME, but she said she just wants to put it all behind her. That she didn't believe anyone would kill Gage, but he'd been slowly killing himself for years. I tried to appeal to his brother but I got the same thing."

"Given everything I've learned about the family, I can't say that his brother's attitude surprises me," I said. "Their mother basically made Graham responsible for another adult and from everything I've heard about him, he's not going to tell his mother no."

Carter nodded. "Graham has always been at her beck and call. Took over as the man of the house when their father bounced, and always took his position seriously. Gage was always the troublemaker. My mom used to joke and say that they'd have been better off if Graham had become a lawyer instead of an accountant, given that Gage had a lot more trouble than money."

Blanchet put his hands in the air. "Then there you have it. Unless I can come up with a solid reason for the ME to do those tests, Gage's body will be cremated. Someone will get away with murder, and there's not a darned thing I can do about it."

"*You* can't," I said, "but I don't operate with the same rules."

Blanchet shook his head. "I don't want you getting into trouble over this. Gage didn't deserve to be murdered, but you don't need any legal problems trying to find answers about a man's death when even his immediate family isn't concerned."

I laughed. "I just traveled to the Middle East with a fake passport and managed to cross the Sea of Oman underwater and then locate a terrorist compound in the mountains of Iran to rescue Carter. There is nothing I could do here that comes close to matching the potential for trouble that was."

Blanchet blinked, trying to take in everything I'd just said, then he gave me a pointed look. "But you weren't in love with Gage Babin. You didn't even know him."

I huffed, hating that he was right.

"I wasn't in love with Gage," I said. "But I'm in love with right and wrong."

CHAPTER TWELVE

AFTER A FITFUL NIGHT, I WOKE UP EARLY THE NEXT morning. Carter was still asleep, so I eased out of the room, careful not to wake him. He'd tossed around most of the night —something I was aware of due to my own inability to sleep— and he'd finally drifted into a decent sleep a couple hours before. Since he didn't have any duties at the moment, I intended to let him rest as long as he could manage.

I went straight for coffee, hoping the caffeine could spur my creativity. I'd tossed around a million ideas in my head— everything from an appeal or even a light begging to the family to press for a harder look, to stealing the body and seeing if I could get my own assessment. The last one wasn't really on the table, but it showed just how desperate I was for a solution before Gage was reduced to an urn.

I hadn't come up with anything new by the time the coffee finished, so I poured a cup and sat back down, praying for enlightenment. But ultimately, there were only two ways to ensure the situation moved forward into an investigation. Either I convinced Jenny or Graham to push the ME for more tests or I came up with a motive for murder that passed the sniff test. I'd already sent a text to Ida Belle and Gertie telling them to head over when they were awake. They could probably help formulate an approach for the first plan, but I wasn't sure about the second.

The reality was, I could see where a ton of people might be aggravated with Gage, especially if they'd been the brunt of a prank, but I couldn't wrap my mind around murdering a man for it. Nickel was mad as heck over his boat, and definitely had a temper and a prison record, but even he wouldn't have killed Gage over the exploding seat. Unfortunately, from where I sat, the two people who benefited the most from Gage's death were Jenny and Graham, the only two people with the clout to push the ME into further action.

I huffed. The coffee really wasn't doing its job. I still had nothing.

A light tap sounded at the back door and Merlin looked up from his bed in the corner and meowed. I opened the door and saw Ronald standing there. I blinked twice, then, deciding I needed more coffee to take it all in, waved him inside as I shuffled back to my chair.

I motioned to his outfit as he poured himself a cup. "That's a lot for 7:00 a.m."

"Honey, this is a lot for 11:00 p.m.," he said as he put his coffee down and started gathering the dress so that he could sit.

It took a minute.

The dress was something straight out of a British historical, but I had no idea of the time frame. I just knew it was huge and pink, with tons of layers and seams and lace, with a tight bodice, and it went all the way to the floor. When he finally managed to sit, the skirt sat fluffed out as wide as the kitchen table. An enormous pink feather boa was wrapped around his neck and hung almost to his knees.

But that wasn't even the most interesting part.

He wore a huge fancy hat covered in the same satin as the dress with matching lace trim. But on the hat and adorning the sleeves of the dress were birds. And not cute stuffed animal birds—these looked like someone had confused the tailor with the taxidermy shop when seeking an adjustment. I was equal parts confused and fascinated.

So was Merlin.

The cat hadn't taken his eyes off Ronald since he'd entered the kitchen. Normally, he gave Ronald a wide berth. Cats liked to be the craziest one in the room, and I think Ronald and Gertie both challenged that notion. I gave Merlin a hard stare, which he saw but pretended to ignore.

"So...?" I asked waving a hand at the dress.

"Oh, right," Ronald said. "I have a big party in NOLA tonight and I always wear a new dress around a bit to make sure it's going to work."

"A big party on a Thursday night?"

"It's a bachelor party, of sorts. The to-be-married are both bachelors, but they're doing one of those ridiculous destination weddings and fly out tomorrow, so Thursday night it is. At least that's what they say. I think it's because they get discounts for booking midweek."

"And you're thinking about wearing this?"

"I'm not sure. That's why I'm testing it now. There's nothing worse than being shoved into satin and lace for hours on end only to find it's itchy or binds in all the wrong places."

"There are *right* places to bind?"

"Certainly, if one has an uneven body part or—God forbid —signs of overindulging in wine, chocolates, or any number of calories that aren't kind to fitted dress. A tight seam can hide a lot. Not as much as spandex, of course, but we do what we can."

I shook my head. "I'm just going to go the Ida Belle route and move from yoga pants to flannel."

Ronald sighed. "Well, it will certainly be easier and cheaper than going the Gertie direction. And a lot kinder to your body, but it would be a waste. Still, I've got decades to reform you. So what has you frowning this early? It's horrible for the skin."

"Then what's the best time to frown?"

"Don't try to change the subject. As much as I would love to have a serious conversation with you about skin care, we both know you're not interested."

"Busted. It's this situation with Gage."

He nodded. "A lot to unpack. I mean, the nun in the boat thing was hilarious. I give him props for originality on that one, but that exploding boat seat was just mean. I assume Gertie is all right."

"You know Gertie."

"Yes. Got more lives than a cat. But I don't see why you need to waste precious face lines over Gage Babin. You didn't know him, did you? And aside from being comic relief at times —assuming you weren't the brunt of his joke, of course—he wasn't a very nice man. I imagine everyone will turn out for the funeral and pretend they're sorry he's gone, but I expect most of them will drive off and rarely give him another thought. Besides, it's not like he didn't bring that heart attack on himself."

"Unless it wasn't a heart attack."

His eyes widened. "You think he was murdered? What do the police say?"

"Blanchet feels the same as me. Unfortunately, the ME has called it natural causes and without a motive, he's not willing to take a closer look. And since Gage is going to be cremated, there's a very narrow window to come up with a motive good enough to convince the ME to act further on the matter."

"Lord have mercy! No wonder you were frowning. Who are your suspects?"

"Everyone?"

He stared at me in dismay. "I'm going to need another cup."

"Let me. By the time you get up and down in that dress, Gage will be sprinkled across a bayou."

"Yes, I'm going to have to reconsider this for the party. It might be a short night if sitting is such an issue, and I'm still working out the bathroom thing, because no way I'm skipping free champagne. The host always has the good stuff."

Since dwelling on Ronald's bathroom thing was even worse than Gage's potential murder, I focused on pouring the coffee.

"So any ideas who might want Gage dead?" I asked as I sat back down. "Not being sad over someone dying is a far cry from actually killing them. And it would have to be someone close to him or they wouldn't have been there for the prank."

Ronald frowned. "True. Good Lord! Now you've got me frowning too. I will not age over someone like Gage Babin. I suppose if I had to throw out a name, then it would be Jenny. I just don't want it to be Jenny because I like her."

"Why would you settle on Jenny? I'm sure he was no joy as a husband, but I have to be honest; she didn't seem the type."

"Oh, I'm sure she's tolerated all manner of bad behavior from the man, but being an immature idiot and a questionable provider is a completely different thing than cheating."

I perked up. "Gage was cheating on Jenny?"

He nodded.

"Why didn't Ida Belle and Gertie tell me that? Heck, why didn't half the town tell me that?"

"Because they don't know."

"Then why do you know?"

"I saw him with the other woman, lips locked and loaded. I

had these new shoes I was wearing to a charity event the next day and completely forgot to break them in. So I was walking down the street—with protective pads on the bottom of course—and I saw Gage leaving her house in the middle of the night."

"You're sure it was Gage?"

"The porch light was off, so I couldn't see their faces clearly, but I know who the house belongs to. He parked down the street in the other direction and didn't turn on his headlights, but I'd know that muffler with a hole in it anywhere. Been complaining about it for months given he passes my house for work every morning when I'm in the middle of meditation."

"Who was the woman?"

"Nancy Allard."

"No! Dean Allard's ex-wife?"

He nodded.

"Well, this just took an interesting turn. I wonder if Allard knows?"

"A week ago, I would have said if he did, Gage would be dead, but here we are."

I huffed. "Here we are. So the next question is, does Jenny know?"

Ronald held his hands palms-up. "Does she *know* know or know? There's evidence knowing and there's being a woman in a relationship knowing. It's my contention that most women's relationship intuition is just as good as a video when it comes to a cheating husband, but that won't exactly stand up in court."

I frowned. "Or to the ME. But it does open the whole thing to suggestion, and that might be enough of a prompt for him to run a couple tests. It's a small amount of money and time spent on something that could turn out to be a big black mark if this whole thing blows up later."

Ronald nodded and started the complicated process of rising, which involved gathering the dress in different spots and sliding his chair away from the table, then getting just the right stance to launch the weight of himself and all the fabric upward, all while having his insides in a vise, because I had seen Ronald in my hot tub and there was no way his waist naturally fit in that dress. I was surprised he hadn't passed out already.

I couldn't help feeling a bit gleeful as I took another sip of coffee. I'd been presented with a credible pitch for the ME before I'd even finished my morning coffee. It was turning out to be a most excellent morning after all.

Then Merlin struck.

I'd been so absorbed in Ronald's story that I'd completely forgotten the cat in the corner, silently plotting his takeover of the enticing dress. And while he'd managed to contain himself while Ronald was sitting, rising had created a lot of movement, and the jiggling birds were too much for the cat to ignore.

He leaped out of the corner, as only cats can do—without warning and straight up and sideways—landing on Ronald's arm. Ronald let out a bloodcurdling scream as the cat straddled his shoulder and locked his claws into place as he ripped one of the birds off the dress with his mouth.

As I jumped up to try to detach the cat, I heard the front door fly open and feet running down the hall. The panicked and probably injured Ronald had started spinning around, and the bulk of the dress slapped me back into my chair. I did a backward rollover and just as I was about to spring up, I felt a wet tongue on my face.

I looked up to see Rambo rear up on Ronald's legs, now wrapped tightly in the wayward dress, then the young hound proceeded to bay at the cat. Ronald, completely constricted by the dress, teetered back and I jumped up to try to catch him. Merlin, apparently deciding things had gotten loud and way too active, launched off Ronald's shoulder with his prize, but the feather boa had somehow gotten wrapped around him, and he swung back toward Ronald like a giant angry pendulum.

His backward trajectory was all it took to send the imbalanced Ronald pitching off into the laundry room. Merlin, still wrapped in the boa, flew across the room and landed on the kitchen curtains. His claws had barely touched the fabric before he did an impressive leap onto the kitchen table, where he slid into the coffee cups, sending them crashing onto the floor. Then he took another jump over Gertie's head and exited the room.

Rambo was locked in on the cat and couldn't care less about the chaos in the kitchen. He took off after Merlin and I heard them both scrambling up the stairs. A couple seconds later, I heard Carter yell and then the sound of the bedroom window sliding up. I ran to the front of the house and looked out the window, catching sight of Merlin as he leaped off the edge of the porch roof and into the oak tree nearby, the feather boa streaming after him as he went. Then he sat there on the branch, the boa draped around him, glaring at the house as if this was somehow all our fault.

Cat logic.

I looked up as Carter walked down the stairs with a wriggling Rambo. He had small drops of blood on his forehead, evidence of the path Merlin had taken when he fled. A pink feather was stuck in his hair. I was rather relieved to see the puppy because given his dedication to tracking, I had no doubt he would have gone right out the window after Merlin if Carter hadn't caught him first. Ronald shuffled into the living room, covered in laundry detergent and with his legs still bound together by the dress. Carter looked at him, handed Rambo to Ida Belle, then went back upstairs without another word. I wasn't sure if he was going to go back to bed or gather his things up and forget he'd ever met me.

It was fifty-fifty at that point.

"Sorry about Rambo," Ida Belle said. "I was going to leash him before we came inside, but then we heard all the yelling..."

"I just think it's nice to start the day with someone else taking the heat," Gertie said.

"Talk about heat," Ronald said. "Carter in boxers and holding a puppy had romantic comedy written all over it."

"I don't think the joke is supposed to be on the hero in those movies," Ida Belle said.

"No," Gertie said, "but I can't deny that it perked up my morning. Jeb has sexier underwear, but I'm afraid his six-pack is more like a case of marshmallows. Still, there's an argument to be made for a little fluff—"

"No!" Ida Belle interrupted.

"Fine," Gertie said. "I'm going to clean up the laundry room and kitchen and put on another pot of coffee. Maybe you and Ida Belle can cut Ronald out of that dress."

Ronald stared at her in dismay. "This was custom made."

"You got ripped off," Ida Belle said.

"You don't even know how much I paid."

"Don't have to."

"You are not cutting this dress," Ronald declared. "While I've decided it won't work for the event I have in mind, the lace and satin alone are worth more than your entire flannel wardrobe."

Ida Belle shook her head. "Like I said, you got ripped off."

"Close Rambo up in my office," I said. "There's a bone in the top drawer of my filing cabinet. Meanwhile, I'll try to figure this one out."

"I have an idea on that," she said as she hurried off.

When she returned, she motioned to me. "Let's lay Ronald and his cat-attracting garment on the rug and try to roll him the other way and loosen the bottom of that dress. Otherwise, he's going to have to wear it forever and either shuffle one inch at a time or hop like he's on a pogo stick."

"The real problem is when all that coffee hits him," I said.

Ida Belle grimaced. "We're not going there."

"Yes, I'd prefer if we didn't," Ronald said. "This is satin. You don't want lines in satin so undergarments—"

"Got it!" Ida Belle said, holding one hand in the air.

"Okay, Ronald," I said. "Hold still, and we're going to lower you like a piece of furniture."

We each took hold of one of his shoulders and lowered him like a giant colorful pole onto the living room rug. Then I proceeded to roll him across the floor while Ida Belle tugged at the tangled dress. It took two passes and a spin when we ran out of living room, but we finally got the dress hanging back where it belonged, although it would take hours of steam and a commercial-grade iron to get the fabric straight again.

"Now go take that ridiculous thing off," Ida Belle said. "And put on something normal for this time of the morning. Sweatpants maybe."

Ronald stared at her in horror, then glanced outside. "I'm not walking out there as long as that serial killer is lurking. And those feathers are ostrich and expensive. Good Lord, he's eating one of them."

I sighed. "He's going to cough that up all over my rug, and pink does not go with the decor here. Head to the back door and I'll get him in the front. It's time for breakfast, and he's going to want help getting those feathers off."

Ronald gave the cat one final glare before huffing off down

the hallway for the kitchen. A couple seconds later, Gertie hurried in with an open can of tuna.

"This should get him moving," she said. "I got the laundry room cleaned. You can toss him in there."

I took the tuna and stepped out on the porch, calling to Merlin. He stopped chewing on the feather and gave me a nasty look that said all of this was clearly my fault.

"If you want breakfast, you'll get out of that tree and head inside. And stop glaring at me. This is all on you."

He blinked slowly, then turned his head away and up, clearly in a snit as only cats can manage.

"Oh, for goodness' sake," Ida Belle said and stomped past me. "Why in the world are you negotiating with that cat?"

She headed for the tree, grabbed the end of the boa and yanked Merlin off the branch. She snagged him as he fell and tucked him under her arm, then hiked back into the house, taking the can of tuna out of my hand as she passed. Merlin gave me a dirty look but was smart enough to remain still.

"You're probably going to have to sell the house and move," Gertie said.

I nodded. "Thank God cats don't have opposable thumbs."

With Merlin secured in the laundry room, and Rambo chewing on a bone in my office, we finally sat down for coffee. I hadn't heard a peep from upstairs and hoped that meant Carter had managed to go back to sleep. While we indulged in some of Ally's cookies, I told them about Ronald and the middle-of-the-night shoe hike.

"Whoa!" Ida Belle said and exchanged looks with Gertie. "That's definitely something that hasn't made the rounds. Maybe Ronald was mistaken. It's not like only one vehicle in this town has a bad muffler."

"True, but besides recognizing the muffler that's been terrorizing his meditation, you know how Ronald is about stature. He's always trying to figure out how to dress people better. If it was someone else with an annoying muffler, he would have been confused that the shadow of the driver and the muffler didn't match."

"So if we assume he got it right, then the big question is whether Jenny or Dean Allard know," Gertie said.

"Exactly," I said. "Unfortunately, I have no way of confirming with either one of them without giving the whole thing away."

"Why not just hand it over to Blanchet and have him run it by the ME?" Gertie asked.

"I plan on it, but I don't know that it will be enough. It's not exactly motive unless we can prove that the people who might have wanted to kill him over it knew about it."

"Gage was a heavy drinker," Ida Belle said. "Surely he would have run his mouth at some point."

"And I thought of that, but he did most of his drinking at the Swamp Bar. If he'd run his mouth there, it would have made it around town at the speed of text."

Gertie shook her head. "This is bad all the way around. Nancy is friends with Jenny. What in the world was she thinking?"

"Maybe we should talk to Red again," Ida Belle said. "Seems like Gage spent most of his time drinking with Red and Dean, and I don't think even Gage would have gotten drunk enough to tell Dean he was sleeping with his ex. But he might have let it slide to Red."

"And Red wouldn't have repeated it," Gertie said. "He would have known the trouble it would cause."

"Like someone murdering Gage?" I asked.

Ida Belle nodded. "Exactly like that." She pulled out her phone. "I can get Red's phone number from Walter. We should talk to him somewhere besides the Swamp Bar."

I nodded. "It's too early to do anything now. What do you say we head out for breakfast? I haven't been to the café since I've been back."

"What about Carter?" Gertie asked.

"I'll check with him but my guess is he'll pass. I can bring him something back."

Gertie clapped her hands. "I love it when we have a lead."

CHAPTER THIRTEEN

CARTER OPTED OUT OF BREAKFAST, AS I'D EXPECTED, CITING a need to go home and feed Tiny and a promise to Emmaline to stop by for an early lunch. So Ida Belle, Gertie, and I had a long breakfast and talked to other customers about Gage's death, the exploding boat seat, and Celia's run-in with Rambo. After breakfast, we made a pass by the bakery to chat with Ally for a bit and managed to consume a pastry each. By that time it was close to 11:00 a.m., and we figured it was a reasonable time to call.

I waited until we were back in the SUV before dialing the number Walter had provided.

"Who dat?" Red answered, in typical Cajun fashion.

"Hi, Red. This is Fortune Redding. We chatted at the Swamp Bar."

"Heck, I know who you are, girl. What can I do for you?"

"I was hoping I could talk with you a bit more about Gage. Somewhere private. Are you available now by any chance?"

"I guess I sort of am. I'm over at Pops Doucet's place visiting. I try to make it by a couple times a week."

'Pops' Doucet was Whiskey and Nickel's father. He had

terminal cancer and according to his doctors, should have exited life well over a year ago. But he was intent on showing them what true Cajun stubbornness could accomplish and was still hanging on. He was mostly housebound and looked after by Nickel and a day nurse who made rounds, but he still managed poker with his friends every week.

"Do you think he'd mind more company?"

"Pretty sure he'd love some more, especially pretty ladies."

"Great. Then let him know we're going to drop by. And we just left the bakery with a box of goodies."

"Pretty ladies and Ally's treats. The only way this day could get better was if you brought us fresh fish and some good knees."

I laughed. "I could probably manage some fish, but the knees are out of my wheelhouse. See you in about thirty minutes."

"He's at Pops's house," I said when I disconnected.

Ida Belle perked up. "Oh. That might work out even better than we thought. Pops is good friends with Miriam Babin and has known Gage and Graham all their lives. Probably knows them better than anyone but Jenny."

"The bonus package," I said. "Swing by my house and I'll grab some of those fillets you gave me a couple weeks ago from my freezer. They're not exactly fresh, but you caught them, so those and the baked goods should get them talking."

We headed for Pops's house with the fish and the box of assorted pastries and cookies and Red had the front door opened, waving us in, as soon as we stepped onto the porch. We followed him into the kitchen where Pops sat at the table, a glass of iced tea in front of him. We all greeted him, and he gave us a big smile and waved at the chairs.

"Pull another chair in here from the dining room," he told Red.

Red fetched an extra chair and then waved at the refrigerator. "I just made a pot of sweet tea. You ladies want a glass?"

As he served up the tea and brought some plates to the table for the baked goods, we made the required inquiries about Pops's health.

"Got them doctors running around in circles, I do. Said I wouldn't make it through the year and that was almost a year and a half ago. I keep asking 'em for a new date as my boxers is getting worn and I don't want to buy more than I need." He laughed. "You should have seen the look on that doctor's face —me asking about my drawers."

We all laughed and Gertie reached over and squeezed his hand. "We sure are glad you're proving them wrong. I swear, you're looking better every time we see you."

He nodded. "Feel better too. Some say it's remission, but that's not what the tests say. Others say it's a last hurrah before it all gives up the ghost. Or I become a ghost is a better way of putting it, I suppose. I don't care either way. Had a decent life, even though it's a bit shorter than some. Served my country, had a good wife and a business, got two sons who gave me hell for a lot of years but seems like they've turned into decent men. That's all I can ask for."

"Got some good friends, too," Red said, holding up a pastry.

"Heck, my friends are better than my boys more times than not, but don't go telling them I said that. They're supposed to boil me up a mess of shrimp this weekend."

We all laughed again, then Red sobered a bit and looked at me. "You said on the phone you needed to talk to me, private like. Anything you got to say to me, you can say in front of Pops, iffin' that's all right by you."

"Actually, Pops might even be able to help," I said.

Pops's eyes widened. "Don't know what I could help with

unless it's got to do with new boxers. Been studying them on that pad thing Nickel insisted on getting me. Have to admit, though, I like those funny videos."

"It's about Gage Babin."

They both frowned and Red nodded. "I figured that's what you was up to. You find out who was helping him with that prank?"

"No. And the ME is ready to call his death natural causes."

Red shrugged. "Shouldn't surprise anyone."

"Except that I'm not sure it is. And without a good reason for the ME to run tests, he's not interested in pursuing things any further. The only way to get him to take another look is to give him motive for a suspicious death. And I have to get one fast because Jenny's going to have him cremated."

Red shook his head. "I can't give you a motive. Truth was, Gage annoyed a whole lot of folk, but I can't see any of them killing him for it."

"Not even Dean Allard?" I asked.

"Dean's got some issues with his temper, that's for sure, but he's not a killer."

"Even though Gage was sleeping with his ex-wife?"

Pops's eyes widened, and I could tell this was news to him. But Red had no response except a tiny flinch of his cheek. Oh yeah, he knew something.

"Your poker face needs some work, Red."

He shook his head. "Thought it was pretty good."

"You probably do fine playing cards with your buddies, but it's nowhere near CIA good. You knew about the affair. How?"

He blew out a breath. "About a week ago, Allard was hassling Gage about his failure to make his limit in quail season. Allard bagged his the first week while Gage ended the season with half the limit. But instead of getting mad, Gage just laughed, and when Allard didn't get the rise he wanted out of him, he called it a night. Then Gage gave me this smug look and told me if Allard only knew what he *had* bagged that season, he wouldn't be puffing his chest out."

"Gage told you he was sleeping with Nancy?"

Red gave me a sheepish look and nodded. "I told him it was a mistake. Dean never wanted that divorce and although he's not the nicest man alive, he loves his kids and tries to do right by them. I never thought Dean cheated on Nancy, and since all that mess about Venus came out, I think he was hoping she'd consider getting back together."

I sighed. Venus was a previous Sinful resident who had been murdered. The list of suspects was long, as she'd ruined a lot of lives. She liked to get married men drunk until they passed out, then claim they slept together and demand money for not telling their wives. Allard had ended up divorced over it and paying child support for his six kids, although now, everyone knew he hadn't done what he was accused of. It was a bad deal all around.

Pops shook his head. "I can't claim to like Dean all that much, but like Red, I was hoping Nancy would give him another chance. He was a fool to get in a position for Venus to take advantage that way, but given his, um, medical issues, Nancy should have known it wasn't true."

The rumor was Allard's parts hadn't been working for a while, so he'd sworn he couldn't have cheated.

"Given the medical issues, I don't think Nancy ever really believed Dean cheated," Ida Belle said. "But he's still an alcoholic, or he wouldn't have been in the position for Venus to take advantage in the first place. I think Nancy took an opportunity to opt out of a marriage she'd been done with for years."

"You might be right," Pops said. "Still, it's sad for those kids. And for Dean, even though he mostly brought it on himself."

"The real problem here is not that Nancy Allard has a bed partner," I said. "She's single and entitled. But another woman's husband—who's now turned up dead—well, that's a problem. Did Dean know about the affair?"

Red frowned. "He never said anything, and honestly, I can't believe he did because if he had, there would have been trouble between him and Gage."

"The man was murdered," Ida Belle said. "Can't get more trouble than that."

"But that affair had been going on for some time," Red said. "Patience isn't part of Dean's character. If he'd known, he'd have done something straight off."

"Like started a fight," I said.

Red nodded. "Given that they were at the Swamp Bar together several times a week and drunk as heck, I just can't see Dean knowing and there not being trouble."

"Maybe not," I said. "What about Jenny? You think she knows?"

"I doubt it," Pops said. "I'm good friends with Miriam Babin. Don't have the energy to visit no more but I chat with her on the phone a couple times a week."

"Does she know who you are?" I asked. "My understanding was she was really struggling with her memory."

"That's true enough. Some days, she doesn't seem to know me from a can of soda, but others, she's just as lucid as she can be and sounds as normal as she ever was. If Jenny knew about Gage, she would have told Miriam. Those two are thick as thieves."

"Even if she knew how ill Miriam was?"

"Then she'd have told Graham. Couldn't no one get Gage in line better than his mother and his brother. If Graham or Miriam had known about Gage tangling with Nancy Allard, he'd have been out on his ear."

"Probably why he kept it quiet," I said. "One of the many reasons."

Red nodded. "Can I ask how you found out?"

"I have a witness."

"Someone seen 'em together?"

"Yes. At a time of night and in a display of affection that would be impossible to take any other way. But don't worry. My source hasn't told anyone but me."

Red shot Pops a worried look. "But if one person's seen 'em, might be someone else has too. You think someone killed Gage over Nancy Allard?"

"Maybe."

"That would be a huge blow to Miriam," Red said. "Don't get me wrong. She knows her son wasn't the best, but I don't think she ever figured him for something like this. An affair, maybe, but getting himself killed over it? That might just send her straight to the grave."

"Ha!" Pops said. "That woman's tough as nails. Her doctors said she'd be dead years ago. They underestimated her, too, just like mine do me. If Miriam knew what Gage had been up to, she'd have found a way out of that facility and would have set him straight, just like she did when he was a boy."

Red frowned. "Maybe. But I still hope this all turns out to be nothing. Maybe the ME is right and it's natural. Then Jenny, Dean, and Miriam never have to know about Gage and Nancy. Wouldn't do any of them any good now."

I nodded, but I only half agreed. If none of the three knew about the affair, then what Red said was true, but I had a feeling it wasn't the secret Gage and Nancy thought it was. And I'd made a decision.

My next conversation was going to be with Nancy Allard.

Nancy lived in the center of the neighborhood, a couple blocks from Ida Belle's place. We headed to her house when we left Pops's, figuring the element of surprise would be a better route on this one than calling ahead. People tended to panic when they were guilty and had no time to prepare. I'd had very little interaction with Nancy—mostly just a hello when passing downtown—but given that she usually had a ton of kids in tow, we didn't exactly have a lot of common ground to spark a move to anything beyond polite greetings. Plus, those kids kind of scared me. They were loud, messy, and always in trouble, and I already had Gertie for all that.

Her minivan was parked in her driveway, so now the question was could we get her alone long enough to ask if she was having an affair with the now-dead Gage Babin. I expected to hear a racket as we approached the house, probably because I always knew when they were in the General Store by the noise level alone, but it was surprisingly silent.

"Maybe she's drugged them all," Gertie said as she knocked on the door.

A minute later, Nancy opened the door and stared out at us. She'd obviously been crying, and she had dark circles under her eyes. I looked behind her, expecting the parade of noise to begin any minute, but the house was strangely silent and impeccably neat. Maybe she *had* drugged them.

"Can we have a chat?" Ida Belle asked.

"I'm not feeling well. Can it wait?"

"Given that Gage is going to be cremated unless the ME has a reason to call his death suspicious, I'm going with no," I said.

Her eyes widened. "What's that got to do with me?"

I shrugged. "I guess I was thinking that since someone might have killed the man you were having an affair with, you might want that person to pay."

She stared at me for several seconds, not even breathing, then finally sighed and stepped back for us to enter. We followed her into the kitchen and took a seat at the kitchen table.

"Your kids aren't here?" Gertie asked.

"Ha," she said, and waved her hand around. "Look at this house. The only time it's this clean is when Dean's got them. It will look and sound like a tornado hit ten seconds after he drops them off."

"So you're not going to deny your affair with Gage?" I asked, getting right to the point.

"Doesn't seem to be a point since you already know."

"So it was common knowledge?"

"God no! But you're CIA. I figure you've got spies and cameras everywhere."

"Former CIA, and we don't just set cameras up everywhere in the hopes of catching people doing bad things. We sort of need a reason."

"It's the government. That's pretty much all the reason they need for most things."

I ignored her somewhat accurate point. "So neither Jenny nor Dean knew?"

"No. Jesus. It's not exactly something I'd brag about down at the General Store or talk about at a church social. I have to live in this town, and so do my kids."

"Not to mention Jenny is supposed to be your friend," Gertie said, frowning.

Nancy huffed. "You think I don't know that? It's not like I feel good about it, because I don't. Never did. Jenny's a fine woman, and yes, we're friends, of sorts, but we're not close. Jenny's a really private person. I don't know that she's close to anyone but the Babin family. But you're right—I owed her better."

I put my hands in the air. "Then I have to ask, why? We all know Dean has his issues, but was Gage really any better? He spent more time drinking with your ex than at home with his own wife. Given that alcohol was a factor in your own divorce, you'll have to forgive me if I don't see the draw."

"You're right, he's Dean all over again, except all the parts were working. Heck, truth be known, Dean's probably more responsible than Gage was. Least he holds down a good job and he's good with the kids. Never drinks when he has them."

I raised one eyebrow, as she still hadn't given me any positive reason for starting up a relationship with Gage.

"Look, it's not like it was some star-crossed-lovers thing," she said. "He just started talking to me one day last summer after dropping my kids off—he and Jenny had been babysitting so I could make a doctor's appointment—and he was flirting with me. I'm not so out of the game that I didn't know what he was doing, but it's just that it's been a long time since someone's made me feel attractive and I missed that attention and, well, the other."

She shook her head. "It's hard to explain because in so many ways, Gage was just like Dean, even worse in a lot of them, but Gage had a different energy. I'm sure Dean is depressed but he won't see a doctor about it, and the drinking only makes it worse. But Gage was upbeat and fun. Being married to Dean was like living with Eeyore."

"Whereas Gage was Tigger?" Ida Belle asked.

Nancy gave her a small smile. "That's fairly accurate in both cases."

"But if it wasn't love, then why betray Jenny that way?" Gertie asked. "You might not have been close, but she's another woman married to an alcoholic cheater. You left Dean for cheating on you. Or at least, assuming he had."

"I left Dean for a lot of reasons. The cheating was just the final straw. And I never wanted to hurt Jenny. I figured it was going to be some quick and done thing and she'd never have to know. It was selfish, but I wasn't trying to ruin her life. I'm not like Venus."

"No one is suggesting that," I said. "But if it wasn't love, then why have you been crying and not sleeping?"

She pursed her lips and gazed out the window for several seconds. "I wasn't supposed to catch feelings, but I did. A little, anyway. Don't get me wrong, I wasn't thinking we had a future or anything, but him dying hurt more than I thought it would. Maybe because it was so unexpected. Maybe because I let myself care more than I should have. Doesn't matter anymore, as it's over."

"It matters if someone killed him," I said.

She shook her head. "I don't believe that. He annoyed people with those jokes of his, but that's no reason to kill a man. His heart was bad—really bad—and he didn't do a thing to take care of himself. One night when we were...you know, he almost passed out from the exertion. And I've got to tell you, it wasn't exactly the stuff X-rated movies are made about."

"And you're sure Dean didn't know?"

"No way! And even if he did, Dean would never... He's a lot of things, but he wouldn't kill somebody."

"Even if a man he considered his friend was sleeping with the ex-wife he never wanted to divorce?"

A slight look of fear crossed her face, and she hesitated before shaking her head again. "No way. He isn't capable, and besides which, he didn't know."

"*I* knew. And I can assure you I don't have cameras mounted around town. If I found out, other people could have as well."

She shook her head, firmly planted in a state of denial.

"Another thing I'm certain of is that Gage had help with

that prank, and since that person hasn't come forward, I have to wonder why. Do you have any idea?"

"No," she said, a little too quickly.

She wasn't lying about not knowing, but I could tell she had her suspicions. And given my line of questioning, they scared her. Dean had denied helping Gage with pranks when we'd talked to him, but I wasn't sure he was being truthful. Maybe he was just trying to avoid being involved in a police investigation. Or maybe he was lying because he'd handed Gage a poisoned beer for sleeping with his ex.

"Dean helped Gage with some of his pranks, didn't he?" I continued to push. "And he was drinking with Gage that night at the Swamp Bar."

"That happened more nights a week than it didn't," she argued. "Unless Dean had the kids, he was in that bar. And since Gage was all but paying rent there and he and Dean were buddies, of course they spent a lot of time drinking together. That doesn't mean Dean talked Gage into some prank trying to work him into a heart attack. It's ridiculous to think."

"What if the climbing wasn't what killed him?"

Her jaw dropped. "What are you—no! No way. If you're suggesting what I think you are, which is outrageous, then there's no way it could have been Dean. Gage wasn't a small man. There's only a handful of people I know who could have hauled him up into that boat."

"I have no doubt Gage climbed into the boat himself. I just don't think he was planning on dying when he was up there. But it might have been someone else's plan."

"I don't believe it. I don't think anyone would have done something like that deliberately, but especially not Dean. If he'd killed Gage, it would have been in a fistfight, and it wouldn't have been what he was trying to do. He's not a violent man, just a sad, angry one."

I studied her for a moment. She was clearly nervous, but I couldn't figure out why. Nothing she'd said so far was a big flaming neon sign. Unless there was something she wasn't saying. Then I remembered Red's comment.

All I know is he never looked that happy when he was headed home.

"Gage came here that night after he left the Swamp Bar, didn't he?"

CHAPTER FOURTEEN

I COULD TELL BY THE TIGHTENING OF NANCY'S JAW THAT I'D hit the nail on the head.

"CIA, remember?" I said.

"Oh man, I don't want no trouble. If the police come here questioning me, then everyone's going to find out. Then the whole lot of hypocrites in this town will come down on me and my kids. I can't afford to move, and the man's dead. What purpose would it serve now for everyone to know? It's only going to hurt the living."

"Blanchet is not the sort of cop that would blow up a bunch of kids' lives over something that could be handled in a private conversation."

She blew out a breath. "Gage came by around two."

"What about your kids? I know Dean was drinking with him at the bar."

"I had my rugs cleaned Monday, so their grandparents agreed to keep them overnight so everything could dry properly. I have to practically beg them for anything to do with the kids—it's Dean's parents that live close, not mine. Normally, Dean would have taken them, but the tides are running early these days, so he would be out on the boat long before they needed to be up for school."

"What time did Gage leave?"

"About four," she said. "I needed him out of here before fishermen and oil riggers start heading out for work, and they start early. He didn't park in front of the house, of course, but once people start driving by, they might see him. Usually, he's gone well before that."

"But not this time? Did the partying go on too long?"

She snorted. "He was so drunk when he got here, he couldn't even...uhm, party. I thought he'd sleep it off for a couple hours, but he just turned on the TV, asked me for some aspirin, then kicked back with my good bottle of whiskey. I told him a fat lot of good it did to take the aspirin if he was going to keep drinking, but he's a man."

We all nodded.

"Who was he meeting when he left?" I asked.

"Far as I knew, he was going home. I didn't even hear about all that boat mess until it started circling around the Sinful gossip train the next morning."

"You're sure he never mentioned a prank he was going to pull?"

"No. But then, I never cared for any of that. He wouldn't have said anything to me."

"I'm surprised Jenny never questioned him about coming home so long after the bar had closed."

Her jaw twitched again, and I knew there was something else she wasn't saying.

"Nancy? Is there something you want to tell me?"

"I don't want to make any more trouble for Jenny than she's already got. I already did her wrong sleeping with her husband."

"Right now, you're the last person to see Gage alive. If you know anything about his mental state or his plans, you have an obligation to tell. If this wasn't natural causes, it might point to the guilty party. If it *was* natural causes, it might explain why he was so stressed his heart gave out, and then the police could put this whole thing to bed."

She stared out the window, then huffed out a breath. "He told me he was going to file for divorce as soon as his mom passed."

"He told you that the night he died?"

"No. About a week before. I asked why he didn't just do it now if that's what he wanted, but he said his mom would cut him out of the will. I didn't put much stock in it because it sounded crazy."

"It might sound crazy, but it's accurate."

Her eyes widened. "Seriously! Well, he was mad as heck about something but wouldn't tell me what. I figured their marriage wasn't great—alcoholics are really married to the bottle—and besides, he was over here with me instead of his wife. But he'd been pretty low-key until that night. Something happened to set him off. Now that I know his hands really were tied on the inheritance, him being so angry makes more sense."

"And you don't have any idea what he was mad about?"

"None whatsoever. We never talked about Jenny or Dean or personal stuff. Didn't do much talking period, if you want the truth. It wasn't a talking kind of arrangement. Now, if you don't mind, Dean will be dropping the kids off soon, and I think it's best that he doesn't find you here."

We rose and headed for the door. Nancy glanced up and down the street as we stepped out.

"Hey," she said. "You're not going to say anything to Dean or Jenny, are you?"

"I don't have any reason to," I said. "But the police are

going to want to talk to you. This isn't going to go away, Nancy. I think you better start working up your story or apology, whatever you feel is needed, because I'm afraid you're going to need them before this is over."

We headed for Ida Belle's SUV and Gertie slammed the door when she got in. Ida Belle shot her a dirty look, then sighed.

"I can't even be mad about the door when I felt like doing it myself," she said.

"What the heck was Nancy thinking?" Gertie ranted. "Jenny is one of the only people in town who will babysit that brood of hers. You don't have an affair with a friend's husband. Even a casual friend."

"You don't have an affair with *anyone's* husband," Ida Belle said. "But them being friends—of sorts—just makes it worse. I don't understand people."

Gertie nodded. "With friends like that... As much as it pains me to say it, even if Carter lost his mind and came calling, there's no way I'd take him up on it."

I smiled. "See, that's a real friend."

Ida Belle frowned. "Gage has never been one to keep his mouth shut, especially when he was mad. If he really told Nancy he was going to divorce Jenny when his mom died, I'm willing to bet he said the same thing to Jenny when they got into it."

"If he did, then that gives Jenny even more motive to kill him," Gertie said. "All those years of carrying a deadweight husband, and then he's going to effectively kick her out of the house she's been paying for and maintaining all these years?"

"Not to mention the years spent caring for Miriam," I said.

Ida Belle nodded, her expression grim. "And if Jenny knew about the affair, that's all the more reason. Insult to injury. The only way she recouped even a small portion of her investment was if Gage was dead."

I nodded. "So we're right back around to the big question —did Jenny or Dean know?"

"Can't be certain without asking," Ida Belle said. "And thank the Lord that one's not on our plate."

Gertie nodded. "But I don't think Blanchet is going to be falling over himself thanking us for the information."

He wasn't.

———

CARTER WAS SCHEDULED FOR DINNER WITH EMMALINE THAT night and I had decided to give the two of them some mother-son time, so I begged off, citing a headache and the over-whelming desire to sit in silence. After all the crap I'd heard today, both seemed like the best option. Carter said he'd prob-ably stay the night at his own house but would call if he changed his mind. I figured he wanted to sleep somewhere there was no risk of being awakened by a cat using his fore-head as a launching pad.

Gertie always made sure I had a chicken casserole in my freezer for nights when a sandwich just wouldn't do and there was no one on hand to cook me anything better, so dinner wasn't an issue. I had just polished off my second helping and was about to grab another beer and settle back in my recliner when I heard a knock on my door.

And not a polite knock. If knocks had feelings, I'd say this one was somewhere between aggravated and exhausted. I figured it was Blanchet.

He didn't even speak when he entered my house—just headed straight for the kitchen, came back to the living room with a beer, and flopped down on my sofa. I never said a word as he took a couple sips, stretched his arms above his head, closed his eyes, and then let out a long-suffering sigh.

Finally, he looked over at me. "If this is what being the sheriff is normally like in Sinful, then I understand why Carter went back to Iran."

"I take it things didn't go so well with the ME when you presented him with the new information?"

"Oh, things went great, until they didn't. I told him about the affair, and that Nancy had admitted it—I just left out the part where she hadn't admitted it to me. Then I launched into how I was hoping he'd agree to run more tests without me having to question Jenny or Dean about it as I wasn't interested in blowing up a bunch of people's lives unless a crime had been committed, especially since there were kids involved."

"And he went for it?" I was a little surprised it had been that easy.

"Apparently, Jenny used to clean for them before his wife stopped working, so there was probably some sense of obligation there. I topped it off with allowing that I might be wrong, which I think swayed him more than the tug of an old obligation."

I snorted. "Yeah. That's where you got him. He's the 'never been wrong' type."

"Well, it was enough to get him to run the standard toxicology panels, which he actually offered to do while I waited."

I straightened. "You have the results?"

He nodded. "That's where things went south. The results were negative for everything, and it's a fairly extensive list."

I stared at him, a little stunned. "What the hell, Blanchet?"

"I know. I've thought about nothing else since he told me. Went over every single aspect of the situation on my drive over here, but no matter what the evidence says, I still can't shake the feeling that man was murdered."

"Me either. You have the beer can recovered from the boat? That had to be the delivery mechanism, right? I mean, no way he took enough poison to kill him, then managed to climb up that ladder, get dressed in that habit, and get in position. And no way he would have risked climbing up in the habit, either."

Blanchet nodded. "If this was murder, then my guess is whoever did it waited until he was set, then popped the top on that can of beer, dumped in the poison, and hiked up the ladder to hand it to him."

"So you can test the remaining liquid for more obscure poisons?"

"There's only a bit of liquid remaining. It would yield two tests, maybe three. That gives me three chances max to guess correctly, and I don't have any idea where to start."

"This blows."

He threw his hands in the air. "Agreed. But what the heck can we do about it? Nothing, that's what. Anyway, I started to just head home and save this bit of cheery information for the morning, but then I figured you'd want to know as soon as possible. And I wanted to thank you for getting me enough to push the ME for the tests."

"You have Ronald and his unwavering desire to wear uncomfortable shoes for that one."

"Then you tell him I said thanks. He scares me a little." He sighed. "It doesn't exactly clear my conscience, but I'm glad the ME did the tests. At least I know I did everything I could. So did you for that matter. Anyway, I guess I'll get out of here and hunt up some dinner."

"I have half a chicken casserole you can take with you."

"Gertie's?"

"Who else?"

"That might just make a really bad day a little less crappy. I'm sorry I couldn't make this stick."

"It's not on you. But if we're right, and Gage was murdered, someone was very clever."

"It's no consolation when the criminals are smarter than the good guys."

———

THE NEXT MORNING, I WAS ON MY THIRD CUP OF COFFEE and still mulling everything over when I heard my front door open and Ida Belle called out. A couple seconds later, they headed into the kitchen and Gertie went straight for the coffee. Ida Belle waved her off when she lifted the pot in suggestion and grabbed a bottled water from the refrigerator instead.

"Already had your limit?" I asked.

"I woke up at 3:00 a.m. and couldn't sleep anymore. Already had my limit and all of Sinful's for that matter."

"Why couldn't you sleep?" Gertie asked. "Walter snoring again?"

"He's never stopped. And I've been friends with you enough years to know how to handle snoring. Besides, Walter's practically a mosquito compared to your chain saw."

"Doesn't seem to bother Jeb," she said.

I laughed. "I'm guessing it's all the activity before the snoring that makes it more tolerable."

"That's true," Gertie said. "He does have trouble keeping up with me. We're working on his stamina, though. The other night—"

"No," Ida Belle said. "I could have been awake since last

Tuesday and still wouldn't be tired enough to listen to *that* conversation."

"So what had you up last night?" I asked.

"All this mess with Gage. I got to thinking about it after you called last night and told us what the ME found."

Gertie frowned. "You mean what he *didn't* find?"

Ida Belle nodded. "Well, all that nothing had my mind whirling and I had stupid dreams. One of them was about Merlin poisoning Gage for putting oregano in his catnip toy. He was still wearing that feather boa, by the way."

Merlin, who'd been sitting on his bed in the corner, pretending to ignore Ida Belle, as she was the purveyor of the dreaded hound, rose and gave her a hard glare before heading to the back door and meowing.

I let him out and Ida Belle raised an eyebrow. "Have I insulted his majesty by reminding him that he was wearing girlie things?"

"I think the irony of being strangled by bird feathers while attempting to nab a bird wasn't lost on him," I said.

"You're giving that cat a lot more credit for deep thinking than he deserves," Ida Belle said. "He's just mad that you took the stuffed bird away."

"Probably. I don't suppose a solution to our problem came to you in these vivid dreams?"

"Unfortunately, no. After the cat and the boa dream, I gave up and headed into the garage. Rebuilt a carburetor for a '69 'vette."

"You don't own a '69 'vette," Gertie said.

"Someone does," Ida Belle said. "I can sell it on eBay for a huge profit. Work like that relaxes me, so I always keep some engine parts around to tinker with."

Gertie shook her head. "I'll stick to knitting and baking. The garage is cold, and I'd have to put on shoes."

"I can't say that I slept overly well either," I said, "but I'm as blank as Ida Belle on answers."

It wasn't exactly a lie. I hadn't slept well and the situation with Gage was definitely part of it, but Carter being 'off' was fast becoming a bigger concern. As Blanchet said, I hadn't been in love with Gage—and right or wrong, he was already dead and I was completely out of ideas.

Gertie gave me a sympathetic look. "It was bound to happen sooner or later. And by that, I mean that someone got away with it, because I believe you're right about Gage being murdered."

"Really? I didn't think you were convinced."

She shrugged. "Maybe I didn't want to be. For Jenny's sake anyway and Miriam's, even though they might not even tell her. But with you, Blanchet, and Carter all in the same boat, it's hard to think otherwise."

"I appreciate that."

"You shouldn't be hard on yourself, though," Ida Belle said. "Neither should Blanchet. It's not like you can force the ME to keep Gage stored until you come up with something else to test for. He'll never agree to testing randomly."

"And I can't really blame him on that one," I said. "Like he said, it would be a waste of taxpayers' money and his time."

Ida Belle nodded. "Sometimes they just slip through the system."

"I can understand it and still not like it," I said.

"The older I get, the more I feel that statement," Ida Belle said. "So what would you like to do today?"

I stared out the window and shook my head.

Ida Belle sighed. "You can't let it go, can you?"

"No. But heck if I know what to do about it."

I heard a tap at the back door, and when it inched open, Ronald peered in.

"Is it safe?" he asked.

"Depends on what you're wearing."

He stepped inside and I blinked. For the first time since I'd laid eyes on the man, Ronald looked absolutely normal. And he was wearing jeans. I was fairly certain I'd never seen him in jeans. Granted, it was skinny jeans, which I still didn't like on men, but nevertheless, denim was actually touching his skin. His shirt was a standard polo, although he'd managed some flair there with the bright turquoise background and fuchsia palm trees. His feet were clad in standard Nike running shoes.

"Are you ill?" I asked as he sat down.

"Why do you ask?"

I waved a hand up and down. "Because you're dressed like you're going to a costume party and the requirement is 'average dude.'"

"It's self-defense. That cat of yours is a menace, and then there's Godzilla to worry about as well. I appreciate that he's nabbed some bad guys and saved Gertie, but he still scares me. The bottom line is I end up with too many damaged garments when I come over here and I run far too much. It's like a whole year of cardio shoved into a single visit."

"I can't believe you even have those clothes," Gertie said. "You *are* still rocking the look with that shirt."

"Yes, well, one can only stray so far from oneself."

"There's coffee if you're interested."

"God no. I've already had a pot and a half. I'll have to drink three gallons of water for my skin to recover, but I needed all that caffeine for my head."

Gertie nodded. "Hangover. I've been there."

"It was worth it," he said. "That party will go down in history. Literally, as the police were called."

"What happened?" I asked.

"Well, as required for bachelor parties, there were games

and prizes. We were playing Pin the Macho on the Male and two people got into a fight over the prize tiara."

Gertie perked up. "Pin the Macho on the Male?"

"No!" Ida Belle said.

Ronald rolled his eyes and patted Gertie's hand. "I'll send you the purchase link. Anyway, the tiara was spectacular. It wasn't real stones, of course, but it was high-quality fakes. And so pretty with all that purple, green, and gold. Most of us weren't even close with our attempts—I mean, who could be after all the champagne and that spinning while blindfolded? But Greg and Peter were both really close, and the vote was split right down the middle. So no consensus on a winner."

"So who won the fight?" Gertie asked.

"That depends on who you ask. Greg ultimately left with the tiara, but that's because his friend Eleanor decided to pin the 'macho' on Peter. And given that she hadn't been spun around and wasn't wearing a blindfold, she was dead-on accurate."

Even though I was a girl, I flinched a little.

"Anyway, Peter dropped the tiara and started screaming like a banshee, and one of the hotel employees called the police, probably thinking someone had been murdered."

"So did they arrest the 'macho' pinner?" I asked, making a note to wear Kevlar if I ever found myself at a party with Ronald's friends.

"Lord no!" he said. "Peter wouldn't press charges. Said it was all an unfortunate accident due to high heels."

Gertie nodded. "You never rat out your friends. Even when they've stabbed you."

"Oh, the culprit isn't friends with Peter, but she was wearing this simply divine Valentino dress, and Peter couldn't bear the thought of her sitting on a jail cell bench while wearing it. A man has to have priorities."

He shifted slightly and pinned his gaze on me. "And although all that was spectacular fun and just as enjoyable in the retelling, it's not why I forced myself into denim and trekked over here this morning. I have gossip for you."

"We verified the affair with Nancy yesterday," I said. "She didn't even bother to deny it."

He waved a hand in dismissal. "Not about that. About Jenny."

I perked up and Gertie practically bounced in her chair. Even Ida Belle lifted her eyebrows.

"Well, come on!" Gertie said. "Spill the tea."

"So before the whole macho male fiasco, there was a magician doing his thing. He had this fog machine he used in one of his tricks, and no way I was letting steam touch my hair, makeup, or dress, so I headed into the hotel lobby for a breather and a break. Judging people based on their attire can be exhausting."

"Then you must be completely worn out living next door to Fortune," Gertie said.

He sighed but I noticed he didn't disagree. "Anyway, I was tucked away in a horribly uncomfortable chair in the far corner, sort of hidden behind a banana plant, when the elevator dinged and Jenny stepped out. I was surprised, of course, because it wasn't exactly the place I'd normally see her, but then a man stepped out behind her and put his hand on her back while leading her to the entrance. They were walking very close together, their heads inclined toward each other, and I could tell the conversation was serious and private."

"You're sure it was Jenny?" I asked.

"Of course I'm sure. She was wearing those ghastly shoes she wears to clean. I know they're supposed to be heaven for feet, but you'd think if you're going to rendezvous with an eligible man that you'd pick something sexier. Anyway, I followed them and watched out the front window as he gave her a hug—a very long, rubbing-her-back hug—then she gave him this dazzling smile and headed off. He was grinning and humming when he walked back inside."

"Can you describe the man?" I asked.

"Why would I have to do that? I know who he was."

CHAPTER FIFTEEN

"WHO?" ALL THREE OF US SHOUTED AT ONCE WHILE RONALD just sat there smiling like the cat who'd swallowed the canary.

"Brent Copeland. He owns the hotel the party was in."

"Her ex-husband," I said. "Well, that's interesting."

Ronald nodded. "I thought so. So now the question is, was Jenny cheating on Gage because he was cheating on her or vice versa?"

"Or neither," I said. "It's possible they could have both been stepping out and neither knew about the other."

Ronald, Ida Belle, and Gertie all gave me a look that adults give to children who don't quite understand.

"Women always know, remember?" Gertie said.

"Right," I said. "But that doesn't mean Gage would know. I mean, he was a man. And definitely the immature, not-emotionally-developed kind."

"Nor did he seem to pay much attention to his wife," Ida Belle said. "Hard to notice something when you're not watching in the first place."

"I assume since you said Nancy admitted the affair that you gave the information to Blanchet?" Ronald asked.

I nodded and told him about talking to Nancy and Blanchet, and the ME's subsequent testing. His expression went from excited to utterly disappointed.

"So it's not murder?" he said and huffed. "And here I was thinking I'd provided the clue that might unlock the whole can of worms. How disappointing."

"According to the ME, it's not murder," Gertie said. "But Fortune, Blanchet, and Carter are all in agreement that something isn't right."

"Well, I don't care how much education and fancy equipment that man has," Ronald said. "If Fortune says he was murdered, then he was. I'm always Team Fortune."

"Can we leverage this information about Jenny for more tests?" Gertie asked.

I thought about it for a couple seconds, then slowly shook my head. "I don't see how. I mean, it's just more motive, and we already had plenty. But what we don't have is an idea about specific poisons to look for, so we're back to the same issue that the ME is not going to start randomly testing Gage's blood for everything."

"Can you at least convince him to keep blood samples for future testing?" Ronald asked. "I mean, shouldn't they be doing that already these days given how many people are cremated?"

"That's a great thought," Ida Belle said. "I was just reading an article about that yesterday and wondered myself what the criteria for storage would be."

Ronald nodded. "It just seems like we're making it too easy to get away with murder if we allow all the evidence to be destroyed. All it takes is a bad ME and criminals are practically skipping around with no repercussions."

"They don't even have to be bad at their job," Ida Belle said. "They could be ill, or exhausted because they just had a baby, or going through a divorce. MEs are still human and subject to all the things that might affect the quality of their work. And if the victim's general health supports their initial findings, why go the extra mile?"

"Especially if the family isn't yelling about it," I agreed. "And they certainly aren't in this case."

Gertie frowned. "We can't just sit here with all this information and do nothing. There's got to be some way to stop the cremation."

"At this point, Jenny is the one holding all the power," Ida Belle said.

"Then let's go talk to Jenny again," Gertie said.

"Why?" Ida Belle asked. "The way things stand now, she's our main suspect. If anyone wants Gage sitting in an urn, it's her."

"I agree that their marriage was sketchy at best," Gertie said. "But if she was back with Brent, she didn't need Gage to die. She could have simply left him and moved back to NOLA. Brent is loaded. He owns a hotel, probably several."

"I can confirm that," Ronald said. "I can also confirm through my sources that he's never remarried since he and Jenny divorced. And although he's been linked with several society women, none of the relationships have ever seemed serious or lasted more than a year. And he's never lived with anyone."

"The plot thickens," Ida Belle said. "But I agree with Gertie—Jenny could have left Gage at any time. Why stick around? The house isn't worth enough to stay in a bad marriage and half belongs to Graham anyway. If she's back with Brent, she's got a place to live and a job. Even if it went south, she'd have been back in NOLA and made connections again if she needed to change directions later on."

I nodded. "Doesn't seem like a good risk for the slight gain, especially if she's already landed the prize fish."

"I *would* go with pure old-fashioned jealousy and insult as a motive," Ronald said. "But those are usually crimes of passion."

"Like the whole macho on the male fiasco," Gertie said.

"Exactly," Ronald agreed. "But if someone got away with murdering Gage, they planned very well. Not only is the murder undetected, but we don't even know how it was achieved. You're assuming it was poison, but who gave it to him? Has to be the same person who helped him up in the boat, right?"

"I think so," I said. "Which is why I think no one has come forward, even though his death has been put forward as natural causes."

"Maybe it was Brent," Ronald suggested. "Could be she wasn't willing to up and leave Gage. She might not have trusted Brent enough, or religious reasons, or even just a long-standing history of basically being a member of the family."

"But Gage wouldn't go out to the highway in the middle of the night with Brent," I said. "He'd be a stranger to Gage at best and the ex-husband of his wife at worst. No way he'd trust him. No. This was someone Gage knew. I suppose Brent could have paid off a local, but I can't see his type taking the risk. He would assume by default that he was positioned to win and wouldn't gamble unnecessarily."

"I really don't want it to be a local," Ronald said. "Unless it's Celia. I'd be fine with Celia."

"Celia's not smart enough to pull it off," Gertie said. "And Gage would have met Brent out on the highway before he even acknowledged Celia's existence. He hated her."

Ida Belle shook her head. "Well, I don't see any way to alibi everyone Gage knew and trusted enough to be out there in the middle of the night with. He was a salesman, after all, and spent far too much time drinking with the good ole boys. And even if we had an exact list, how many are going to have an alibi that can be verified?"

I nodded. "They'll all say 'I was home alone sleeping.'"

"Exactly," Ida Belle said.

"Maybe we should talk to Graham," I said. "I know he wasn't exactly a fan, but Gage was his brother. And by all accounts, Graham is a mama's boy. Surely if there was a chance that Gage was murdered, Graham would want to know. If not for his own sake, then for his mother's."

"Even though he might not plan on telling her?" Gertie asked.

"After talking to Pops, I don't know that they will go that route," I said. "He seems to think she's still firing on all cylinders more times than not. If that's true, then at some point, she's going to ask why Gage stopped visiting. If Miriam has enough of her mind left that she can question his absence, Graham will have to tell her something because then it becomes a principle thing. And you both said Graham is highly principled."

Gertie sighed, then looked over at Ronald. "Okay, so let's take this another direction. I don't suppose you know if Graham has a male he's pinning the macho on back in NOLA?"

Ronald shook his head. "We don't run in the same circles. He's worn that same tired suit cut for decades. I don't think he'd fit in with my people at all. And why on earth would it matter if Graham's macho pinning?"

Gertie shrugged. "The rumor that he's in love with Jenny has been floated since they were kids. And most of those floating that sentiment think she married the wrong brother. I was trying to find out if that's a viable option."

"Ah!" Ronald nodded. "Then Graham would be a suspect

instead of lovely Jenny. I can appreciate your desire, but unfortunately, I know next to nothing about the man."

"We could always go talk to him," Ida Belle said. "It might not accomplish anything, but you never know what people might say under stress. We can always offer our help with planning a service and ask him about anything Jenny might need as we don't want to bother her while she's grieving."

"That's a good approach," I said. "So a conversation with Graham is first on our agenda. Ronald, call up your friends and see if they have any gossip on Brent and Jenny. If they were openly hugging right out on the street, then it's not exactly a secret."

"I know just the person to call," Ronald said. "He absolutely lives for this."

A timer went off on Ronald's phone and he jumped up. "That's my cue. Time for meditation."

And with that, he hurried off.

Gertie shook her head. "How in the world does he meditate after all that macho and murder talk? I'm so amped up, I feel like going for a jog. And I never jog."

"I better hop in the shower," I said. "After we talk to Graham, I'd like to have another chat with Dean Allard. He's the only person with as much emotional motive as Jenny."

———

Since I liked the element of surprise, I didn't want to call ahead and schedule with Graham, but we also couldn't be sure he'd be at home. So we waited until late morning, then Ida Belle called the accounting firm where Graham was a partner and asked about getting an appointment. She was told he was expected to be out for a week or better due to a death in the family, so the odds were good he was at home.

We made a quick pass by Jenny's house and spotted only her car in the drive and none parked at the curb, which meant she was at home and Graham wasn't at her house. So we headed over to Mudbug and located Graham's house. It was a Victorian, just a couple streets back from the main street, and it looked like something out of a Disney story.

"Wow!" I said as Ida Belle pulled up to the curb. "This is gorgeous. It makes my house look sad by comparison."

The house was several light shades of blue and looked like an ocean. White trim that looked like lace was all over, perfectly setting off all the blue. The railings were custom ironwork, with tons of beautiful scrolling. Two huge magnolia trees stood out front, and I could see the spots already cleared out of the beds where spring flowers would be planted against a backdrop of azalea bushes.

"You could do this," Ida Belle said. "Change out the trim that's there now and add some more for embellishment. Then change up the siding and trim paint. It does look like a Beach Barbie dollhouse."

I laughed as we headed up the walkway. "Perfect description. Now that I've got the interior where I want it, I might have to look into an exterior remodel."

"Careful," Gertie said. "You're on the verge of sounding domestic."

"I'm still a lifetime away from taking up knitting or baking, so I think I'm safe," I said.

Ida Belle rang the bell and when the door swung open, I got my first look at Gage's brother.

Fortyish. Six foot two. A hundred eighty trim pounds. Good muscle tone. Literally wearing slacks without a single wrinkle and a long-sleeved button-up shirt—tucked—while at home on leave and he'd finished off the look with uncomfortable dress shoes. His hair was perfectly in place, and his hands had soft, unblemished skin that Ronald would have had a fit over. Threat level low unless he had information on financial shenanigans that he could use to tip off the IRS.

But even though I wondered if he'd discovered a fabric that didn't wrinkle, or had been standing ever since he'd gotten dressed, that wasn't what had my eyes widening. It was how much he looked like Gage, but didn't, all at the same time. It was incredible to see what two different lifestyles could do to the same body and face.

"Ladies," Graham said, looking a little surprised. "I haven't seen you in ages. Please come in and tell me what I can do for you."

"Actually, we're here to find out what we can do for you," Gertie said and held up a baking pan. "And to deliver a casserole, of course."

He gave her a warm smile. "There's nothing like your casseroles, Miss Gertie."

I held out my hand. "I'm Fortune Redding, a good friend of Ida Belle and Gertie's. It's a pleasure to meet you, but I'm very sorry about the circumstances."

He gave me a sad nod and a weak handshake. "I've heard a lot about you—all good, of course—taking down the bad guys and all. And thank you for the food and the condolences. Would you ladies like a glass of tea? I've just finished a fresh brew."

We all nodded and followed him down a hallway to the kitchen. I bypassed the kitchen table and went straight for the window, staring outside at the patio, complete with desk, hot tub, custom grill area, and wood-fired pizza oven, all surrounded by incredible landscaping. I couldn't even see any of the surrounding houses. It was like a private oasis.

"This is awesome," I said. "Do you mind if I take a couple pictures? I would love something like this in my backyard."

He looked pleased. "Go right ahead. I did all the design

myself, including the landscaping. And I handle the planting every year. I find it relaxing to move around in the dirt after sitting at a desk staring at a computer all day."

I snapped a few shots, then joined the others at the table. A couple seconds of silence passed, and then Graham gave me a curious look, probably because I'd been studying him.

"I'm sorry for staring," I said. "But no one mentioned that you and Gage were identical twins. It's sort of uncanny... I mean, the resemblance is huge, but yet not quite the same."

He nodded. "It's amazing what a poor lifestyle can do to the same set of DNA. Gage looked a good ten years older. His diet, the aversion to exercise, and all the drinking were bound to get him at some point. When our mother was diagnosed with heart issues a decade ago, I did my research and found out how it's often inherited, so I immediately changed my diet and incorporated more cardio. Gage, unfortunately, never took it seriously."

"I'd say that's more the rule than the exception," Ida Belle said.

"I'm sure you're right," Graham agreed. "I review people's financial health every day and it's shocking the scant level of care most give it." He looked at Ida Belle and Gertie and smiled. "I have to say, it's good to see you again. I'm afraid I don't get over to Sinful much anymore now that mom isn't living there."

Gertie nodded. "Used to see you, Miriam, and Jenny at the café after church service. It's been a while now."

"It has, but I appreciate your coming here to pay your respects. And the casserole is an absolute blessing. But to be honest, his death didn't surprise me any more than my mother's will when I get that phone call. And I can't think of anything I need help with at the moment."

"Oh, we knew you'd have it all under control," Ida Belle

said. "You were always the most capable person in your household, even when you were a child. But we wondered if Jenny might need help. We've paid our respects with her and asked, of course, but Jenny has always kept to herself. It's hard to know if she could use some support but won't ask. We figured you would know better than anyone if that's the case."

"Jenny, of course," he said. "You ladies are from a generation that treats things with dignity and social grace. Such a lost art, don't you think?"

"Definitely," Ida Belle said.

"I've talked with her several times since I was...notified. And I've been to the house to check on her every day. She's always been a strong woman. I suppose some would argue that being married to Gage either required it or created it, but you knew Jenny's mother, so you already know she came by her fortitude long before she took on my brother."

"Yes, she had a rough go of it as a child," Gertie said.

"I'm afraid being married to Gage didn't improve her situation much," Graham said. He shook his head, and I could see the frustration. "Time and time again I tried to compel him to be a better husband. Even though I shouldn't say things like this, I'm glad they were never able to have kids. Can you imagine how that would have gone?"

"Will she be okay financially?" Ida Belle asked. "I hope Gage had life insurance at least."

"Ha," he said. "When I approached him about it, he claimed it would cut into his drinking and fishing money, and that if anything happened to him, he knew I'd take care of Jenny. The longer they were married, the less he seemed to care."

"What about the house?" Ida Belle asked.

"Legally, Gage's share passed to Jenny on his death, with the other half being mine, but I don't want any of it. I'll be transferring the deed to Jenny as soon as we're able to sort out the legalities. I've already got my attorney working on it."

Gertie squeezed his hand. "That's really good of you."

"Jenny is more to me than just a sister-in-law," Graham said. "We grew up together. My mother practically raised her and then she took care of my mother for a lot of years. If it wasn't for Jenny, I would have already gotten Gage out of the house and sold it."

"How's your mother doing?" Gertie asked. "Jenny told us about her memory issues. We were really sorry to hear it."

His expression shifted to one of considerable grief and he slowly shook his head. "Her mind is drifting away a little more each week, and her stamina is practically gone. Last month, they insisted she start using a wheelchair full time. They don't want to risk her falling."

"I'm so sorry to hear that," Ida Belle said. "But I'm glad that you're taking better care of yourself than Gage and your mother did. I'm rather surprised Miriam didn't take things more seriously early on."

"You don't know?" Graham asked, looking slightly surprised.

Ida Belle and Gertie shook their heads.

"My mother was adopted."

"We did not know that," Ida Belle said. "But then, people kept personal things personal back in her parents' day."

"She just found out herself a few years back. Her biological and adoptive parents were long gone when an old aunt did a deathbed confession. Since her adoptive parents never had heart problems, she'd always assumed she was in the clear. Well, as much as anyone else without family history is."

"That's a real shame," Gertie said. "If she'd had some information, then she might have been able to take preventive action."

Graham nodded. "It was a closed adoption, but the old aunt gave up names. Both her biological parents died young. Both with heart issues, I'm afraid. That's why I figured given her issues at a relatively young age, and the history of heart trouble on my father's side of the family, it was best not to take risks with my own health."

"That's the smart route for sure," I said.

"Have you told her yet?" Gertie asked.

He shook his head. "I talked with her doctor, and he said her mind wasn't the problem although she might forget sometimes. He has some concern about the stress it will put on her heart, but he's going be present when I tell her, in case she needs medical aid. We were waiting on the ME to issue his opinion first. But now that we have it, I guess we need to plan on doing it soon, even though I'm not sure she'll be capable of attending the service."

"You're not afraid someone else will get to her first?" I asked.

"The few people she's still in contact with wouldn't risk her health that way, but her doctor notified them all about our plans going forward."

I nodded, wondering how to segue into Gage's affair when the doorbell rang.

"I guess I should expect occasional visitors given the situation," he said. "Excuse me for a moment."

Because the kitchen wasn't far from the living room and sound sometimes echoed down hallways, we all remained silent while Graham answered the door. I heard low voices but couldn't make out what they were saying. Then Graham reentered the kitchen with Jenny in tow.

CHAPTER SIXTEEN

THERE WAS AN AWKWARD SILENCE FOR A MOMENT, THEN Jenny gave us a weak smile and sat as Graham poured her a glass of tea.

"I didn't expect to find you ladies here," she said.

Gertie glanced over at Graham. "Caught red-handed, I suppose. We were here to offer our support and see if Graham knew of anything we could do to help you, as we figured you wouldn't ask yourself."

She forced a laugh. "I've never been good at asking for what I need. Except when it comes to business. I guess you can't be good at everything, right?"

Ida Belle glanced over at me, and I gave her 'the look.' The one that conveyed my approval for what I knew she was about to do. Because it's exactly what I would do if I were Ida Belle. It just wouldn't work if it came from me.

"Can we help planning the service?" Ida Belle asked. "I'm afraid at our age, you know all the major players, so to speak. I know you have Graham, but neither of you is well versed on this sort of thing."

"There won't be a service," Jenny said.

Gertie frowned. "Not even a celebration of life? Or a small gathering?"

"What's the point?" she asked. "Spend a lot of money for a man few people really liked, except his drinking buddies, and they won't come unless it's open bar."

"I don't think that's true," Ida Belle said. "Gage had plenty of friends, and I'm certain they'd come to the service."

Gertie nodded. "Besides, people will come out of respect for you."

"Well, I don't want to deal with it," Jenny said. "People are a lot of effort for me. They always have been. Gage never understood that, as he wasn't happy unless he was surrounded by a crowd."

"Not even a viewing?" Gertie asked. "You wouldn't have to be there. I'm sure everyone would understand."

"Unless people want to march through the church and look at an urn, there won't be any point," she said, her agitation starting to show. "Even when Gage made a decent paycheck, he always found a way to blow it, and funerals are expensive. The medical examiner said I have to remove his body by Monday. I can't bring him home and prop him up in his boat, although he'd probably think that was just fine, especially given the way he decided to exit. I'm doing the best I can. I don't need more grief over it."

Graham stared at her, clearly dismayed. "Jenny, you know I'll pay for whatever you want."

She shook her head. "I won't take money from you. I know Gage did and I'm certain he's never paid you back. This is my responsibility. He was *my* husband."

"And he was *my* brother."

"It's not your decision to make," she said firmly. "Gage will be cremated, and we can sprinkle him over the bayou or at the Swamp Bar so he can do his final resting at the place he loved most. But his last poor decision will not cost you or me any more than we've already given him."

"What about Mother?" Graham asked.

"You know as well as I do that her doctor wouldn't allow her to attend or we'd be burying two people instead of just one. I'll have the newspaper do a nice write-up that she can put in her Bible."

Graham looked surprised, but I'd already figured out that he wasn't the kind of man who argued over this sort of thing, especially with a woman. "Whatever you decide," he said.

"That's what I want," she said. "Cremation only. No service, no viewing, no celebration, no nothing. I want this chapter of my life over with. I'm just asking that you give me a month to move out of the house."

Graham's eyes widened. "Move—what are you— Good Lord, Jenny, I would never take your house. It's *your* house!"

"It's half yours."

"Legally, yes. But God knows, it would have disintegrated into dust without you keeping it up. I already have my attorney working out how to transfer my interest to you."

She shook her head. "Don't do that. I don't need a place to live anymore. Not here. I'm leaving Sinful. The truth is, I've wanted to for a long time."

Graham gave her a helpless look. "I know being married to Gage wasn't easy, but if this is the way you felt, then why didn't you divorce him?"

"Because right before I walked down the aisle, Miriam asked me to promise her I'd take care of Gage. I just had no idea what it would cost."

Graham's expression shifted from helpless to dismayed. "She had no right to ask that of you. And you should never have agreed."

"Miriam is the only parent I've ever had. She was the first

person who truly loved me. And she loved Gage, faults and all. I agree she roped you and me into propping him up and it wasn't right in either case, but I wasn't going to break that promise. My word is one of the few things I own free and clear. But now that my debt to her is officially paid, I'm going back to New Orleans."

Graham looked completely overwhelmed. "I'm so sorry, Jenny. If I had known—"

"There's nothing you could have done about it," Jenny said. "I made a promise and I kept it. But I'm still young enough to try to make something of my life. I'm not going to lock myself in my house in that tiny town and slowly die. New Orleans has more opportunity for me with my business and for me personally."

"Of course, if that's what you want, I understand," Graham said, but I could tell he was still in shock over the whole thing. "If there's anything I can help with—work contacts in New Orleans. I know a lot of people and could get your name around."

She reached over and squeezed his hand. "Let me get settled first."

"Sure, okay."

Jenny rose from the table. "I've got to get going. I'm meeting with Timmy Benoit this afternoon about repairing that mess Gage made with the deck. That's where Gage's 'funeral' money is going."

"I can make the repair," Graham said.

"I know you can, but I don't want you to. Gage screwed it up big-time, trying to do it himself. If he'd listened to you and just poured a concrete pad off to the side for the hot tub, it wouldn't be a problem. But since he's torn half of it up, I'm just going to have the whole thing ripped out and pour a concrete patio with some steps down from the sliders. It will be cheaper, and the house will sell better with no wood back there to worry about."

"I'm sure," Graham said, "but I can handle the repair and the costs."

She shook her head. "Timmy said, given the situation, he'd do it for just a bit over cost. He's going to start on Monday, so it will all be taken care of before I move."

I took one look at the determined expression on Jenny's face and knew that no argument Graham could formulate would be good enough to change her mind. Given that Graham knew her far better than I did, I assumed he knew as well.

"Okay," Graham said, sounding a bit helpless. "Let me know if I can help."

Jenny nodded. "I have a small cleaning early tomorrow morning for one of my seniors, then I'm going to head out to NOLA. I need to start looking for a place to live. I'll probably stay over until Sunday. I need to get away from here for a bit."

"I understand," Graham said.

"I'm so sorry I unloaded all of this on you at once," Jenny said, "but with the situation with the medical examiner, it couldn't wait. I'll let you know when the ashes are available."

She gave us a nod and headed out of the kitchen. I figured Graham would see her out given that his manners were light years beyond most men in his age group, but instead, he remained seated, a shell-shocked look on his face. I couldn't really blame him. It was a lot to take in for one conversation, especially given his twin had just died and it sounded as though his mother wasn't far behind.

"Are you okay?" Gertie asked him.

He hesitated before answering. "Yes. I'm just surprised. I never considered Jenny would leave Sinful. I think I need a minute to catch up."

I glanced over at Ida Belle, who narrowed her eyes a bit at me. Out of everything she'd said—the cremation, the lack of any kind of memorial service, the comments on her financial position—the one thing Graham had focused on was her moving.

I supposed given how poorly Gage had behaved during his life, Jenny's declarations shouldn't have been surprising. After all, those closest to people who made poor choices usually bore the brunt of them. And it certainly seemed as if Graham and Jenny had been carrying Gage for a long time.

But it only made me even more suspicious of everyone involved.

"I know this is an intrusive question," I said, "but have you ever considered that your brother's death might not have been due to natural causes?"

Graham stared at me for a moment, as if he hadn't really heard the question. Then it clicked and his eyes widened. "Of course not. Why would you even suggest that?"

"A gut feeling. I was first on the scene, so to speak. And assessing that kind of situation is something I was trained and experienced in during my time with the CIA."

He shook his head. "While I can appreciate the skills necessary for your previous work, perhaps your experience has also lent you toward assuming the darker side of human nature."

"Without a doubt," I agreed. "But that doesn't make my intuition inaccurate. You're a numbers guy. I assume you play the market?"

He nodded, looking somewhat confused with the shift in topic. "With a discretionary fund set aside for that purpose."

"Haven't you ever made an investment that looked completely wrong on paper, but you just had a feeling it was going somewhere?"

"Well, yes, but that doesn't mean anything. It's just blind luck."

"I don't think it is. I think some people have a natural intuition about certain things. And even though you wouldn't be able to tell someone why that investment was a good one because the numbers didn't exactly back you up, there was something about it that clicked with you. Maybe your subconscious mind processed something that your conscious didn't. But I'll bet it's happened to you far more than once."

"It's the stock market. Making any risky investment is tantamount to walking down a line of slots at a casino, randomly shoving in dollars and hoping for a jackpot. Which is exactly why it's a discretionary fund that I use for such investments. It's money I can afford to lose."

"You do know that the person who helped Gage with that boat prank has never come forward, right?"

He sighed. "That doesn't surprise me. Gage's friends were of the same caliber as him. And since I have to assume they were both drunk, that's two people driving intoxicated, trespassing, and I'm sure there's some sort of private property law they broke by him getting into that boat. None of the people Gage called friends are going to volunteer themselves up for charges, especially when I have zero doubt it was all Gage's idea and he's no longer here to take his share of the blame."

I could see I wasn't getting anywhere with him given a logical argument, so I moved for the emotional one.

"Did you know Gage was having an affair?"

His eyes widened and I could tell he wanted to deny it, but it was too late. In that flicker of a second, his expression had given him away, and he knew that I knew.

"I didn't know," he said.

"But you'd heard something. Did Jenny tell you?"

"What? No! It was a neighbor of the other party involved.

He saw something that looked, well, improper and felt he should let me know."

"And how can you be sure this neighbor didn't tell Jenny?"

"He wouldn't do that to her. That's why he called me."

"If one neighbor saw, what are the chances someone else did as well?"

"Slim," he said hopefully.

I shook my head. "I have a witness who doesn't even live on the same street as the other party, which takes 'slim' right off the table. So I know, and you know, and at least two other people witnessed something that had them telling us. You're the numbers guy. What are the odds that gossip made it around to Jenny and Dean Allard?"

He sucked in a breath when I said Allard's name, and I knew he had been hoping I was fishing and didn't have facts.

"We've already talked to Nancy," I said. "She didn't deny it. And it wasn't a one-off, either. This started up last summer. My guess is they were a lot more careful at first but have gotten lax enough that some people have seen things they weren't supposed to."

The blood rushed out of Graham's face, and he ran one hand over his head. "Oh my God. I rather hoped he'd been mistaken with what he'd seen. I asked Gage, of course, but he denied it."

"Did you really think he'd tell the truth? Especially given that if Jenny left him, he'd be homeless. We know about the stipulations your mother placed on the house."

Graham put his hands in the air, a helpless look on his face. "What do you want me to do? I talked to the medical examiner. He said Graham died of a heart attack. And they did some sort of testing for poisons. I assumed it was because it was odd circumstances and the police requested it. But they were negative. He was very clear on that point."

"They don't test for everything."

"I understand that, but I don't know what you want from *me*. I don't know anything about poisons, assuming you think that's what happened, and my knowledge of the affair was secondhand at best. What can I possibly do?"

"You could see to it that Gage isn't cremated. If his body is destroyed, and evidence surfaces later that indicates foul play, there will be no way to test for other poisons."

His jaw dropped and he stared at me for several seconds, then slowly shook his head. "It's not my decision to make. You heard Jenny. She's resolute in how this is to be handled and I don't have any legal standing. Even if I did, it sounds like you're asking me to preserve my brother's body so that it can potentially be used to convict Jenny."

"I'm asking you to preserve his body so that it can be used to convict the person who killed him. We don't know who that was, and if Gage is cremated, we might never know."

He stared down at the table, frowning, his brow scrunched in thought. Finally, he looked up at me and shook his head. "Maybe it's for the best."

"Even if he was murdered?"

"Nothing can bring him back. And if I'm being honest, his passing gives Jenny a chance at a normal life. A good life. She deserves it."

"I find it hard to believe that you're the kind of person who'd be okay with someone getting away with murder, much less the murder of your twin."

He sighed. "I'm not okay with it. Far from it. But life experience has taught me that my mental health depends on not worrying or dwelling on things I can't control. I have no knowledge, experience, or legal standing here. The ME has already run the panels. Even if I were to push for more testing, where would I tell him to start?"

"You could ask that blood and hair samples be stored," Ida Belle said. "It would allow testing later on if the truth ever surfaces and you have something specific to test for."

"That's interesting," he said. "And something I've never thought of, but it seems a reasonable compromise. I'll talk to Jenny about it and the ME, but I'm guessing that we're ultimately all bound by her wishes."

The fact that he was right only made it more frustrating.

He looked at me and gave me a rueful smile. "I appreciate that you're trying to help. Your dedication to justice is as high as mine to equity. I wish I could do more."

"Me too," I said, and taking his words as a dismissal, I rose from my chair.

"Thank you, ladies, so much. For the casserole and for checking in," Graham said.

"Of course," Gertie said. "If there's anything we can do for you or your mother, let us know. I guess Jenny is set and doesn't need any old women interfering with her plans."

He nodded. "I think we all got a bit of a surprise on that one, but I'd rather see her determined and optimistic than the alternative. I've seen too much of that already."

We made our way out, silent until we climbed into the SUV, then we all exploded at once.

"Can you believe it!"

"First time I've been surprised in forever!"

"That took a hard turn!"

We all huffed in unison, then Ida Belle fired up the SUV and pulled away.

"It was all going so well," Gertie said. "You were making a connection with Graham, and he seemed to be opening up a little."

"Then Hurricane Jenny blew in and he put on the storm

doors," Ida Belle said. "I'm still a little surprised he admitted to knowing about the affair."

"His expression gave him away," I said. "And he knew that I knew. He still tried to play the 'can't be sure' card, until I gave Allard's name and said I'd heard it from someone other than a neighbor."

"I think that spooked him a bit," Ida Belle said.

"Oh, it definitely spooked him," I agreed. "The question is why? Is he afraid someone will tell Jenny, or worse, is he afraid Jenny already knew and that gave her motive?"

"But did it?" Gertie asked. "She flat-out refused to take the house and Graham was clearly offering it up, completely unencumbered. It's not a palace, but it's paid for so it's worth a decent amount of money."

"She'll still get Gage's half of the proceeds from the sale," Ida Belle said. "That's plenty enough to get her going in NOLA."

"But she could have had it all if she'd just waited to drop the moving bomb until after Graham had transferred the entire house into her name," Gertie said. "And he put that out there before she said she was moving. Why not wait a bit longer?"

"Maybe she feels she's waited long enough," Ida Belle said. "She's been married to Gage what—ten years or better. And she was taking care of Miriam for a good portion of that as well. Jenny's given some of the best years of her life to that family. And you heard her—her promise has been fulfilled. The debt is paid."

"But why kill him?" Gertie said. "If Miriam is as close to death as everyone seems to think, why take the risk? Like you said, she's been living that way for over a decade. Why not wait a few more months? That would make more sense."

"It would," Ida Belle said. "To us. And to anyone sane, but who knows how long Gage's poor treatment of Jenny has been festering. And no one can be sure that Miriam will pass anytime soon. Look at Pops. He was supposed to exit over a year ago and looks better now than he did when they declared him terminal."

"She still could have waited a couple weeks and gotten the whole house in her name," Gertie argued. "Why take the risk for half the profit?"

Ida Belle shrugged. "Maybe she doesn't need a lot of money because she's got someone on the line who has plenty of it."

CHAPTER SEVENTEEN

WE HEADED BACK TO SINFUL, PLANNING TO FIND DEAN Allard and see if we could get anything out of him. I had no intention of telling him about the affair, but I was hoping with some well-placed prompts I might be able to spur a reaction and figure out if he was aware. It was early afternoon, but Ida Belle had already checked with Walter, who said the tides were supporting early-morning fish runs, so most of the fishermen had headed in before noon.

With any luck, we'd catch Dean at home, which was a mixed bag. It was private and the conversation I wanted to have didn't need a bunch of drunks hanging around for it. But he could also easily close the door in our faces and refuse to talk at all.

I was pleased to see Dean's truck in the driveway and hoped the chicken casserole we'd brought as a bribe would get him to open the door. We rang the bell and waited, then rang it again. Finally, I heard shuffling inside, then the door opened and Dean glared out at us. It was clear he'd been asleep, so we weren't exactly off to a good start. Since the fishermen headed out before dawn, they usually caught a nap when they returned.

"What do you want?" he asked.

"Conversation," I said, and motioned to the casserole. "In exchange for food."

He looked at the casserole, then up at Gertie. "Is that one of your chicken casseroles?"

Gertie nodded.

He stared at us again, then back at the casserole, and for a second, I wondered if he was going to grab the thing and slam the door, but finally, he stepped back and we headed inside.

The house was a disaster, but then Dean didn't exactly strike me as a homemaker. And to be fair, except for the beer and half-eaten sandwich on a table by the recliner, the majority of the mess looked as though it was made by kids. We followed him back to the kitchen and Gertie presented him with the casserole. He lifted the tin foil on one end and took a sniff, then almost smiled.

"If I could cook worth a d...darn, I'd ask you for this recipe," he said. "Best casserole I've ever had."

"Just as well then," Gertie said. "The recipe is a family secret."

"Best leave it to someone in your will then," he said. "This town might dry up if your chicken casserole and Francine's banana pudding disappear."

Gertie shook her head. "I'm not planning on dying."

He stared at her for a second, then let out a single laugh. "That doesn't surprise me one bit. I'm not much for conversation so say what you need to say and let me get back to my nap."

"I wanted to ask you about Gage," I said.

"What about him? He was a drinking buddy, a lousy fisherman, and annoyed a bunch of people with those pranks of his. Not much else to say. He wasn't what you'd call complicated."

"Complicated enough that someone might have killed him."

He shook his head. "The only person who believes that is you. I paid my respects to Jenny. She said they told her it was natural causes. Shouldn't surprise anyone. All that drinking and his mama's heart problems—he knew what the things he was doing was going to get him."

"You were there drinking with him most nights, weren't you?"

"Got no heart problems in my family. Gage's mama was told to sit down and rest long before she hit sixty. Now she's up in that home. If I had that staring down at me, I might do things differently."

"Fair enough," I said, deciding to try a different tactic. "But things might be easier for the police to wrap up if they knew who was out there that night with Gage. There was no way for him to get into that boat without help, and the ladder was in his truck, which was stashed in the trees a bit down from the boat display. Someone put it there."

"What's all that got to do with me?"

"You sure you weren't the one helping him?"

"I already told you I wasn't. And if I was, why would I lie about it?"

"To avoid charges for trespassing, driving drunk, and damaging personal property? Just to keep the cops from questioning you, maybe?"

He shrugged. "They wouldn't bother with charges, and they can talk to me all they want. Doesn't change anything. The only person responsible for Gage dying is Gage. He's been working on it like it was an Olympic event for years now."

"What if the person who helped him with that prank knew all of that and was hoping for exactly that outcome?"

He stared at me for several seconds, frowning. "You think someone talked him into that prank hoping he'd have a heart attack? That's pretty far-fetched."

"Is it? Everyone knew about his drinking and his mother's heart problems. They knew he sat at a desk all day, didn't bother to do anything to keep in shape, and that his diet was crap. Is it really that big of a stretch? Maybe it was wishful thinking and then when it actually happened, they got spooked. Because no one's stepping forward, that's for sure."

He stared down at the floor for a while and I could tell he was contemplating what I'd said. But I had no way of knowing if that was because I had hit the nail on the head, or if he was wondering which one of his friends or neighbors had sent Gage up that ladder trying to kill him.

"Let's say I give this wild idea of yours a go," he said finally. "It has to be someone mad enough at him to try it on. And I can't think of anyone who fits the bill. Gage annoyed the hell out of me, but if I killed everyone who annoyed me, wouldn't be no one left in the whole parish."

"What about his wife?"

His eyes widened. "You think Jenny was out there in the middle of the night, holding ladders and praying her husband had a heart attack? If that's where you're headed, then you don't know the woman at all. She's the salt of the earth. Couldn't ask for a better wife, even though Gage didn't do much to deserve it."

"Which is exactly my point. What if she finally got tired of it all? Or maybe there was that final straw."

I registered the tiniest flicker of fear in his expression—so minute even trained CIA agents might have missed it.

"What final straw?" he asked.

"Gage was having an affair," I said, making it a statement, not speculation.

His eyes widened. "And you think Jenny knew?"

"Women usually do. Did you know?"

"I don't like talking ill of the dead, even Gage, but he made some noise in that direction a couple of times."

"What kind of noise?"

"Comments about keeping his bed warm—in a way that you knew he wasn't talking about his wife. I figured he was making stuff up to brag like guys do to other guys, but if you're certain..."

"I am, which makes things messy for anyone who might be upset about it...starting with Jenny and ending with anyone who might take offense to the woman he was having the affair with."

I saw the flicker again—fear, anger—I couldn't be sure.

"Who was it?" he asked.

"I can't say."

He studied me for a couple seconds, trying to figure out if I literally meant I couldn't say or I wouldn't say.

"I think it was just big talk," he said finally. "You know how guys get when they've been drinking."

"That's usually about who caught the biggest fish," Ida Belle said. "Not who was cheating on his wife."

He shrugged. "Gage didn't play by nobody's rules but his own. But I think you might be chasing after gossip. And even if it was true, there's no way Jenny was out on the side of that highway in the middle of the night, trying to spur her husband into a heart attack. I'd bet money on that and I ain't got any to lose. Now if that's all, I'd like to finish up my lunch and get back to that nap."

I knew we weren't going to get anything else out of him, so

we trailed out. As soon as we got into the SUV, Gertie asked the question I'd been asking myself.

"Was he lying? Did he know about Gage and Nancy?"

"I can't be sure," I said. "He's tough to read. Anger can mask a lot of things, and Dean Allard is a very angry man. I saw something a couple times—fear maybe—but that still doesn't mean he knew. Not for certain, anyway."

Ida Belle nodded. "The way he asked you who it was... I couldn't tell if he already knew and was trying to see how much you knew or if he had suspicions and was trying to get you to verify or negate them."

"Exactly," I agreed.

"Where to now?"

"It's hot tub time. Maybe the steam will clear my brain."

———

THE HOT TUB WAS GREAT FOR MY NECK AND BACK. I TENDED to tense when I was trying to work out a problem, and this one had my back muscles flexing on overtime. But sadly, it didn't offer up any new insight as to how to keep Jenny from destroying what was likely our only good evidence. We could hope that Graham could talk her into preserving blood and hair samples for later testing, but if Jenny had been the one out on that highway with Gage, the chances of her agreeing to it were absolutely nil.

For that matter, if Graham really was in love with Jenny and had even a single ounce of suspicion about her, then he'd never ask. Or maybe Graham was the one out on the highway with Gage. Maybe he'd gotten tired of waiting for Gage to keel over and had decided to help him along, so he could have the only woman he'd ever loved, besides his mother.

I sighed as I stepped out of the shower and grabbed a

bottle of lotion. I loved the hot tub, but it was hell on my skin. Not that I was worried about it in a Ronald sort of way. It was just that when it got really dry it itched. And it always itched more at night. If I scratched in the middle of the night, half asleep, Merlin took that as an invitation to play and would pounce on my hand moving under the covers. The body part I was scratching determined just how awake I became after he made his move.

So lotion it was.

At least it didn't smell like roses or strawberries. I'd been insistent on zero smell when I'd asked Ronald to pick something out for me. His initial excitement at my desire for a skin product had been short-lived after I'd given my requirements, but he'd still offered up a brand that did the job and didn't make me smell like a whorehouse or a bakery.

I was headed downstairs when my front door opened and Carter stuck his head in. He spotted me on the stairs and gave me a halfhearted smile. I plastered on one myself, but at the same time, I felt my heart sink.

Every day, he seemed more distant than before. Physically, he was improving rapidly, but the mental strain was starting to show more and more. I'd tried to remain upbeat around him, hoping to see the old Carter begin to emerge, but he seemed to be moving in the opposite direction.

It was time to address things head-on.

I grabbed us some beers and headed back into the living room. He'd already sat back on the couch and took the beer from me and set it on the table without even taking a sip. I sat next to him, turned a bit so I could look directly at him, and went for it.

"What's wrong? I hoped it was fatigue and a need for decompression, but every time I see you, you're more checked out than the time before. You know you can talk to me,

Carter. Jesus, I'm one of the only people in Sinful who has a clue what you went through."

He nodded. "I know. But I need to work it out for myself before I can tell you."

I held in a sigh. It was frustrating, but I couldn't exactly force a grown man to talk. The terrorists hadn't been able to, and they'd tortured him.

"Are you feeling okay physically? Do we need to get a second opinion on anything?"

"No. I'm feeling pretty decent, except for my ribs. Still can't take a deep breath or sneeze without cussing the entire world, but Cassidy said everything is ahead of schedule as far as healing goes."

I nodded, trying to figure out my next angle of attack. Maybe if he wouldn't just offer it up, I could get enough pieces out of him to put it together myself.

"Have you talked to any of the men in the unit?"

"A couple of them."

"How is everyone doing?"

"Good. No one had permanent injuries. Not the physical kind anyway. One of the men had his arm broken. They're iffy on if he'll regain full range of motion, so that could affect his future with the unit. But they're all benched now anyway."

"Oh?"

He nodded. "There's an investigation."

This was news to me, but it began to explain what Carter was dwelling on.

"Are they going to question you?" I asked.

"I'm sure. I was debriefed before I came home, of course, but I expect they'll show up here at some point, wanting to go over it all again. They wanted me to go back to DC, but I refused."

I struggled not to let my anger show. Why would they

expect an injured soldier, who'd been held hostage and tortured, to travel to them? They could darn well get their abled bodies on a plane and come to him.

"I'm glad you refused," I said, unable to say more lest I get going and couldn't stop.

He stared at the TV, but I knew if I turned it off and asked him what was playing, he wouldn't be able to tell me.

"I called it off," he said suddenly.

"Called what off?"

"The mission."

I sucked in a breath. Jesus! No wonder he was stressed. But if Carter LeBlanc, the most honorable man I'd ever known, had gone against a direct order and aborted the mission, he'd had good reasons.

"Why?"

"It wasn't right. I can't tell you why—and I don't mean I don't know; I mean I can't tell you."

"I get it. But you had reason to believe the mission was compromised."

"And I was right. If we'd continued..." He shook his head. "Let's just say I wouldn't be sitting here now. And none of those men would be sitting in their homes either."

"Then you did the right thing."

He frowned. "Yeah."

But he didn't sound convinced.

"Have you heard from your father?" he asked.

"What? No! Why would you even ask that? He's not exactly the kind of man who calls to make sure his daughter got home safely."

I hadn't told Carter about the card I had tucked away in my safe. If I did, when he was questioned about him—and I was certain he would be—then he'd be forced to either lie or give up my secret. He'd already lied about enough concerning his rescue and I knew it was hard for him, even though it was necessary.

I, on the other hand, had no problem lying. The CIA had made me a professional. But if this whole thing ended up in court, I wasn't certain Carter would be able to lie under oath, while I'd do it without hesitation and very, very well.

"Your father came to our rescue in Iran," he pointed out.

I nodded. "He also let a fifteen-year-old kid think her father was dead for thirteen years. Let's not give him any father of the year awards just yet."

"True." Carter stared off again, silent for several seconds, then he looked back at me, locking his gaze on mine. "He said something to me before he disappeared."

I frowned. "What?"

"He said, 'You weren't supposed to be here.'"

"Of course you weren't supposed to be there. You'd been captured."

"Exactly. But it was an odd way of putting it."

"It was probably nothing. We were all seconds away from death."

He nodded. "You're probably right."

But now, I wondered.

CHAPTER EIGHTEEN

I WOKE UP EARLY THE NEXT MORNING AFTER A FITFUL NIGHT of mixed-up dreaming. I'd been back in the Middle East for part of it, but Harrison and I were both dressed like nuns. And we hadn't rescued Carter. He'd had a heart attack. Jenny had been vacuuming the church while the funeral service was going on and then Graham had presented me with a bill.

I bolted up so quickly that I startled Merlin, sending him flying out of the room.

I checked my watch. It was only 5:00 a.m. but no way I was going to try to sleep again after that. For all I knew, the next dream might have Carter replacing Gage in an affair with Nancy Allard, and Harrison and I might be wearing Ronald's bird dress. I headed downstairs without bothering to change or brush my hair or teeth. I wasn't expecting anyone that morning and if anyone showed up unannounced that early, they deserved whatever they saw.

I put the coffee on and plopped into a chair, then grabbed my laptop and scanned the news for the area. When the coffee was ready, I shoved the laptop back and blew out a breath. I didn't know what I'd been expecting. A headline news story about who killed Gage Babin and how they did it, maybe? But it was all the normal stuff for the area—the weather, the fishing outlook for the year, how much revenue Mardi Gras had brought to NOLA—nothing that sent a flare up telling me where to take this investigation next.

Until it did.

I grabbed my phone and sent Ida Belle and Gertie a text.

Pack an overnight bag and head over here when you get up. We're going to NOLA today to spy on Jenny.

I tossed my phone on the table and hopped up to pour myself a cup of coffee, feeling energized. It probably wouldn't amount to anything, but I always felt better when I was doing something. Sitting around was like a quiet death to me. If nothing else, we could confirm that Jenny and Brent were back together and that he was the likely catalyst for her sudden move.

My phone dinged and I picked it up. I should have known Ida Belle would already be awake.

Thank God. I spent all night trying to come up with something.

I grinned. Somewhere deep, deep in our family history, Ida Belle and I had to be related. Maybe eighty-sixth cousins, forty times removed. I downed my coffee and ran upstairs to shower and pack. Gertie probably wouldn't stir for another couple hours, but I wanted to be ready to roll as soon as they pulled in my driveway.

I was also still worried about Carter, and our conversation the night before had replayed a hundred times in my mind. I wished he could share everything with me. Then I might have a better idea how to help, or if I even could. But I knew if I ever found out what actually happened in Iran, it wasn't likely to come from him. He'd gone home not long after asking me about my father. I'd asked him to stay, but he'd cited needing to feed Tiny and fix some eggs that were going to expire if he didn't eat them last night.

Both statements were true, I'm sure, but they were weak excuses at best. Still, Carter and I were our own people and we'd never pressure each other into doing things we didn't want to do—that went double for our relationship. But if I was being honest, I didn't like thinking of him sitting in his house alone, dwelling on all those things he couldn't say.

I took a really long shower, covered my body in my lotion, then pulled on comfortable running clothes, because cardio seemed to happen even when it wasn't on the schedule. I popped my lotion and some other toiletries into a duffel bag along with three sets of spare clothes, because...Gertie. Then I zipped the bag up and dumped it next to the front door. I fed Merlin breakfast and was just finishing up my own when Ida Belle and Gertie came walking in at not quite 8:00 a.m.

"I kicked Jed clean out of bed this morning when I got your text," Gertie said.

"I didn't know he was coming over last night," I said. She'd been in the hot tub at my house until after six.

"He had to pick up some parts at the boat store over here —at least that's his story." She grinned. "It was a booty call."

"No," Ida Belle said, shaking her head.

"Anyway, the text came in and when I saw the time, I grabbed the phone. Then I let out a shout and my leg just went along with it. Nailed him right in his rear. He's a side sleeper and was already on the edge, so he just rolled right off. I ran around to help him up, but there he was, all naked, and I'd just mopped the floor—"

"I said no!" Ida Belle repeated.

Gertie rolled her eyes. "My point is my morning is already off to a fine start. And here I was afraid we'd all be sitting around, waiting until what was considered a decent hour before we could drown our sorrows. But instead, you've come up with a plan of action."

"I don't know how much action my plan will entail," I warned. "Or if it will amount to anything at all."

"It's still better than sitting around depressed over the whole thing."

"That we can agree on."

We took our time over coffee and some of Ally's cookies and then when we figured Jenny might be done with her morning cleaning job, we headed out to keep watch and make sure she left town. She lived on one of the many connecting streets between my house and Ida Belle's so even if she saw us drive by, she shouldn't think anything of it. We'd just wave and smile and keep driving.

Her car wasn't in the driveway when we pulled onto her street, so Ida Belle parked at the curb in front of one of the Sinful Ladies' homes. The windows of the SUV were tinted so dark that no one could see inside, and we had a clear view of Jenny's house from there. After ten minutes had passed, I wondered if we'd missed her, but then I saw her car approaching from the other end of the street.

She pulled in the driveway, jumped out, and hurried into her house. A few minutes later, she was back outside with an overnight bag that she tossed into her car. She glanced down the street in both directions before climbing into her car then driving off.

"You want me to follow her?" Ida Belle asked.

I considered for a moment. "No. That looking around was strange. Whatever she's up to, she's already jumpy. Your vehicle parked here wouldn't necessarily spook her given that one of the Sinful Ladies lives here, but there's no way we could follow her all the way into NOLA without her noticing."

"She doesn't know my motorcycle," Ida Belle said.

"Wouldn't take long to get it and I could easily catch up to her on the highway."

"Yes!" Gertie declared. "Finally! I can't believe I gave you a motorcycle and you have yet to let me ride it."

"You are not riding with me all the way to NOLA," Ida Belle said as she started up the SUV and drove down the street after Jenny turned the corner. "Call it—you want me to get the motorcycle?"

"No," I decided. "If she's going to meet Brent, like we suspect, then we should be able to track her down later."

Ida Belle nodded. "Then she'll think she's in the clear."

"How long are we going to wait before heading after her?" Gertie asked. "Are we assuming she's headed for the hotel that Ronald saw her at? Brent's family owns several of them."

"We'll start with the one Ronald was at. That might be Brent's home base. And since it was after regular business hours when Ronald spotted them, he might even have a suite there. I made a list of the other hotels the family owns this morning. If we don't spot her car parked near that hotel, then we'll work down the list."

I frowned as we drove by Jenny's house, something else coming to mind, but I wasn't sure it was a risk worth taking.

"What are you thinking?" Ida Belle asked.

"I was thinking that I'd love to get a look inside Jenny's house, especially since we know it's empty."

"Oh!" Gertie said, and clapped her hands. "I love when we do the B&E thing."

"Don't ever say that in front of Carter or Blanchet," Ida Belle said. "Or Walter for that matter. The man has lost more hair in the eight months he's been married to me than he has in the past decade. You think she'd be foolish enough to still have the poison on hand?"

"You wouldn't think so, right? But then how many times

have we seen foolish win the race? But it's not only that. I'd like a look at her computer for starters. If I could access her email, it might give us some insight into what's going on with Brent and maybe whether or not she knew about Gage and Nancy."

"What about Dean Allard?" Gertie asked. "You haven't given up on him as a possibility, have you?"

"I hate to say it, but I like Jenny for this more than Dean," Ida Belle said. "I get that Gage was fine having drinks with Allard at the Swamp Bar—probably even got off on it given that he was bedded up with Dean's ex—but was he so drunk that he'd enlist Allard to help him with a prank?"

"Could have been Dean's idea," Gertie said. "And Gage would have jumped on it."

"Anything's possible, but I tend to agree with Ida Belle," I said. "Unless Allard has found Jesus or a really good therapist, I can't see him being able to hold his fists back from Gage's face as soon as he found out about the affair. And I don't see any indication of the creativity required to stage that prank."

Ida Belle nodded. "So, you planning on breaking into her house in broad daylight?"

"Don't have to break in. The back patio door is broken. I noticed it when we were there last time."

"You can't just stroll up the walk and into the backyard," Gertie said. "Well, you could, but I figured the point of this sort of thing was not being seen."

I grinned. "Did you not notice whose house shares a back corner with Jenny's?"

Ida Belle's eyes widened. "Carter's."

I nodded. "And I happen to know that he's having breakfast with Walter at the café today and then is supposed to help him move some stuff around in the storeroom."

"You're right," Ida Belle confirmed. "Perfect. So unless a

nosy neighbor just happens to spot us out their window and calls him, that's plenty of time to dig through Jenny's stuff."

"Especially with three of us," Gertie said.

I shook my head. "Just me."

"Why do you get to have all the fun?" Gertie complained.

"Because I'm the only one who can scale a six-foot fence without a ladder. It's not like I can haul one into Jenny's yard. If I have to make a quick exit, you being stranded on the other side of the fence would definitely give the whole thing away."

Gertie gave me a smug look. "You're not the only one who noticed things at Jenny's house. Gage has an old doghouse in that huge mess he has piled in that corner. And there's a stack of wood beside it. I can climb right up, no problem."

Ida Belle didn't look completely thrilled with the idea, but she shrugged. "It would be easier with three people searching. At least one of us could always have an eye out a front window in case Jenny returned."

It took less than a second to come up with a hundred ways this could go wrong, but before I could change my mind, I nodded. "Carter should have headed out by now. Make a pass by his street and let's see if his truck's out front."

"I thought he'd finally gotten his garage cleaned out and was parking inside," Gertie said.

"Crap. You're right. I'll have to do a little surveillance."

"Or..." Ida Belle said, and pulled out her cell phone and put one finger to her lips as she turned it on speaker.

"Are you on your way to Francine's yet?" she asked when Walter answered.

"We just sat down," he said. "Is something wrong?"

"No. Not at all. I just heard that Francine was supposed to make blackberry cobbler this week. If she did, would you get us half a pie to freeze? We ate the last one a week ago."

"Of course."

She smiled as she pulled away. "House is empty. Well, except for Tiny, but he won't be a problem."

Gertie laughed. "Remember that first time Fortune had a run-in with Tiny and lost some of her hair?"

"I think you and Tiny remember it more fondly than I do. Having an extension ripped out is no joke."

"Having them put in is no joke either," Ida Belle said. "Sometimes, when I consider all the things you've done, I put that one up there in the top five bravest things."

Gertie sighed. "It's a good thing Ronald isn't here. Statements like that would send him right into a depression."

Since no one would blink at the sight of Ida Belle's SUV parked at Carter's house, she pulled right up front, and we walked normally up the sidewalk and I let us in. If anyone happened to mention seeing us, I'd just say we'd stopped by on our way out of town to check on Tiny, since I knew he was dining with Walter then helping him at the store and might be a while. He'd know it was nonsense, and if he could tear his thoughts away from Iran long enough to consider everything, he might even have a good idea what we'd been up to.

But he wouldn't have proof.

Tiny greeted us at the door, his entire body wagging his pleasure at seeing me, then he ran for the pantry, where his dog snacks were housed.

"You can only have one," I said as I retrieved a chew stick for the massive rottweiler.

He grabbed the treat and headed for the couch without so much as a backward glance.

"I see where I rank," I said.

Ida Belle shrugged. "Typical man. Someone after food."

We pulled on gloves and headed out back and over to the corner of the lot. We were lucky because Carter had a nice sized oak tree near the fence in the back and it would be no problem to climb up and over. I gave Gertie a bit of a boost into the tree and held my breath as she crept out on the limb and then kinda slid over the fence. I heard her grunt a couple of times but then I heard a thud and Ida Belle, who was waiting in the tree, gave me a thumbs-up before she dropped onto the other side.

I made quick work of the fence and we hurried to the patio door, and I was relieved that it slid right open. I briefly wondered if Jenny hadn't realized it was broken or simply didn't care, but either way, we were in. I spotted her laptop on the kitchen counter where it had been when we visited and parked myself on a stool in front of it.

"You guys tackle the rooms," I said. "I'm going to try to figure out the password. And make sure at least one of you always has eyes on the driveway."

They headed off down the hallway and I opened the laptop, wondering how I would be able to guess the password of a woman I'd only spoken with twice and didn't really know. Then I saw the sticky inside the laptop and laughed.

Anothernew$&#password*

I could appreciate the plight. I was constantly updating my password list that I kept in my safe. As often as I was required to update my password, and as difficult as they required me to make them, I was certain the average business had better cybersecurity than the CIA.

I typed what I saw on the sticky and did a fist pump when it opened. I immediately clicked on email and went to work scanning. I didn't find anything of interest in the inbox, but then, I didn't expect she'd have an email discussion about how she planned to kill her husband. I switched to trash and started scrolling until I spotted one that stood out, mainly because it had one of those spammy limited time offer descriptions and was from an email address that looked computer generated at random. But it had gone into her inbox instead of spam, where most things that looked that way went, and it had been read.

I clicked on it and saw in the message today's date and the words 'same place.' I did a quick trace on the email and found it coming from a server in NOLA. So this was how she and Brent were communicating. Seemed like a lot of effort to hide things if there was nothing to it. I took a pic of the email with my phone, then did a search for others from that email address but came up empty.

I shifted to text messages and found they'd all been cleared except for a single one today from the cremation service. I read the message and frowned. If we didn't figure out a way to stop it, Gage's body would be picked up first thing Monday morning and cremated the same day. I left text messages and shifted over to personal documents, clicking through the folders and opening anything that looked like it might be important, but the only thing I was certain of when I'd gone through everything was that Jenny had been carrying Gage financially for their entire marriage.

According to the tax documents I found, her cleaning business did quite well, but with her husband not pulling his weight on the earning end, but exceeding expectation on the spending side of things, it didn't leave much left over for Jenny. I shook my head as I ran through months of expenses listed out in spreadsheets that I'd have bet money the meticulous Graham had created for her. The expenses were highlighted in different colors, each representing the type—home, groceries, repairs, and other regular things, then a bright pink for Jenny's personal expenses and a bright blue for Gage's. Those personal expenses trended 90 percent blue.

Even with no life insurance, Gage had given Jenny a significant raise by dying.

I popped a flash drive into the laptop and copied over some of the files, praying that Jenny wasn't the type who checked her log. I was about to close it and help dig through the rest of the house when the laptop signaled an incoming email. A brief description popped up in the top right corner stating something about a prescription being ready for pickup.

It probably didn't have anything to do with the case, but since I was already there, I popped into the email again to read it, then frowned and did a quick search on my phone for the shortened code to figure out what the prescription was for. I had an idea but I wanted to be sure.

Birth control injections!

I sat back in my chair, trying to put this into perspective. Miriam had told Gertie that Jenny and Gage had tried for years, even checking into fertility treatments but ultimately unable to afford them. Granted, there were a lot of reasons a woman might be on birth control, especially as she got older and hormones got less predictable. But I knew Gage had wanted a big family and Miriam had wanted to be a grand-mother. What if Jenny had only pretended to be on board with their plans?

Not that I could blame her for wanting to forgo mother-hood. Clearly, she'd already had one child to take care of in the form of a grown man. A baby would have only added to her already enormous list of responsibilities, not to mention the additional strain on already stretched finances. Even the always-proper Graham had commented that it was a good thing they hadn't had children.

But what if Gage had found out and that was the reason he'd told Nancy he was going to divorce Jenny as soon as his mother passed? It had to have been something recent and something big to have set him off the way Nancy described, because otherwise, Gage had no reason to want to change his life. His domestic life and the majority of his finances were taken care of by his wife, leaving him free to drink and fish and essentially amount to nothing. It was a luxury very few people had.

But if he'd really wanted to be a father, then finding out Jenny had taken steps to ensure he never became one would have certainly enraged him.

I took a picture of the email, marked it as unread, and closed everything down, leaving the laptop exactly as I'd found it. I had just hopped off the stool when Gertie came flying down the hall, almost running into me, Ida Belle right on her heels.

"Carter's truck just went by!" Gertie yelled.

Crap!

We rushed out of the house and sprinted across the lawn to the back corner, navigating as quickly as possible the mess of crap Gage had heaped there. Ida Belle went over the fence first in case Gertie needed help out of the tree, then Gertie scrambled up the stack of lumber and took a flying leap onto the doghouse.

And Gertied.

CHAPTER NINETEEN

J<small>UMPING ONTO ANY STRUCTURE THAT HAD BEEN BUILT AND</small> maintained—or not maintained—by Gage Babin wasn't the smart move. The roof collapsed and her legs fell through. I rushed up the lumber pile and started to pull her up, but I didn't have the leverage I needed at that angle and height, and couldn't risk standing on the doghouse to get it, as clearly, it was falling apart.

"You're going to have to go down through it," I said.

"What happened?" Ida Belle yelled over.

"Gertie," I yelled back.

That was really all the explanation that was needed.

A few seconds later, Ida Belle peered down from the tree.

"Good God!" she said. "We better hope Carter is stopping off at Emmaline's."

"Houston, we have a problem," Gertie said.

"You think?" Ida Belle asked.

"I can't go down," she said. "That idiot put this roof on from inside. All the nails are facing up. I'd be stuck like a voodoo doll."

Ida Belle started gesturing to one of the many piles of junk. "Toss me up the end of that rope."

Immediately understanding what she had in mind, I snagged the rope and tossed one end up to Ida Belle, who located a smooth area where two branches met and looped the rope over. I had already fashioned the other end into a harness and Gertie got it secured under her arms. Ida Belle tossed the other end of the rope down to me and I gave it a slow tug to test it.

"Let her rip!" Ida Belle said.

I would have preferred a slower extraction, but time was working against us, so I leaned back and let my arm strength and body weight lift Gertie out of the doghouse. But either I was stronger than I thought I was, or heavier—pride had me going with the former—because instead of inching out as I thought she would, she hung there for a second, then all of a sudden, she came loose and shot up as though she'd sat on another exploding seat.

I fell onto the ground, dropping the rope, and sprang back up in time to see her land clear of the doghouse and onto one of the junk piles. When she popped up, there was rust-colored liquid dripping from her hair.

"What the heck did I land in?" she asked.

"Something a shower will fix," Ida Belle said. "Hurry up!"

Gertie shook her head, slinging the stuff everywhere, and climbed back onto the lumber where I boosted her up onto the fence. Then Ida Belle helped drag her into the tree. As soon as I was certain she was secure on the other side, I vaulted over the fence and did a roll before popping up and running for the back porch behind Ida Belle and Gertie.

I didn't see Carter anywhere, so I opened the patio door and Tiny came loping out, ready to play now that he'd had a snack. At least he had his priorities straight. Gertie grabbed the water hose and squirted her head, but there was no way she was going to get that crap out of her clothes. Ida Belle shrugged off her windbreaker and threw it at Gertie, whose yellow T-shirt was now drenched and looked as if it had been sitting in rusty pipes for a year.

I heard Carter's truck approaching and waved at her hair. "He's about to pull in. Do you have a wig in your purse?"

She shook her head. "I took it out to style it and there was this situation with the curling iron. It was a fluke."

"Of course it was," I said. "My agency is going to spring for spares, then you're never allowed out of the house without at least one of them."

"I can just say I was going to fill Tiny's bowl and got myself in the face."

"With rust-colored water?" Ida Belle asked. "Your hair is practically burnt orange."

Tiny, hearing his name, rushed over and dropped his ball at Gertie's feet. She reached out and yanked the bandanna from around his neck and tied it over her head. We'd barely flopped into chairs when Carter opened the patio door.

He looked at the three of us, then around the backyard, then back at Gertie and narrowed his eyes. "Are you wearing Tiny's bandanna on your head?"

"I really liked the color," Gertie said.

He raised his eyebrows. "Red?"

"I'll buy you a whole pack of new ones," Gertie said. "I did this deep conditioning on my hair yesterday and sitting out here in this weather was drying up the ends."

He looked over at Ida Belle and me and we both shrugged. After all, we were probably the last two females on the face of the earth that someone should ask about split ends.

Knowing he'd been outplayed, he switched tactics. "So what are you guys doing here exactly?"

I tossed the ball into the middle of the yard and Tiny scrambled for it. "Playing with Tiny.

I knew you were doing breakfast with Walter and then helping him at the store. We were out, so we figured we'd swing by and give Tiny a run."

"So you're just out riding around for no reason?" he pressed.

He knew good and well he wasn't getting the whole story, but he hadn't hit on what playing with Tiny in his backyard might be hiding. Since he'd been so caught up in his thoughts over Iran the night before, I hadn't told him about Jenny's moving bombshell or her planned trip to NOLA. Hopefully, he wouldn't make the leap to shared fence corners and find out Jenny wasn't at home. It wasn't so much that I cared if Carter knew what we were up to personally, but any evidence we might have gained hadn't followed proper channels, which could make things sketchy if Blanchet ever managed to put a case together.

Bottom line, Carter and Blanchet both had to be kept in the dark. At least until we had proof.

"You got everything done fast," I said.

He nodded. "It wasn't much to move. Just bulky and took two people. The store got busy right about the time we finished up so I headed out. Lots of people asking about Gage."

Ida Belle nodded. "People count on Walter for the local information."

"He said he doesn't know anything," Carter said. "I mean, as far as the service goes."

Ida Belle glanced over at me and gave me a barely imperceptible shake of her head, meaning she hadn't told Walter about our visit with Graham.

"I don't think any decisions have been made yet about the

service," Ida Belle said. "We paid Graham a visit yesterday to see if there was anything we could help with and he never mentioned a date."

Gertie nodded. "I know Gage was a trial to his brother, but they were still twins. I can't imagine this has been easy on him."

"Probably not," Carter said. "How's he doing?"

"Seems all right, but it's hard to tell," Ida Belle said. "Graham was always the proper, stoic one of the family."

"True," Carter agreed. "If they hadn't looked so much alike, I would have sworn Graham was switched at the hospital. He doesn't really fit with the rest of them. Don't get me wrong, Miriam is a nice woman, but Graham comes across as a higher social station."

I nodded. "If I hadn't known who he was and had met him out somewhere, I would have assumed he was part of New Orleans society. He's got that refined look and speech. Anyway, I guess we'll get out of your hair. Since we've been sitting here talking, Gertie and I decided we need a shopping trip for funeral clothes, so we're heading to NOLA. Might stay overnight if we can't find anything today. You know me and shopping."

He narrowed his eyes at me. "I *do* know you and shopping, which is why I'm having a hard time believing that's what you're going to do. And Gertie has a bigger wardrobe than a Kardashian."

"True," Gertie agreed, "but the vast majority is not fit for a funeral."

"The vast majority is not fit to wear outside your house," Ida Belle corrected.

"Anyway," Gertie continued, "there were a couple of incidents and I need to retire my two standard funeral dresses."

I held in a laugh. Carter wasn't about to ask for more information on that one.

"And you?" he asked me. "Did you have an incident with your funeral dress as well?"

"Not unless you count wearing the same dress to every funeral I've attended since I moved here. And that's not exactly a small number. Ronald claims I've moved past frugal and am hurtling toward disrespectful. I don't care, of course, but if Gertie needs to shop anyway, I might as well add another option."

It was clear that Carter didn't believe a word we were saying, but he also couldn't figure out why we'd be going on an overnight trip to NOLA when a man might have been murdered and all the major players lived here. As long as he didn't find out that Jenny was off there on holiday, then we'd be good.

He must have decided that it wasn't worth the effort to try to figure it out, because he leaned over and gave me a kiss. "Try not to get into any trouble."

"Who? Us?"

"Detective Casey can't bail you out of everything, you know."

"It's shopping. How bad could it be?"

He laughed. "Remember when you went shopping for that dress for the New Year's Queen contest?"

"That was different. Celia won't be anywhere near us."

We headed out and as soon as we jumped into the SUV, Gertie ripped off the bandanna and leaned forward to look at her hair in the rearview mirror.

"I've got to get in the shower right away and get this off," she said. "I can't go anywhere with rust-streaked hair. I look like old plumbing bled on me."

"Head to my house," I directed Ida Belle. "Gertie can shower and change there."

"Why there?" Gertie asked.

"I have a bad feeling about that hair. It might call for a Ronald intervention, so might as well go where he and his supplies are readily available."

After three shampoos, using three different products, the rust color hadn't budged so much as an inch. If anything, it was now shiny. Ida Belle lifted a couple of strands to inspect it.

"We could always cut the streaked ends off," she said.

"You're not cutting my hair! I've seen you cut snowflakes with the kids at Sunday school. It's not pretty."

"I think it's time to get Ronald involved," I said and pulled out my cell phone.

Hair emergency. Need you asap!

I swear I had barely hit Send when I got a return message.

Omw. Don't panic!

He must have run all the way over because the back door opened, and he dashed in as soon as I finished reading the message to Ida Belle and Gertie. He took one look at Gertie's hair and shrieked as though he'd just spotted a ten-foot spider. It was especially dramatic as he was wearing a *Gone with the Wind* dress, complete with parasol. Obviously he'd panicked over the words *hair emergency* and had bolted out the door in what he was already wearing, which led to so many other questions.

"No jeans?" I asked.

"I put them through the shredder," he said and waved a hand at Gertie.

"Sit!" he commanded, and hurried over to inspect her hair, muttering to himself the entire time.

"What did you do?" he asked finally.

"We'd rather not say," I said.

"Well, what *is* it?"

"I don't know," Gertie said.

"How can you not know?"

"Because she fell in something while we were somewhere doing something we can't talk about," I said.

He threw his hands into the air and flopped into the chair next to Gertie, then started waving himself with a stack of napkins.

"I have no words," he said. "I never understood what my gran was referring to when she said she had the vapors. I do now."

"We have something important to do this afternoon in NOLA and we need to blend," I said. "Can you fix it?"

His jaw dropped and he stared. "I'm a fashionista, not a sorcerer. Or Jesus. You remember how he walked on water and rose from the dead after a week? This is harder."

He stared at Gertie's hair for a while longer, shaking his head. "Without knowing what it is, it's next to impossible to know what to use to neutralize it. The wrong product could make things worse."

"How could it be worse?" I asked.

"Before I learned from professionals, I turned my hair green," he said. "And then there was the time that I burned it all off right down to my scalp. Thank God I didn't do my eyebrows to match. I plucked them once over a decade ago and the hair still hasn't grown back in, which is just my luck now that big eyebrows are in fashion."

He put one hand over his heart and took in a deep breath, then slowly exhaled. "I don't suppose you can pop back over to that secret place this happened and see what it is?"

"Not unless we want problems with the law and the property owner."

He sighed. "You're such a hard person to be friends with. A normal hair emergency is about humidity or not having the right styling wand."

"So you can't fix it," I said.

"I'd be afraid to even try."

"Okay, then plan B. Do you have a wig she can borrow?"

He narrowed his eyes. "Things that Gertie borrows often become destroyed or police evidence, but I'll check my synthetic hair collection. I have a lovely pink one—"

"No." I shook my head. "Remember, I said we need to blend."

His eyes widened. "And you're going to NOLA... You're investigating! Are you going to spy on the hotel king? I want to come!"

I stared and motioned to his dress. "Blend?"

He slumped back in his chair, as much as the tight fabric allowed anyway. "I guess I should have held up on that jeans-shredding thing. But it's just as well. I've got a blister on my foot from those abominable shoes I wore to the party. I really need a long soak and to limit my walking for a day or two. You people run too much."

"Only when people are shooting at us," Gertie said. "And from alligators and bears, and anything else that can eat you. And when there's an explosive about to go off."

Ronald stared at her in dismay. "And that's okay?"

"We've factored it into our daily lives," Ida Belle said. "Maybe you have something you wore for a costume party. You ever played the grandma from *Little Red Riding Hood*?"

"No, but I went to a cosmic party as a sexy three-hundred-year-old alien."

"Nothing sexy," I said. "Blending, remember?"

He waved a hand in the air. "Honey, you're going to NOLA. Butt naked with lit firecrackers on your head would blend."

Gertie perked up. "That's a great idea for a Medusa costume."

"Maybe with a fire-retardant bodysuit," Ronald said. "Have to hide those stubborn fat areas."

"And your unmentionables," Ida Belle grumbled.

Ronald pushed himself out of the chair and the dress sprang out, filling half of my kitchen. "I'll go see what I've got. I'm sure I can come up with something."

"I'm happy to pay for it," I said.

"The wig's on me," he said as he squeezed through the back door. "I'll have my *therapist* bill you."

———

ON THE DRIVE TO NOLA, WE FILLED EACH OTHER IN ON what we'd found at Jenny's house. Ida Belle and Gertie didn't seem surprised with Jenny and Gage's financial state, but they hadn't realized it was so bad.

"Miriam really did that girl a disservice, getting her to promise to take care of Gage," Gertie said. "At some point, you need to accept your kid is a dud and let them sink. Hitting bottom is the only thing that turns some of them around."

"I think Gage would have hit bottom and drowned down there," Ida Belle said. "And I'm sure Miriam knew that, which makes it even worse that she roped Jenny into that mess. She knew Jenny would never go back on a promise to her."

"Especially given how indebted Jenny felt," Gertie said. "It's one thing if you want to carry your useless kid through life, but you shouldn't ask other people to sacrifice themselves at the altar of your poor choices."

I nodded. "And all that helps explain the next bit of information I got."

I told them about the birth control.

"Smart," Ida Belle said. "She might not have been able to get away from Gage as long as Miriam was still alive, but she could ensure she wasn't tied to him the rest of her life through a kid."

"Not to mention the additional financial, physical, and emotional strain it would have been," Gertie said. "It doesn't appear Gage showed up much as a husband. I can't imagine that would have improved as a father, regardless of how much he thought he wanted kids."

"Men want kids because women are usually doing the bulk of the work," Ida Belle said.

I nodded. "You know what I don't understand? Why was she with him in the first place? I mean, I get that he was probably a decent-looking guy before alcohol and poor diet got the best of him, because Graham is an attractive man. But it sounds like Gage has always been the class clown, never taking any responsibility. So why marry him? Why not marry Graham instead? Seems like he would have been the better choice."

"Gage was a charmer," Gertie said. "Even as a boy. When he was a rascal in school, he could often talk himself out of trouble with the teachers. That's probably why he went into sales. If he'd taken it seriously and laid off the alcohol, he probably would have been quite successful."

Ida Belle nodded. "Add to that he was the opposite of Jenny—outgoing where she's an introvert—and people are often attracted to their opposites. Brent was an attention-grabbing party boy when she met him. But ultimately, I think she felt safe with Gage and he's the brother who pursued her."

"Exactly," Gertie agreed. "Even if she'd been interested in Graham, Jenny would have never made a move his direction. It simply wasn't in her personality makeup to do so."

"People are so complicated," I mused.

"People *make* things complicated," Ida Belle said.

"I wonder if the rumors about Graham being in love with Jenny have any truth to them," I said.

Ida Belle frowned. "I remember seeing Graham off to the side at Gage and Jenny's wedding reception and thinking, 'That's not exactly a look of joy on his face.' He was putting forth his best manners with people, of course, and smiling the whole time, but I had the feeling it was plastered on."

"So he wasn't a fan of the marriage," I said.

"It didn't look like it," Ida Belle said.

"But that could have been just because he knew Gage wouldn't treat Jenny right," Gertie said.

"And it could also be because Graham thought he could treat her better," I said.

"If Graham has been carrying a torch for Jenny all these years, it might explain why he never married," Ida Belle said.

I nodded. "It also gives him a motive for murdering his brother, especially since Graham was aware of Gage's affair."

"Crap," Gertie said. "I hadn't taken it that far, but you're right. With Gage gone, Graham might have thought Jenny would make the next safest move."

"Which is why he was so shocked when she announced she was moving," Ida Belle said. "The man was so taken aback he didn't even escort her out like he did us."

"I noticed that," I said, rolling all the possible scenarios over in my mind. Finally, I had to stop because I was getting nowhere. "Okay, let's table all that for a moment and you guys tell me what you found."

"The living room was devoid of anything interesting, including a personality," Gertie said. "They haven't changed a single thing in there since Miriam decorated it back when Noah came over on the ark. I assume they kept it that way for her."

"Or Jenny didn't want to spend all the money they didn't have on upholstery, rugs, and sofa pillows," I said. "Having done some changing of the color guard myself, let me just say that I'm in the wrong business. Those decor people are making a killing."

"True," Gertie said, "but Miriam's bedroom and bath are still completely intact as well. And I mean everything. Clothes, shoes, books, jewelry, nail polish, even an old coffee mug on her nightstand. The bathroom still has a bar of soap in it and expired prescription meds in her cabinet. It looks like no one has been in the place since the day she moved out. See?"

Gertie showed us some images of the room she'd taken.

Ida Belle glanced over and frowned. "It's like a shrine, but she's not dead yet."

"Maybe they were hoping for a miracle," I said, "and didn't want to change anything because it felt disrespectful."

"Or like they were willing her into the grave," Ida Belle said.

"But why not clean her room up at least?" Gertie asked. "Why not toss the coffee mug in the dishwasher or throw away that old bar of soap? Jenny cleans for a living and so did Miriam. It just seems strange to me."

"I agree," I said. "But there's been no shortage of strange since I moved here."

"If I had to guess, that's on Gage," Ida Belle said. "A lot of people around here are superstitious."

"So washing out a dirty mug would somehow trigger a negative event, but all the pranks he played wouldn't," I said, shaking my head. "Only in Sinful does that make sense."

"Well, that's all I've got," Gertie said. "There was one more room used as a guest room, but it was set up like a motel, so nothing in it but the basic furniture. Clean as a whistle though. Did you come up with anything, Ida Belle?"

"A whole lot of nothing," she said. "I found the checkbook and some old bank statements—probably before everything was digital—but nothing that adds to what we already know. I will say that Jenny lived a very spartan life. Her wardrobe is leaner than Fortune's and that's saying something. There was one exception, which I found interesting."

"What's that?"

"She had a small jewelry box—a kid's jewelry box, and it was old. There was a plain gold necklace and one with a crucifix and a pair of diamond earrings. Tiny diamonds, so probably real. And then the usual assortment of costume jewelry. Her wedding band was also in there."

"That *is* interesting," Gertie said.

"I haven't gotten to the interesting part yet," Ida Belle said. "I noticed the bottom of the box moved when I shifted the jewelry around, so I took it all out and there was a secret panel beneath."

She pulled her cell phone out and passed it to me. "I took a picture."

I pulled up the last picture taken and stared. "Wow! That's some serious ice."

Gertie leaned forward and I showed her the bracelet. "No way she'd go to the effort to hide it if it was a fake."

"Or if it was from her husband," Ida Belle said.

"A gift from Brent?" Gertie suggested. "He has the pocketbook."

"That's the logical assumption," I said. "The question is was it gifted back when they were married or more recently?"

"Why hide it if it was from before?" Gertie asked. "Gage could hardly complain about a gift her husband gave her when they were married."

"To keep him from hocking it," Ida Belle suggested.

"Oh yeah," Gertie said. "That makes a lot of sense. Interesting that she's kept it all this time."

"Maybe it was always part of her exit strategy," Ida Belle

said. "I bet it would bring a nice sum. She might have been planning to use the money to start over after Miriam died."

I considered this for a moment. "But did Jenny consider her promise to Miriam null and void when Miriam died?"

Ida Belle frowned. "Good question. Because if the answer is yes, then she had no reason to kill Gage. She just had to wait for Miriam to pass."

Gertie nodded. "So unless Jenny felt an obligation to care for Gage the rest of *his* life, that seriously reduces her motive."

"Unless Brent wasn't willing to wait around for Miriam to die," I said. "Miriam's already been around longer than originally predicted. And with the constant advances in medication, she could be around for years to come."

"True," Gertie said. "Or maybe Graham knew he couldn't make a play for his brother's wife unless Gage was dead."

Ida Belle shook her head. "We really don't know enough about Graham, do we?"

I stared out the windshield, trying to figure how to get more information on what was most certainly a very private man with a perfect public image. Then before I could change my mind, I motioned to Ida Belle.

"Go to Mudbug," I said.

Ida Belle changed lanes and took the exit without question, but when we stopped at the end of the access road, she looked over at me, one eyebrow up.

"I don't have a plan," I said. "I just have this feeling that we should watch him for a bit."

"What about Jenny?" Gertie asked.

"If she's going to see Brent, then we'll be able to find her just as well later as we could now."

Ida Belle put on her blinker and made the turn. I watched as the cypress trees zoomed by and wondered, yet again, if my instincts were on point or completely off-kilter.

CHAPTER TWENTY

IDA BELLE FOUND A SPOT TO PARK AT THE END OF THE BLOCK behind a plumber's van. I'd pulled a ball cap down low on my head, put on sunglasses, and taken a jog down the street. I made the block, then jumped back into the SUV.

"Well?" Gertie asked.

"His car is parked out front, same as when we were there yesterday."

"I have a feeling it's going to be a long afternoon of watching that loose sticker flap on the plumber's van," Ida Belle said. "What are you hoping to see?"

I shrugged. I couldn't give her an answer because I didn't have one. But I had this overwhelming feeling that I needed to be here to see something. Still, maybe it was a waste of time when we could be in NOLA tracking down Jenny.

I was just about to tell Ida Belle to forget it and go when a sleek white Mercedes sedan drove past us. I motioned to Ida Belle to pull around the van, so we had a clear view of the house. If this car turned out to be nothing—like the last six that had passed—then we'd head to NOLA, and I'd chalk this whole thing up to another misfire of my intuition.

As Ida Belle swung around the plumber's van, the Mercedes pulled into Graham's driveway.

"I don't know that car," Ida Belle said.

"Me either," Gertie said as a tall, distinguished-looking man climbed out. "But I know the man.

Midfifties. Six foot two. A hundred eighty-five pounds. Trim build. Expensive suit. Perfect haircut. Looked as dangerous as a box of kittens.

"That's Richard Mayfield III," Gertie said. "His father founded the CPA firm Graham works at. He's the senior partner."

Ida Belle sighed. "So nothing."

I nodded. "Let's go. I don't know what I was hoping for, but the longer we sit here, the less I think something is going to materialize."

She continued down the street toward Graham's house, figuring since he had company he wouldn't be looking outside, but as we passed in front of his house, I saw two silhouettes in the living room window.

"Stop!" I said, and Ida Belle slammed on the brakes. I jumped out of the SUV and yelled, "Park around the corner," as I dashed behind a hedge between Graham's yard and his neighbors'.

I crept down the hedge, then bolted down the side of Graham's house, around the back, and to the other side until I reached the side wall window of the living room. I heard low voices coming from inside but couldn't make out what they were saying. Then the voices went quiet, and I eased up and peered into the window, hoping to verify what I thought I'd seen when we passed.

Graham and his boss in a clench. A romantic clench!

I ducked down again, skirted the house and headed back to

the sidewalk where I jogged around the corner and jumped into the SUV. Ida Belle and Gertie gave me expectant looks.

"Is Mayfield married?" I asked, clearly confusing them both.

"Yes," Gertie said. "To a particularly loathsome but well-connected woman who comes from old money."

And suddenly, certain things made perfect sense. "Well, that explains why they're keeping their relationship a secret."

"Mayfield and Graham?"

"You're kidding me."

They both reacted at the same time.

I nodded. "I thought I saw the silhouette of them in a clench, but I wanted to verify."

"And you're sure it wasn't just a consoling hug?" Gertie asked.

"If I saw Carter hugging Blanchet like that, I'd be retrieving my toothbrush from his bathroom. There was also kissing. And not European-greeting kissing either."

Gertie shook her head. "Well, I guess I can't say that it's completely surprising. We've probably all had that thought cross our minds about Graham at some point."

Ida Belle nodded. "But I'm certain no one picked Mayfield as the object of his affection."

"What are the odds that Mayfield's wife knows her husband is gay?" I asked.

"Given that he's still breathing, I'm going with slim to none," Ida Belle said.

Gertie nodded. "Her family is rigid when it comes to reputation. They've been married for over thirty years and have four kids. If this got out, it would be a scandal the likes of which that family has never seen."

"Got it," I said. "But it does explain two things—why

Graham left NOLA for Mudbug and why he's never been romantically linked to a woman."

"Which means he was never in love with Jenny," Gertie said with a sigh. "There goes his motive for killing Gage."

"I'm certain he loves Jenny," Ida Belle said. "He's obviously just not *in* love with her."

"But is that enough to kill his brother over?" I asked. "She's not his flesh and blood. Gage was."

Ida Belle shrugged. "Doesn't mean anything to a lot of people. And besides, Gage was a thorn in his side as well. But I agree. If a romantic interest in Jenny is no longer on the table, I don't think he has a strong enough motive for murder. Looks like we're back to Jenny."

"And Dean Allard," Gertie said. "For that matter, maybe it was Nancy. We only have her word about Gage divorcing Jenny, and she admitted she'd developed feelings for him. Maybe she told him as much, and he said it would never happen."

Ida Belle nodded. "She wouldn't be the first woman scorned to decide if she couldn't have him, no one else could either. And she *was* the last to see him."

"But why admit that if she was the one who killed him?" I asked.

"Because she thinks someone saw him leaving her house that night," Ida Belle said. "You never told her *when* your source saw them."

"And then there were three," Gertie said.

"I don't know," I said. "It's a flimsy motive, at best, and I don't really like her for this."

"Let's get to NOLA and find Jenny," Gertie said. "I know it looks really bad for her, especially with the cremation and her moving and being seen with Brent, but I really don't want it to be her."

I nodded. I didn't either. I had only had two interactions with her, but I liked her. And based on what I knew about her life, I felt sorry for her. The first time we went to her house, her grief had seemed genuine. I knew now it was no great love affair, but that didn't mean she had stopped caring about Gage altogether. Given their history, it would take a lot to completely erase all her feelings for him.

Or maybe she'd just been upset because of what Gage's death would do to Miriam.

Was it grief or guilt? I wished I knew.

———

THE HOTEL WAS NICE, THEREFORE EXPENSIVE, BUT I STILL opted for two rooms, connected. The snoring wasn't an issue, but three women and one bathroom was. Even if two of the women didn't spend a lot of time getting ready. Technically, I didn't have a client, which meant it wasn't a business expense, so I just put it on my personal card and we headed for the elevators.

We'd made small talk while checking in—saying we'd stayed once before and asking if the Copeland family still owned the place. When the clerk verified that they did, Gertie asked about Brent as she'd met him when he was a child. The clerk had smiled, as people tend to do when talking to nice senior ladies, and informed her that Brent was all grown up and the manager of this hotel as well as two others.

The rooms were gorgeous with great views of the French Quarter. It only took us a minute to dump our bags, then we got to work. Gertie and I hauled out binoculars and started scanning the parking lot across the street, figuring it would save us some walking time if we could spot Jenny's car from our room. There was a parking garage on the other side of the hotel, so if we came up with nothing here, we'd take a walk through the garage next.

Ida Belle made a call to the hotel from her cell phone, asking if the manager was in because she'd like to speak with him in person about handling a high-profile event. The receptionist had tried to transfer her to the events coordinator, but Ida Belle had remained insistent and had finally learned that Brent would not be working again until Monday.

I was about to decide I'd misplayed our hand by assuming Jenny would come here when I spotted a car that looked like hers in the back spot of the parking lot.

"There," I said. "Right side, all the way in the back."

Gertie swung over. "It's a white Accord. Can't see the plates from here though. And I didn't make note of the wheels."

"Me either, but there's Mardi Gras beads hanging from the rearview mirror just like Jenny's."

"Not exactly an uncommon occurrence in these parts."

"True. We'll check the plate to be sure."

But I was pretty sure it was her car, which made me happy, especially after Ida Belle's phone call. We were just getting ready to head out when my phone rang. Ronald. I put him on speaker.

"So I got some juicy info from my friend about Brent Copeland," he said. "Apparently, Brent got off into the cocaine scene years ago, maybe as far back as his twenties. His parents tried everything but couldn't get him straightened out."

"That would explain why no relationships," Ida Belle said. "Most addicts are already married."

"Might also explain why he and Jenny divorced if it went that far back," Gertie said.

"That would do it," Ronald said, "but about a year ago, Brent was partying in Miami with college buddies and one of them died from an overdose. Given money and some family political connections down there, he managed to get off with no charges, but apparently, it was the catalyst he needed. He checked into one of those country club rehabs but unlike most, he did the work. He's clean now."

"And in touch with Jenny again," I said. "Anything else?"

"Yes. He had an expensive penthouse in the business district but sold it after rehab and took a suite at the hotel where I attended the party. My buddy says he threw himself into the business and doesn't even drink anymore. His parents are thrilled."

I smiled. "So am I. We're checked into the hotel right now, and I think we just spotted Jenny's car in the parking lot across the street."

"Oh! I'm so jealous!" Ronald exclaimed. "But my feet simply couldn't handle an adventure right now. Be safe. And no more hair emergencies. I'm out of synthetic wigs that meet the 'blend' requirement you insist on pushing."

"Maybe we'll pick up a couple new wigs while we're here. Thanks, Ronald."

"I think it's safe to assume that's Jenny's car," Gertie said, "which means they're both in residence. I wonder if Jenny has a room or if she's staying in Brent's suite."

"She'll have a room," Ida Belle said. "For appearances if nothing else. But that doesn't mean she's staying in it."

I nodded. "Either way, they're both in the hotel, so we have to be careful traipsing around. If Jenny spots us, the jig is up."

"True, but what exactly are we hoping to accomplish now?" Ida Belle asked. "We know Jenny is here. We know Brent is here. The date matches with the email you saw. Short of videoing them in a clench like Graham and his boss, what else can we do?"

"I'd love to get that picture. But you're right. We verified my suspicions without even leaving the room." I looked over at Gertie's hopeful expression and sighed. "I guess we go shopping."

Since our goal was to go unnoticed, we were all wearing jeans and plain shirts with tennis shoes. Because Jenny was staying in the same hotel, Ida Belle had ditched her signature flannel and opted for a solid navy T-shirt. Gertie had toned down her usual bright colors to what she called the most boring shade of dark green ever invented. Paired with the short-haired and conservatively styled silver wig Ronald had lent her, she looked like any other grandmother you'd pass on the street.

We'd all brought hats and sunglasses, so we gathered those up in case we needed to disguise ourselves further and headed out. We'd just exited the elevator and started across the lobby when I spotted Jenny and Brent coming from the restaurant. And we were in line to completely intersect.

"Hide," I said.

CHAPTER TWENTY-ONE

I bolted for the gift shop like a Christmas shopper running for a TV on sale for $100. Ida Belle had been right beside me, so she was on my heels as I rushed inside and peered out the window into the lobby. Gertie had been a few feet in front of us and had already passed the door to the gift shop. She froze for a second, then caught sight of Jenny and Brent. I hoped she'd turn around and follow us, but Gertie never took the easy way out.

As Jenny and Brent started to turn her direction, probably headed for the elevators, she took a running leap into an unattended cleaning cart just off to the side of the main walkway. Unfortunately, the cart either had no brakes or the attendant had failed to activate them. The cart shot off from its spot near the wall and headed right into the lobby.

So far, Jenny and Brent were blocked from view of the runaway cart by the concierge's booth and a fountain, but if I didn't catch it before it rolled into the seating area, it was all over. I bolted out of the shop, pulling my cap down as I went, leaped over a luggage cart, and sprinted for the cart.

Gertie had managed to upright herself and was now

clinging to the front of it, getting a clear view of her impending disaster. As the cart was almost within my reach, she stood up—I have no idea why—and the cart tipped forward, slamming into the back of a couch. Gertie fell out of the cart and rolled over the back of the couch, landing upright next to an elderly couple, probably taking half of the remaining years they had off their life.

I managed to grab the cart before it tipped over, which would have made enough noise to send everyone running this direction, then ran around the couch to grab Gertie, giving a prayer of thanks that Ronald had insisted on securing her wig before we left. Now we had to get out of there before a hotel employee came to see what the commotion was.

"It's too darn loud in here," the man sitting on the couch said. "All this noise is giving me a headache."

The woman pulled a bottle of aspirin from her purse and handed him pills. "You're not getting out of seeing this play, so don't even try."

He grunted and tossed back the pills as I grabbed Gertie's arm and vaulted her off the couch.

"We're going to miss our plane," I said by way of explanation to the startled couple and dragged her down the hallway toward the restrooms.

Ida Belle hurried in right after us, and Gertie leaned against the counter to catch her breath.

"Good Lord, that was a wild ride!" she said. "But at least they didn't see me."

She gave us a triumphant grin as if she'd just won a gold in the Summer Olympics.

Ida Belle threw her hands in the air. "Why didn't you just turn around and walk the other direction? Millions of old women are walking around with that same hairstyle and none of them are you. It's not like we're wearing jerseys with our names on the back. How was she going to recognize you?"

Gertie sighed. "Buzzkill. Anyway, since I was off riding the maintenance cart, I didn't get a good look at them."

"Since I was off chasing the maintenance cart, neither did I."

Ida Belle shook her head. "Thank God there's three of us. They were walking and talking and smiling, but no hand-holding or any other indication of a romantic relationship. But when they got on the elevator, he pushed a button and she didn't, and when he looked over at her, he wore that same look I see on Carter's face when he looks at Fortune, assuming she hasn't done anything to annoy him."

I nodded. "You think he's still in love with her. How did she look?"

"A bit flushed, like he'd just given her a big compliment—which is all it might take given that she's been married to Gage. I can't imagine she's had too much of that over the years."

"But no stars in her eyes?"

Ida Belle considered this. "I can't really say. But she was happy, which is a look I haven't seen on her in a long time."

"She's had a lot to process this week," Gertie said.

"That's not all," Ida Belle said. "When they walked past the gift shop entry, a delivery person opened the door and took some time to maneuver boxes inside. I heard part of their conversation. He said, 'Are you sure you don't want me to go with you now?' And she said, 'You've already done enough, but I'll call you as soon as I get there.'"

"Where's she going?" I asked. "And what's he done?"

"Maybe he's helping her find a place to live," Gertie suggested.

I shook my head. "He said do you want me to go with you

now—implying that if not now, he'd go in the future. And why would she call him when she got there if she was just going to look at a place to rent?"

"It does sound strange," Ida Belle said. "And I was careful to remember the exact phrasing for that reason. I also managed a quick shot of them while they were walking toward the elevators, but I don't know that it proves anything."

"It's proof of what Ronald saw," I said. "That way, it's not his word against theirs or ours, since us being here is a bit sketchy."

"But does it matter?" Gertie asked. "They aren't exactly trying to hide. Anyone who's been in the hotel at the same time could probably back up what we saw. It doesn't prove Jenny killed her husband. Heck, it doesn't even prove she was having an affair, although I'll admit it doesn't look good."

I frowned. Something was bothering me about the entire thing—something other than the looks and the conversation—but I couldn't pinpoint what it was. I hadn't really gotten a good look at Jenny and Brent before I dashed after Gertie, so I doubted that was it. Besides, something had been niggling at me the whole ride to NOLA. But what was it?

And then it hit me!

I grabbed Gertie's shoulders. "Did you take a picture of those prescriptions in Miriam's bathroom?"

"Yes."

"Show me!" I could feel my excitement building. That feeling that always came over me when I was about to have a breakthrough.

She pulled up the photo and handed me her phone. I enlarged it, reading one pill bottle after another, then let out a whoop so loud both of them jumped.

"That's it!" I yelled.

I pulled out my cell phone and called Blanchet. "Call the

ME and tell him to test for digoxin. Tell him you have motive, means, and opportunity. All you need is confirmation. Yes, I'm sure."

When I hung up, Ida Belle smiled.

"You think someone gave him Miriam's old meds and it caused a heart attack," Ida Belle said.

I nodded. "We know he already had heart problems, and he wasn't healthy. Too much digoxin would have been toxic."

"Especially with all the drinking and the climb up into the boat," Ida Belle said.

I nodded. "And poor kidney function and dehydration are both factors in digoxin toxicity. Want to bet Gage had both?"

"That's so clever," Gertie said, then frowned. "But it puts it square on Jenny, doesn't it?"

"I'm afraid so."

"What put you onto it?" Ida Belle asked.

"It was the older couple that Gertie almost landed on. He complained about a headache and the woman handed him pills and he just took them without even looking to see what they were. Add that to the drinking, the climb, his anger at Jenny, and his excitement over the prank, and you come up with a heart attack."

"But Nancy said she'd given him aspirin at her house," Gertie said.

"I imagine they didn't do much good given that he started in on the whiskey along with them," Ida Belle said.

I nodded. "So if someone offered him aspirin later, he wouldn't have turned them down. He might not have even remembered he'd already taken some given how much he'd been drinking."

"And they could have doubled up and offered the pills and a dosed bottle of water just to be sure, then taken the bottle with them when they left. Unless you think they dosed the beer."

"I doubt it," I said. "That beer can and the liquid could be kept in evidence for years, unlike Gage's body. It probably went like you said. We've been assuming he would have started to seize immediately, but the digoxin would have taken a bit of time to go through his system."

"So he would have had time to climb into the boat and get situated," Gertie said. "Then couldn't Nancy have given it to him earlier?"

"Possibly, but then she would have been risking him dying in her house," I said. "Especially if they got up to their normal business later on. I'm sure the exertion was the final straw that set things off, so all of it was a gamble."

Ida Belle nodded. "Gage dying in her home would be the last thing she'd want. Besides, what would Nancy's motive be? Even if she asked Gage for more in their relationship and was in a rage over his refusal, we don't know that she has access to digoxin. It's not the most common of medications anymore. And people taking it need to be closely monitored."

Gertie's face fell with every word Ida Belle said. "And they wouldn't have let Miriam bring it to the nursing home, which is why it was still there in that shrine of a bedroom suite."

Ida Belle nodded and looked over at me to explain. "The homes order the residents' drugs themselves so they can monitor usage. They don't allow your personal stuff to come in unless they can't get your meds filled in time, and even then they take control of them to ensure proper dosage."

"But if Gage was so mad he was going to divorce Jenny, then why would he let her help him with a prank?" Gertie took one last stab at defending Jenny.

"Gage was mad a week ago," Ida Belle said. "Maybe Jenny came up with a cover or maybe Gage was just blowholing like he always did. Maybe Jenny suggested the prank as a way to smooth things over."

Gertie sighed. "I still don't want to believe it."

"I'm not happy about it myself," I said. "But the alternative is to let her get away with murder."

Gertie shook her head. "Even though I know the evidence lines up, I just can't picture her out on the side of the road with him, handing him those pills and praying they killed him."

Ida Belle raised one eyebrow. "Even though she probably knew he was coming from his mistress's house to meet her?"

"Exactly," I said.

It wasn't the answer we'd wanted. But it ticked all the boxes.

CHAPTER TWENTY-TWO

It was two brutal hours of pacing the floor in our room before I heard from Blanchet, and he was practically shouting.

"You're a genius! His blood had enough digoxin in it to cause a heart attack in a horse. The ME is bouncing between being apologetic and mad at himself for missing it. I did some reading on it while I was waiting and it's a real doozy. I don't think he did anything wrong, which makes me wonder exactly how many people have gotten away with killing someone like this."

"Back when it was commonly used, I'm sure more often than we'd like to know," I said. "Are you sure Gage was never prescribed the medication?"

"I'm sure. The ME finally got his medical records from the hospital for that ER visit. The doctor noted that he had an arrhythmia and told him he should see a cardiologist."

"Which he never did."

"Of course not. You said you had motive and opportunity... tell me."

I filled him in on Jenny and Brent's reconnection and that Miriam had been prescribed digoxin.

"And you saw the meds *in* Jenny's house? When?"

"Uh, yes to the first question but you probably don't want to know the details to the second."

"Good God! Am I going to find any forensic evidence of you guys in there?"

"We're not amateurs," I replied, a bit offended.

"Sorry, I'm just not used to having qualified outside help. Okay, given the cause of death, I'll be able to get a warrant to search the house today—I hunt with a judge who won't mind giving me a signature on a Saturday. I need to retrieve the medication before she ditches it."

I nodded, frowning. Why *hadn't* she ditched it already?

"You've got time," I said. "She drove out this morning for an overnight trip, and the med was in Miriam's bathroom medicine cabinet after she left. We followed her to NOLA."

"Graham owns the house now, right?"

"Probably, at least until Gage's interest is legally discharged to Jenny."

"So he could let me inside."

"I wouldn't contact him. He'll warn Jenny. She's like a sister to him, and he cared about her a lot more than he did Gage from what I can see. But there's something else that might be a problem."

I told him the piece of conversation Ida Belle had overheard.

Blanchet cursed. "You think she's leaving town?"

"I don't know, but if that's the plan, then Copeland has the means to get her most anywhere. And if Graham tips her off..."

He cursed again. "Okay. First things first, I'll get the search warrant and execute. When I have what I need, I'll contact the NOLA police and ask them to hold her for questioning. Can you get eyes on her in case she tries to leave the hotel?"

"I can try. Oh, and Blanchet, her patio door doesn't lock. Don't go breaking down the front door. It will just be something else Graham has to repair."

JENNY'S CAR HADN'T MOVED FROM ITS ORIGINAL PARKING space, so if she'd gone somewhere earlier, she'd either walked or gotten a ride. I hoped it wasn't a ride to the airport. We headed downstairs, figuring we'd check the bar and restaurant for any sign of Brent or Jenny and then take up seats in the lobby. The couch that Gertie had fallen over gave us a view of the front doors but was tucked back enough that it offered a bit of camouflage.

On the elevator ride down, I got a text from Blanchet.

Jenny was issued a passport two months ago.

Crap! I showed Ida Belle and Gertie the text and we gave one another grim looks. Everything we'd discovered pointed not only to Jenny being the killer, but to premeditation with a plan to get out of the country if everything unraveled. She'd only tossed a small bag into her car when she'd left her house that morning, but then, for all we knew, she might have a trunk full of luggage she'd loaded the night before. Maybe that's the reason Ida Belle had found her clothing collection so sparse.

What if she'd already gone and I'd figured it out too late?

We checked the bar first, mostly for easy elimination, because we figured they wouldn't be in there given Brent's life changes. Then we checked the restaurant, but it was only 4:00 p.m. and the place wasn't crowded. Too late for lunch. Too early for dinner. We couldn't exactly waltz up to the front desk and ask for her, so we headed to the couch in the lobby for a stakeout, under the assumption that she was still somewhere in the hotel.

We spent nearly two hours rooted on the same piece of furniture, trying to look casual, and when I finally couldn't stand not moving any longer, I jogged across the street to make sure Jenny's car was still in the parking lot. It was. That bit of activity took all of ten minutes of my time, but at least the cool air had perked me up a bit. It also reminded me that we hadn't eaten since breakfast. I headed back inside and rounded up Ida Belle and Gertie.

"Let's go to the restaurant for dinner," I said. "It's not crowded and there are tables next to the windows. If she exits the hotel, we'll see her."

"Thank God!" Gertie said as we headed off. "I'm starving. When was the last time we ate?"

"Fortune and I ate this morning," Ida Belle said. "You ate this morning, then had a sandwich on the way to NOLA, two bags of chips and a hot dog in the room, and most disturbingly, a Red Bull in the elevator."

Gertie nodded. "Exactly. I've depleted my purse stash."

"You also swiped three baskets of peanuts from the bar while getting us sodas," Ida Belle said. "I'm not sure where you're going to put dinner unless it's in the newly created space in your purse."

Gertie waved a hand in dismissal. "I did a lot of running."

"You ran from Jenny's back door to the fence. It's a standard lot, not a cattle ranch."

"Three and a half, please," I said to the hostess.

The young girl beamed at me. "Oh, are you pregnant?"

"No," I said and jerked my thumb at Gertie. "She's just really hungry."

Ida Belle snorted, and the hostess looked confused but grabbed three menus and we followed her into the restaurant.

"Can we get a table by the window?" I asked.

"Of course," she said. "A large percentage of our hotel reservations are here for a big wedding tonight in the ball-room, so the restaurant is unusually quiet for Saturday dinner."

We took our time over the meal. One, because the kitchen was moving rather slowly—probably catering the big wedding in the ballroom—and two, because when we left the restaurant we had to head back to the lobby couch. It was reasonably comfortable for short-term sitting, but it hadn't been made for a stakeout.

I knew Blanchet had to get the warrant, initiate the search, log the evidence, and then make a call if he determined every-thing added up to detaining Jenny, and all of that would take time, but I was getting antsier by the minute. I kept pulling my phone out to check the display, hoping a text or call had come in and I'd somehow missed it.

"You're going to wear out your phone putting it in and out of your jeans like that," Ida Belle remarked.

I sighed. "I'm not good at sitting still."

"Patience is a virtue," Gertie quipped.

Ida Belle shrugged. "So are honor and courage, which she has in spades. You can't win them all."

Gertie laughed. "I wasn't suggesting she acquire new personality traits. I'm so bored I'm ready to get a job here just to have something to do."

I stared at her for a couple seconds. "Maybe that's it."

"What?" Ida Belle asked.

"Maybe Brent is hooking Jenny up with a job. At Graham's house she said she needed to come here to look for a place to live, not for work. What if she already had a job lined up?"

"Hotels also need good managers for housekeeping, especially someone trustworthy," Ida Belle said.

"I definitely like that idea better than Jenny killing her husband and then trying to flee the country," Gertie said.

"Yes, but if Jenny didn't kill Gage, then we're back to the beginning," I pointed out. "Because someone did."

I had been so wrapped up in my thoughts on the potential of another killer that I almost jumped when my phone signaled an incoming call. I yanked my phone out of my jeans again and hurried to answer. It was Blanchet!

"I've got the meds. Only one set of prints on them and they match what I pulled off personal items in Jenny's bedroom and bathroom once I excluded Gage's. I've already talked to the NOLA police. They're sending someone over to take Jenny into custody and hold her for me for questioning. I'm about thirty minutes out. Please tell me she's still at the hotel."

"I haven't set eyes on her since this afternoon. But her car is still in the parking lot, and we've been watching the front entrance since I talked to you earlier."

"That's as good as I can ask for. NOLA is sending a Detective Casey. I told her you were on-site and assisting me with the investigation. She laughed and said, 'Of course she is.' I take it you know her?"

I immediately felt better knowing that Casey was going to handle Jenny's detainment. "I've crossed paths with her a few times. She's solid. And she seems to like me, so that's a plus. Her boss hates me though."

"He'll get over it. Anyway, sounds like Detective Casey will have everything under control, but stick close. Once she has Jenny in custody, head to the police station and I'll meet you there."

"The captain is not going to allow me to question a suspect," I said.

"No, but he can't say anything about you listening while I question her. Not when you've provided the information for the arrest. You'll know if she's lying better than I will. And you've got more background on all of this to catch any inconsistencies I can use."

He disconnected and I relayed the conversation. Ida Belle nodded, her expression serious, and Gertie looked downright depressed.

But we'd known it was coming.

———

I SETTLED UP WITH OUR SERVER, LEAVING HER A HUGE TIP since it was a slow night, and we headed back to our perch in the lobby. That way, I'd see when Casey came in and whether or not Jenny tried to exit. I wasn't exactly sure what I would do if she started to leave, though. I'd already assumed tackling her in the lobby wasn't a good option. But if she was pulling a runner, she was hardly going to stop and have a conversation, especially when I shouldn't even be there. She'd know right away what I was doing. I just hoped she was ensconced in a room upstairs and wasn't planning on making any big moves tonight.

Fortunately, it didn't take Casey long to get there. I popped up as soon as she walked in, and she gave me a nod when she saw me approaching.

"You were quick," I said.

She grinned. "I double-timed it when I heard you were involved."

"Most people would be offended by that statement, but I'll just take it as you knowing me too well. But my involvement in this one has been fairly quiet. Not a single call to the cops, and we've been here since around lunch."

"Look at you—wanting credit for things civilians are *supposed* to do," she said, and laughed. "Give me the rundown."

I gave her a brief explanation of the crime and the evidence. She nodded when I was done.

"Combine the test results from the ME and it's definitely enough to haul her in for questioning," she said. "Do you anticipate any issues detaining her?"

"No. She's not the type."

"But you think she killed a man."

"I think there's a good chance she did, but I can't help but like her. I know that makes no sense."

"It does to me. Some of the most charming people I've met were killers. Was the husband a good guy?"

"No. He was an alcoholic and a cheater. But he still didn't deserve to be murdered."

She nodded. "Let me round up the manager and get him to call her down. They don't like it when we enter rooms and drag people off in handcuffs. The clientele find it distasteful and go posting negative reviews online."

"Part of your job is catering to tourism now?"

She snorted. "Part of my job has *always* been catering to tourism. Once I've got her detained, head to the station and wait in the parking lot. I'll call you in once I've got her in a room. That way she won't spot you, so if this all turns up nothing, you don't have personal drama with Sinful residents."

She headed for the front desk, and I went back to our secluded couch and relayed our conversation to Ida Belle and Gertie.

"I hate this," Gertie said. "If we didn't need to leave right after, I'd go back to the room. I don't want to see her hauled out in handcuffs."

"You can wait in the car," Ida Belle said. "But you can NOT move the car. You can't even start it. You know what? Maybe you could just take a bathroom break. We'll call you when it's over."

Gertie shot Ida Belle a dirty look but took her advice and headed for the restroom. Casey was talking to a distinguished-looking man in nice slacks and a dress shirt and tie, and I assumed it was the assistant manager. He didn't look happy, but Casey had made it better for the hotel than she'd been required to.

He motioned to a clerk, and they passed him the phone. He spoked to someone and nodded to Casey as he handed the phone back over the counter. He must have wanted to put some distance between him and what he considered a rude violation occurring in his hotel, because he headed behind the counter to stand with the clerk.

I couldn't blame him for being edgy. He had just called down a woman the owner was involved with on some level to face the police. I felt a little sorry for him and hoped Brent wouldn't take out his feelings on the poor man for just doing his job.

The elevator dinged and Ida Belle and I looked over as Jenny and Brent both exited. Crap. I couldn't help but think this would have gone down easier if she'd been alone. They both strode to the registration desk, and the manager got paler as they approached until finally, I thought he might pass out. Brent looked a bit annoyed but mostly curious when he questioned the man.

The manager motioned to Detective Casey, and Jenny's eyes widened and she took a step back. Detective Casey must have explained why she was there, and Jenny seemed to slump against the desk. Brent rushed to her side and put his arm around her to help prop her up, but there was nothing he could do to prevent what was about to happen.

Casey stepped in front of her, and I saw her slip her handcuffs from her pants. When she'd finished cuffing Jenny, she removed her jacket and draped it over Jenny's wrists. I'd liked Casey before, but her compassion in this instance put her even further up in my estimation. Casey was good people.

She took Jenny's elbow and they walked toward the exit, as if they were two friends on their way out for a night on the town. Brent hurried after them and they stopped just on the other side of the plants that blocked their view of us on the couch.

"Don't say anything," Brent said. "I'm calling my lawyer. He'll be there right away. I'm not going to let things fall apart again. You've worked too hard."

Jenny gave him a tearful nod and she and Casey left. Brent pulled out his cell phone and hurried for the elevator, his expression a cross between worry and determination.

"Well, that's it," Ida Belle said, looking as depressed as I felt.

I nodded. It certainly was.

CHAPTER TWENTY-THREE

WE'D BEEN IN THE POLICE STATION PARKING LOT FOR ABOUT twenty minutes when I saw Blanchet pull in. He spotted Ida Belle's SUV and headed over.

"I just talked to Casey and told her I was pulling in," he said. "She's moving Jenny into an interrogation room with cameras. I want you three in the monitoring room. If you see anything I miss or think of anything I need to ask, call. Casey will be in the room with you and can facilitate."

Blanchet took off as we climbed out of the SUV and headed for the police station. No one rushed and I couldn't help but feel that this was the outcome that none of us had wanted.

"You know," Gertie said, "in addition to being depressing, this whole thing is anticlimactic. No gunfire, no explosions, no charging beasts of death. It's like we weren't even involved."

Ida Belle sighed. "She goes three days without a near-death experience and thinks we're doing it all wrong."

Detective Casey was waiting for us up front and signaled to the desk clerk to let us back.

"We lucked out," she said as we followed her down the hallway. "The captain is on vacation this week."

"Tell him I'm sorry I missed him," I said.

Casey grinned and waved us into a room with two monitors and several speakers set up on a wall and chairs facing the screens. Casey turned on the equipment, and Jenny popped up on the screen. She was in the interrogation room alone, and I could tell she'd been crying. She was pale and her hands shook as she reached for the cup of water that had been left for her. At least they'd taken the handcuffs off, but then the woman didn't look as if she had the energy to flee a tortoise. Quite frankly, she was so pale that I was afraid if she tried to stand she'd pass out.

Casey studied her for a moment, then shook her head. "I have to say, I've booked my share of killers, but this one doesn't fit the mold. And it's a big and varied mold."

"I know," I said. "Did she say anything on the ride over?"

"Nothing relevant. She just asked me what happens when we get here."

"Makes sense. Most people haven't been detained by the police or questioned like this."

"It doesn't help that the general public gets all their information from the TV."

I nodded and then the door to the interrogation room opened and Blanchet walked in. Jenny didn't look surprised to see him, so I assumed Casey had explained that they were holding her on the authority of the acting sheriff. Casey clicked on the speaker so we could hear the exchange.

"What's going on?" Jenny asked as soon as he walked in. "Why have I been arrested?"

"You haven't been arrested," Blanchet said as he sat across from her. "You're being detained for questioning."

"But why? The detective didn't explain anything."

"Because it wasn't her place to do so. She was only instructed to detain you and wait for me. There's been some developments in my investigation of Gage's death."

"What investigation? He died of a heart attack."

"That's correct, but his heart attack was not due to natural causes."

"I don't understand."

"Gage had a toxic amount of digoxin in his system."

Jenny's eyes widened. "And you think I gave it to him? No! I would never!"

I studied her closely and had to admit I didn't detect any ambiguity in her statement. And the news that Gage had indeed been murdered seemed to shock her. Or she was a great actress and just shocked that she'd been caught.

"I executed a search warrant before having you detained," Blanchet continued. "I retrieved a bottle of digoxin from your mother-in-law's medicine cabinet. Yours were the only finger-prints on it."

"Because I used to give her the meds," Jenny said, clearly starting to panic. "You have to be careful with them because too many—"

She gasped and swayed a bit in her chair before clutching the table to steady herself. The magnitude of what Blanchet had told her had sunk all the way in.

"Are you saying you didn't administer the medication to your husband with the intent to harm him?" Blanchet asked.

"I didn't give him anything at all. Couldn't have even if I wanted to. Gage never listened to me. I'd been riding him for years to see a cardiologist, but even living with Miriam and seeing the genetics he inherited firsthand didn't sway him. He might not have been a great husband, but that's hardly a reason to kill a man."

"It might be if that husband was draining you financially,

was cheating on you, and intended to file for divorce once his mother passed, leaving you essentially homeless."

Jenny's jaw dropped and I wasn't sure if she'd known about the cheating and the plans for divorce or not. Or one but not both, or was simply surprised that Blanchet knew.

She shook her head. "Those are good reasons to leave someone, not kill them."

"I agree. Unless you made a promise to a dying woman and divorcing Gage would have been breaking it."

She sucked in a breath. "If Miriam had known what Gage was doing, she would have let me out of that promise."

"Would she?"

"Yes," Jenny said, but she didn't look convinced.

Neither was I. Miriam had spent the majority of her life covering for her son's shortcomings. I didn't believe for a minute she'd let Jenny off the hook, especially knowing she wasn't going to be around much longer to prop him up.

"There's also the fact that you have a new man lined up," Blanchet said. "Or maybe I should say have rekindled your relationship with your ex-husband. I'm doubtful a man like Mr. Copeland would wait around for long. Not with all his options."

"What? No! I'm not in a relationship with Brent."

"Then why are you here staying in his hotel? And this isn't the first time."

She sat back and ran one hand over the top of her head. "Brent had a drug problem for a long time. It's the reason I divorced him. But last year, he finally hit bottom and got clean. As part of his therapy, he had to apologize and attempt to make amends for the things he did. He contacted me to apologize, and he asked me if I'd be willing to attend a counseling session with him so that his therapist could get my take on our life together back then. Because of the drugs, Brent's memory was sketchy on a lot of things."

"So you dropped everything and headed over here because of a few 'I'm sorries'?"

"Of course not. Brent gave me his therapist's number and we had several conversations about what he felt I could bring to the table. Then I met Brent in person, and I could tell he was sincere. I agreed to attend a session and the therapist was so happy with everything we worked through that I've attended a few more. As a *friend*. Someone who cared about Brent once and wants him to get better and stay that way."

"You had a very expensive bracelet hidden in your jewelry box. I doubt your husband bought it for you."

"It was a gift from Brent—from back when we were married. I hid it because if Gage found it, he would have pawned it and wasted the money. And it wasn't his to make that choice."

"Uh-huh. What about the trip you were planning with Brent?"

She looked genuinely confused. "What trip?"

"You just renewed your passport a couple months ago and it had been expired for years."

"Because I was going to take a trip to France. I've always wanted to go and Gage wouldn't hear of it. I've been doing side jobs and saving the money for two years."

"You were going to go to France by yourself?"

"Women travel alone all the time. When it came down to it, I was alone in Sinful."

"If Mr. Copeland is only a friend, then why did you tell your brother-in-law that you're moving to New Orleans?"

"Because I am. I've spent some of the best years of my life tied to a man who didn't appreciate me, living in a town with limited opportunity. When I told Brent about Gage's death, he said that if I ever considered moving, he'd be happy to hire me to manage housekeeping at one of the hotels."

"I'm supposed to believe you're only here for a job?"

"You can check with HR. I dropped off the paperwork today. I start in two weeks, so I was here today looking at an apartment. You can call the owner and check. He talked to Brent and verified my employment when I met him to look at it."

She teared up. "I was supposed to be starting over. And now this. Just when I thought my life was finally going to be mine again—Gage is still ruining it."

She started sobbing now and put her hands over her face. Blanchet sat silently.

"If you let them break down, they might start telling you the truth," Casey said. "It's called questioning but sometimes the smartest thing you can do is remain quiet."

I nodded, but my heart clenched at the sight of the woman who appeared to be on the verge of collapse.

"What do you think?" Casey asked.

I shook my head. "I don't know. She's got motive and opportunity. And she's the only one who really benefits from Gage's death."

"What about the brother? Is there anything to inherit?"

"Not really. He already owns half of their childhood home, which is where Jenny and Gage lived. But he intended to transfer his share to Jenny. He's got plenty of money."

"Single? In love with his sister-in-law?"

"Gay. But we only found out by accident. It might be the best-kept secret in Mudbug."

Casey shook her head. "Then it doesn't look too good for your girl. She ticks all the boxes."

I nodded.

"Wait." Jenny dropped her hands and stared at Blanchet.

"You said my fingerprints were on a bottle of digoxin. But there were two in that cabinet."

"Are you sure?"

"Positive. I'd just picked up a refill, and there were still a few left in the previous bottle when we moved Miriam to the nursing home. I didn't know she wasn't allowed to take them with her, or I wouldn't have gotten the refill."

"Why didn't you throw them away?"

"Gage told me not to touch anything in the room. He believed his mother was going to get better and come home. He wouldn't even let me clean in there. It was like he thought cleaning things up would make her die quicker."

Blanchet sat back in his chair and crossed his arms. "Let's just say I believe you. Who else had access to the room?"

"No one but me and Gage."

"No visitors? Repairmen? What about your brother-in-law?"

"Gage changed the locks when Miriam went into the nursing home. Graham would never enter our house without being invited in, but Gage changed them anyway. I think it made him feel in control. He didn't when Miriam was still living there."

"So given that, you see where my problem lies? If you and Gage were the only ones with access, and you appear to be the only one who benefits from Gage's death…"

He put his hands up.

Jenny frowned and shook her head, muttering to herself. Then her eyes widened. "What if Gage took it himself?"

"Why would he do that?"

"Because he was too stupid to go to the doctor. But if the meds helped Miriam, maybe he thought…"

"That's some serious speculation."

"I don't think so. I walked into the kitchen one time and

saw him taking something. I asked what it was, and he said it was aspirin. I remember thinking that was odd because I'd taken the last of our aspirin the night before. And I know for certain his heart was bothering him. He couldn't even mow the lawn anymore without taking several breaks, and his symptoms were the same as Miriam's when she pushed too hard."

"So you think he was self-medicating?"

"I wouldn't put it past him. He was pigheaded, and in his mind, he was never wrong."

I looked over at Ida Belle and Gertie. "You think that's possible?"

Gertie nodded. "It's more than possible."

"His 'species' has an unfortunate habit of thinking they know more than doctors," Ida Belle said.

Casey snorted. "But he'd have to have taken a handful of pills to get to those levels."

I nodded. "But we'd speculated earlier that someone could have given him a round, then because he was so drunk, they could have dosed him again because he would have already forgotten that he'd taken any. We could have arrived at the same outcome with him dosing himself."

Ida Belle nodded. "And men like Gage think if one is good then five is better."

Casey picked up the phone and handed it to me, and I asked Blanchet to come out. I told him the scenario we were proposing, and he was silent for several seconds, then blew out a breath and cursed.

And I knew why. Reasonable doubt.

"You need to think like a defense attorney," I said. "Question the people who were closest to Gage. See if any of them saw him dosing."

Casey nodded. "It's the first thing her attorney will do. And if just one person saw Gage popping pills, the case won't even make it past the grand jury."

"But the people closest to Gage are my other suspects," Blanchet said. "I don't want to provide a potential killer with an easy legal out."

"Start with Nancy," I said. "I don't like her for this for a lot of reasons but mostly because of her kids. But she's seen Gage in an intimate setting and when he was the closest to relaxed and being himself instead of putting on for other people. Then I'd talk to Red. He has absolutely no dog in this hunt. And people tend to forget he's around, so he sees and hears a lot. Skip Dean Allard. He's still a possibility as far as I'm concerned."

Ida Belle and Gertie both nodded.

Blanchet pulled out his phone. "Leave her in there," he said as he walked out.

"This is getting interesting," Casey said.

A sergeant poked his head in the door. "Detective Casey—there's an attorney out front. Says he's here for Jenny Babin."

Casey shook her head. "He's going to be pissed when he finds out she's been talking. I best go show him back."

A minute or so later, Casey escorted a man wearing a suit that probably cost as much as my hot tub into the room, then left them to it. Then she popped back in with us and shut down the equipment.

"Do you know the attorney?" I asked.

Casey nodded. "Defense attorney to the rich and privileged. And he's good. Blanchet will need to have this tied down solid or that guy will unravel his case in no time."

"Sounds like you're speaking from experience."

"Unfortunately. Most of his first offenders—or first time caught—get off with a fine and maybe probation, but rarely any time. It's usually enough to scare them out of a repeat offense. Except for the drug stuff, of course. An addict is going to be an addict. But a couple times, he's torn my case apart and they went on to do worse. It sucks when you know they're bad to the core but you don't have the evidence to prove it."

She shook her head and frowned. "At least your girl doesn't fit the model for a repeat offender."

"A man's still dead," Ida Belle said.

Casey shrugged. "And he'll still be dead even if she rots in prison. If you do this job long enough, you learn to pick your battles or you'll make yourself crazy. You can't control the system. You can only control the job you do and your reaction to it when things don't go like you want them to."

"I don't think I could do it," Gertie said. "I think I'd be all vigilante and end up in a cell next to some of the people I arrested."

"There's legal and there's fair," Casey said. "And too many times, they're not the same thing. Blanchet might be a while. Let's go grab some bad coffee."

CHAPTER TWENTY-FOUR

WE SHIFTED TALK OVER THE COFFEE—WHICH WAS AS BAD AS Casey had promised—and spoke about everything but the case. Gertie asked about Casey's daughter and how college was going, and I wanted to know when she was going to be up for a promotion. The woman was excellent at her job.

She laughed at that question and said she needed some of the old-timers to die off or retire, and she wasn't going to admit which she was hoping for in some cases. I wondered if the captain was on that 'die off' list but didn't ask.

We were on our third round of coffee and Gertie was already halfway into her second snack from the vending machine when Blanchet walked in. His expression was a combination of frustration and resignation. He plopped into a chair and sighed.

"I take it you got verification?" I asked.

He nodded. "From both of them. Not 100 percent, of course, because neither of them tackled him, took a picture of the pills, and googled them, but it's more than enough to support Jenny's version of how it could have happened."

Casey shook her head. "Better you know now before you

put the case up to the DA's office. It's in turmoil since this one"—she nodded at me—"caught the ADA shady-business adjacent." She inclined her head toward Blanchet. "Matter-of-fact, that was *your* case, wasn't it?"

"Don't remind me."

"So what did they say?" Gertie asked.

"I called Nancy first and asked her if she'd ever seen Gage take prescription meds. She immediately said no, but then she said, 'Nothing in a bottle anyway.' I asked her to explain, and she said one night after a 'particularly vigorous round'—her words—Gage was winded and red. He said he just needed to get some air and something to drink and sat up. She went into the connecting bathroom but could see into the bedroom through the mirror. She said Gage watched until she went into the bathroom, then reached inside his pants pocket and pulled out some pills. Then he tossed them in his mouth and downed them with water that was on the side of the bed. She walked out just as he swallowed and said he looked almost guilty. But at the time, she took it to be embarrassment over his stamina and figured he was just taking aspirin."

"Same as he told Jenny," I said.

Blanchet nodded. "But when he went into the kitchen for a beer, she got curious and looked in his pocket. She said there was a sandwich bag of pills in there, but again, she just figured it was aspirin and he didn't want to carry around a bottle in his pocket. I asked her to describe them and it's a match for the digoxin."

"And Red?"

"Similar story—to Jenny's, not Nancy's."

"Thank God," I muttered.

"Red said he's seen Gage reach into his jeans pocket on several occasions and pull out pills, which, like everyone else, he assumed were aspirin."

"But there were no pills or sandwich bag in his jeans pocket at the time of death?" Casey asked.

"No. But it won't matter," Blanchet said. "The defense will just say he took them all, and since he probably took the last of them once he was up in the boat, he probably tossed the sandwich bag and it blew away."

Casey shook her head. "Your case just fell apart."

"I know," Blanchet said.

"Do you still think she did it?" Casey asked.

"Honestly, no. But I'm still having trouble letting the whole thing go. Fortune and I knew his death wasn't natural causes, and she worked her butt off to figure out what caused his heart attack and get motive."

"So it still feels unresolved," Casey said. "I get it. But that's how some of them go."

"I know," Blanchet agreed. "But I've never liked it."

"What about your other suspects?" Casey asked. "Any of them have access to digoxin? If you pressed, they might fold if questioned."

"Ha!" Blanchet said. "The lock on her patio door is broken. Who knows for how long. Anyone could have walked in their house and lifted that other bottle. And it's not like that was the only place in the parish where you could get hold of some. I'll verify that the prescription was refilled right before Miriam went into the home, but honestly, I don't see that there's anything else I can do at this point."

Casey nodded. "You want me to cut her loose?"

Blanchet rose. "I'll do it. I'll give her the usual don't-leave-town speech because we might have further questions."

"Her attorney is there now," I said.

"Great," Blanchet muttered as he headed out.

"Looks like our work here is done," I said. I thanked Casey for her help, and we headed out.

"Let's hurry back to the hotel and check out before Jenny gets back," I said.

"Good call," Ida Belle said and pulled out of the parking lot. "I don't want her to know we were the source of all her troubles tonight."

"Is it wrong that I'm happy about how it turned out?" Gertie asked.

"No," I said. "I like Jenny. I didn't want it to be her, and Gage overdosing himself is not only plausible but likely given everything I've learned about the man. Nancy and Red corroborated Jenny's story separately, and I can't see where either of them had something to gain with Gage dying."

Ida Belle glanced over at me. "But?"

I sighed. "I don't know. There's still something bothering me. Maybe it's just the uncertainty."

"Maybe," Ida Belle said, but I could tell she didn't believe that any more than I did.

We made quick work of checking out of the hotel and were on the highway back to Sinful when Blanchet called to let me know that Jenny had been cut loose.

"She said she's going back to the hotel," he said, "so you guys might want to think about clearing out."

"We're already headed back to Sinful."

"Good. I'll get together with you tomorrow to fill in any of the blanks on this, but I'm going to have to file the paperwork and put it to rest. I just need to have a conversation with Graham and inform him of the updated cause of death, then see if he has anything to add in that regard."

"Jenny didn't want to tell him?"

"I asked, but she said it wasn't the kind of message you delivered over the phone, and she wasn't sure when she'd go back to Sinful. I got the impression that if she didn't have to, she'd never step foot in town again."

"I can't say that I blame her. Everyone is going to find out about the affair if they haven't already. And no matter what proof you have, people will speculate about Jenny because of it."

"Yeah. I'm on my way out myself. I'll give you a call tomorrow."

I put my phone back in my pocket and stared out the window. Everything made sense. Gage's stubbornness was widely known. Look at the mess he'd made of their patio because he wasn't willing to take Graham's advice about the hot tub. And he'd lived with his mother and seen her struggling but refused to see a cardiologist, knowing good and well that he had heart issues. Not to mention the ER doctor had told him he had heart problems that needed to be addressed.

Then three separate people, one with motive, one with very limited motive, and one with none at all, had all reported that they'd seen Gage taking pills he'd kept in his jeans pocket. His blood alcohol content left no doubt as to exactly how drunk he was. And finally, Gage playing a prank was no surprise. It was what he was known for. It all added up to an accidental death, caused by the dead man himself.

The only thing we still didn't know was who had helped Gage with the prank, and I figured we never would. No one was going to voluntarily offer themselves up as the person who helped Gage kill himself, even though it appeared to have been an accidental overdose. I figured guilt would have someone admitting it eventually when they'd had a few too many at the Swamp Bar, but for now, it was going to remain a mystery.

"What a stubborn stupid fool," Gertie said.

"I wonder what Graham's going to make of this new information," Ida Belle said.

"Probably the same thing I just said," Gertie said. "It's not like he didn't know exactly what kind of person his brother was. Gage ignored more good advice from Graham than he did anyone else."

"It's still a lot for him to process," Ida Belle said. "Look how upset he was yesterday about Jenny moving."

I nodded, then frowned. Ida Belle was right—Graham had definitely been upset, but not when Jenny said she was moving. Not exactly. He'd been surprised but that stood to reason. He had progressed to upset, though. I could still see the look that flashed across his face, but when was it?

Then it hit me. And statements people had made over the last several days flooded back in.

There's always gossip. The trick is figuring out how much truth lies in it.

He knew what the things he was doing was going to get him.

Says something about a man when a dead father is more useful than a live one.

I'm sure he'll do what's best for his mother. He always has.

I sucked in a breath as it all came together. But that couldn't be it, right? It was a stretch—a huge, giant, gaping stretch. But something told me I'd finally discovered that piece that brought it all together. I pulled out my phone and accessed my photos, then located the one of Graham's backyard—the one with a sunken hot tub.

"We were wrong," I said. "This wasn't about Jenny, romantic entanglements, or the pranks."

"What was it about then?" Gertie asked.

"Bad childhoods, unhealthy attachments, unreasonable obligations, and the deck."

"What?" Ida Belle gave me a look as though I'd been hitting the sauce.

I glanced at my watch and realized it was close to midnight. "Hurry! This isn't over."

"Where are we hurrying to?" Ida Belle asked. "And what are we trying to prevent?"

"Jenny's house. And we're going to stop Graham from removing a body that's buried under the deck."

Gertie's eyes widened. "What body?"

"If I'm right, his father's."

THE NEIGHBORHOOD WAS QUIET WHEN WE PULLED ONTO THE street. Not a single leaf stirred. I spotted a truck parked a few houses down from Jenny's with a NOLA sticker on it. Anyone could be visiting from New Orleans, but I had a feeling the truck was a rental. And I would have bet money I knew who rented it.

Ida Belle parked several houses down and we crept across the front lawns to Jenny's house. I stopped at the fence to listen, because Graham would have heard a vehicle and paused what he was doing until he was certain whoever had stopped on the street had gone inside. We stood completely still and after a few minutes, I heard the sound of a shovel in dirt.

Gertie held up her fingers like a gun and pulled the trigger and Ida Belle put her hands up in the air, giving her a what-the-heck look. It took me a couple seconds to realize Gertie was asking if I thought Graham had a gun, not suggesting we shoot him, as Ida Belle had taken it.

Either way, the answer was no.

I motioned for them to stand near the gate to tackle him in case he decided to run, then I took the spotlight from Ida Belle and eased the gate open. Like everything else at the house, it was in need of maintenance, and the screech the rusty hinges made probably carried two parishes over in the still night air. Since I'd given myself away, I ran toward the deck, ready to shine the light on him. He jumped up and in the moonlight, I got a look at Graham's clearly startled expression, but instead of rushing for the gate, he ran inside the house.

Good God!

The last thing I wanted was a standoff, especially since Gage had a fairly large collection of weapons inside. But then I heard a door bang and realized Graham had run through the house and exited by the front door. I ran for the gate and heard people scrambling in the front yard, then the sound of feet pounding on the pavement.

I rounded the corner just in time to see Gertie dive to tackle him, but Graham had some NFL skills we'd been unaware of. He stiff-armed her midair and she flew into the mailbox, tearing it completely out of the ground then crashing onto the front lawn. Ida Belle managed to grab hold of one of his arms and was trying to prevent him from getting into the truck.

He had the door open and had just gotten his arm free from Ida Belle when I pulled out my gun and fired two shots—one into each back tire. Then I turned on the spotlight, right in his face. He covered his face with his hands, sank to the ground, and started sobbing.

Blanchet's truck rounded the corner, and I could hear the engine rev as he sped down the street and slid to a stop next to us. He jumped out and took in the scene. Gertie was still laid out in the front lawn on top of the mailbox, which was now wearing her wig. The tires on the truck were still hissing out air as they flattened. And Graham was collapsed on the pavement, slumped against the truck, still crying.

Blanchet shook his head. "When you texted me to get over here as soon as possible, I specifically said whatever was going on, to wait."

"He was going to get away," Gertie said as she came staggering up.

"I know where he lives," Blanchet said.

I shrugged. "Saves you the trip. Besides, it's not like he's dangerous."

"Unless he's handing you pills," Ida Belle said.

Blanchet sighed. "I think you need to explain what the heck is going on."

"Better yet," I said, "I'll show you."

Blanchet cuffed Graham to his vehicle, then we headed into the backyard. I shone the spotlight at the torn-up patio, and Blanchet stepped closer to look inside the hole Graham had been digging. I heard him curse as I stepped up beside him.

And saw the human hand sticking out of the dirt.

CHAPTER TWENTY-FIVE

IT WAS A LONG NIGHT FOR BLANCHET. HE HAD TO WAKE UP Deputy Breaux and get him to take Graham into custody. He wasn't exactly sure what the charges were going to be at this point, but when you're caught digging up a body in the back-yard of your former home, there were probably options. Regardless, Blanchet could hold him while he got a forensics team in and tried to sort it all out.

I'd already given him my theory on who the dead guy was. I was doubtful about dental records, but a DNA test would easily show his familial link to Gage and Graham. Between the gunfire, Blanchet's sliding stop, and Graham handcuffed to his vehicle crying, people had flooded outside onto their porches and lawns, trying to find out what was going on. We'd helped Blanchet establish a perimeter and hung around until Harrison and a couple other deputies arrived to keep people away. Then Blanchet told us to head home and he'd have us come in and give formal statements the next day.

I was too amped up to sleep, so I headed to Carter's house. I figured I'd wake him up, but I wanted him to hear it all from me before his phone started pinging with text messages. He was actually still awake with some old movie playing and listened as I ran down the entire day.

When I was done, he shook his head. "I knew you didn't stop by here to play with Tiny, but I didn't even think about my yard having access to Jenny's house."

"Why would you? You didn't know she was going to be out of town, or that we would think we could find some evidence in there."

"True, but wow, what a load of stuff for Blanchet to process. He's probably cussing me for roping him into filling in."

"Honestly, I think he's loving every minute of it, but don't tell him I said so. He just doesn't strike me as the type of guy who takes well to retirement. Not full time, anyway."

Carter nodded. "Maybe if he ever relocates closer this way, I'll have him sign on as a consultant."

"Hey, you've never signed me up as a consultant."

He laughed. "Why would I? You're already doing it for free."

I laughed along with him. "Well, since I've done all the damage I can for today, what do you say I grab a shower and we head to bed. I might just be tired enough to sleep."

"Great idea. Except for maybe the sleeping part."

The next morning came too soon, but no matter how hard I tried, I couldn't force myself back to sleep any longer than 8:00 a.m. As predicted, Carter's phone had started going off with texts about an hour before, but he'd deliberately left it in the living room, so I could only hear the faint chime in the distance. He stirred when I got up but didn't wake, so I slipped into the kitchen and set coffee on to brew. He wandered out about the time it was ready.

I didn't expect to hear from Blanchet first thing. He had a lot to get in order and our statements weren't as critical as all the other balls he was juggling. But every hour that ticked by had me more and more antsy. Had Graham confessed? And if so, to which murder? One, both? Even though I'd put together a lot, I still had so many unanswered questions.

Carter and I headed over to my house after feeding Tiny and ourselves breakfast. He'd stopped in to feed Merlin for me the night before, but I knew the cat would be in a snit if his breakfast was late. He'd shown his disapproval at my absence by shredding an entire roll of paper towels in the kitchen. It looked as though it had snowed. Carter took one look at the disaster and headed into the garage to put together some shelves I'd bought for an unutilized corner.

I'd fed the cat, cleaned the kitchen, explained the whole thing to Ronald, answered at least a hundred texts from Ida Belle and Gertie, and ignored a hundred more from other people before Blanchet showed up. Since he was wearing the same clothes as the day before, I had to assume he hadn't been home yet.

"You want something to drink—coffee, energy drink?"

He shook his head as he slumped into a chair in my kitchen. "I've already had more caffeine than my monthly allowance in the last twelve hours alone. At this point, I'm not even sure illegal stimulants would give me a spark."

I figured he was there to give me the debriefing, so I yelled for Carter to come in from the garage. I convinced Blanchet that a sugar high from Ally's cookies and a fresh batch of sweet tea would be a plus while he talked and set him up.

"First things first," he said. "The body under the deck belongs to Saul Babin. Believe it or not, he had seen a dentist who was happy to go in on a Sunday and dig up the records."

"Did Graham confess to killing him?" I asked.

"No. Graham hasn't said a word. He had a nervous breakdown of sorts last night in jail and we had to ship him off to the hospital. Someone—probably several someones—let Jenny know what was going on at her house and she sent her attorney down here to make sure he was protected. I can't even question him until the doctor releases him."

I nodded. None of that surprised me.

"The whole thing is going to be a mess," Carter said. "Graham was a minor when Saul disappeared. Unless the ME can pin down time of death within a close range of years, you have no way of proving when it happened. He worked off the books and his family's the type who would deny seeing him if he was sitting right next to them, so you can't even be sure you've got last sighting accurate. Not with them, anyway."

"Oh, it's a bigger mess than you can even imagine," Blanchet said. "So I'm busy putting together the information for the DA's office, because if we're going to charge him with something it needs to happen soon. And I got a call from Miriam Babin telling me she wants to confess to murdering her husband."

"What?!" I shouted.

Carter just stared.

"Apparently, the Sinful gossip train was in full force because someone called and told her what happened."

"Probably Pops. Whiskey's father," I explained to Blanchet. "They're old friends. I bet he told her about Gage too."

"So, of course, I stopped everything and drove over to the nursing home to take her statement. She claims her husband was abusive and one night when the boys were staying at friend's houses, he got drunk and started to tune her up. The beatings had gotten more aggressive, and she was afraid that one night the boys would come home and find her dead. She managed to get away from him and ran into the living room and grabbed a granite bookend off the shelf. When he came after her, she clocked him right in the forehead, killing him."

"And that matches the injury on the skull?" Carter asked.

Blanchet nodded. "Hell, she even kept the bookend. We should be able to match it to the wound."

"So where does Graham come in?" I asked. "Did he come home and help her hide the body?"

"Not according to Miriam. She says she never realized Graham knew what she'd done. She said Saul had been building a deck out back and she pulled the body out there and buried it. The posts were already in place, so she just hired someone to finish the job after he 'disappeared.'"

"But if Graham came home then surely he heard or saw his mother out back," I said.

"She claimed her husband always had the TV on blast, and Graham's room was at the front of the house, so he wouldn't have seen into the backyard. When she went back inside, she saw his backpack next to the front door and realized he'd returned. She checked and he was in his bedroom asleep and reeked of beer, so she assumed he'd gone straight to bed and never knew."

"But obviously he did, or he wouldn't have known to get the body out," I said. "And I'm sure that's why he told Gage he couldn't put in a sunken hot tub since he has one himself."

"Oh, he absolutely knew," Blanchet agreed. "*Or* he came home and caught his father beating his mother and cracked him in the head himself. Either way, when Jenny said she was going to hire someone to pull up the deck and pour concrete, he knew that the body would be discovered."

I nodded. "Jenny said the deck repair would start Monday, and then said she'd be in NOLA through Sunday, so Saturday night was his chance. That's what finally struck me about that conversation between him and Jenny. He was surprised when she said she was moving, but that wouldn't have necessarily been a bad thing. Once she was out of the house, he could have moved the body at his leisure and then put the house up for sale. It was her stating that the deck repair would start on Monday that caused him to panic."

Blanchet nodded. "The thing I don't understand is, if Graham really didn't kill his father, then why did he care about the body being discovered? He could have played dumb about the whole thing."

"Graham would never let his mother be exposed that way," I said. "He's devoted to her completely, and in my opinion, in an unhealthy way."

"That's true," Carter said. "But I still have my doubts about the way Miriam said it went down."

"So do I," Blanchet agreed. "But it would be a hard sell when I've got the victim of a known abuser claiming responsibility for his death."

I shook my head. "You know that also means that Graham might have killed Gage to prevent him from discovering the body. Graham could have easily gotten in through the broken door and taken the meds, and he would have known they were there. And I'm certain he knew the back door was broken because when I accosted him, he ran inside the house instead of for the gate."

Carter nodded. "And that's not the only place Graham frequented where he had access to the drugs. He was at the nursing home all the time. If meds there came up missing, no way they'd let that information get out."

Blanchet sighed. "Yeah. But that's just something else I can't prove. I've got three separate witnesses saying Gage was dosing himself, and if I dug around, I could probably come up with more. And the bottom line is, we don't know for sure. Maybe Gage *did* overdose accidentally. But if that's what happened, I guarantee you that whoever was out there with him setting up that prank is never going to come forward. And maybe Graham *did* witness something his mother did, then jumped into bed so that she'd think he didn't know. Maybe he figured his father had it coming. Sounds like he did, quite frankly."

"I don't think anyone's going to disagree with that statement," Carter said. "And in her version it was self-defense. But why didn't she call the cops? According to my mother, everyone knew he beat her, and she would have had marks that confirmed what had happened."

"I asked her that," Blanchet said. "She said Saul's family would have come after her if they'd known, and she was afraid they would hurt her boys or that they'd be taken away from her and left with his family to raise."

Carter nodded. "That makes sense. His family is as bad or worse than he was. Well, there's no way the DA's office is going to bring up charges against an abused senior who's already terminal. That's not a good look for promotion and we all know that's why they go in for the job."

"No," Blanchet said. "I don't know that he's going to want to make anything of Graham's situation either. The original crime happened when he was a minor. He kept quiet all these years, but I can't see where he needs to be removed from society. He's not exactly dangerous, and honestly, he didn't make it thirty minutes in our lockup before he collapsed. Given that family's history of heart issues, he wouldn't make it a week in prison."

"He might not even make it through a trial," Carter said. "They'll probably plead him out on some lesser charge and call it done. Do you think you could break him in questioning?"

"Doubt it. His attorney will have already instructed him on what to say. And I have no doubt Miriam has already talked to the man and given him her side of the story."

I stared out the window, watching the tide going out.

Maybe everything had gone down exactly as Blanchet had theorized. Maybe coincidence had finally played a legitimate role in an investigation, and Gage's death had just been an unfortunate incident that unraveled a long-kept secret.

"Are you going to be able to live with this outcome?" Blanchet asked me.

"I think we have to. And like you said, we don't know what happened."

Blanchet narrowed his eyes at me. "Don't we?"

I sighed. "Probably. But we can't prove it. And even if we could, what would it gain? Miriam and her boys were better off with Saul dead, and the law wouldn't have punished her for defending herself anyway."

"What about Gage?" Blanchet asked.

"He was a bad husband and friend and a burden to his wife and his brother, but he didn't deserve to die. On the other hand, you could argue that his drinking, diet, and refusing to see a doctor and get the proper medication were all going to come to a bad end, probably sooner than later."

Blanchet nodded. "So everything ended up where it was eventually going to anyway. I guess I can live with that."

"We don't have a choice."

CHAPTER TWENTY-SIX

TWO WEEKS LATER, IDA BELLE, GERTIE, AND I HEADED OUT in my boat for an afternoon of fishing. Well, they were fishing. I was going to read. It was seventy degrees, the sun was shining, and there was absolutely no reason to stay inside.

Even Gertie's hair had recovered from our recent adventures. Blanchet allowed us onto the crime scene to take samples of that rusty liquid which Gertie took to New Orleans to her hair expert Genesis. She gave Gertie a stern lecture—similar to Ronald's—about her dismal treatment of her hair, but got it back to normal after a couple hours of work.

The Babin drama had gone down as Blanchet had predicted. No charges levied against Miriam. Some minimal charge against Graham—mostly just to show that they'd done something—and a fine. No jail time and no probation.

Graham's actions and Miriam's confession had exonerated Jenny of anything to do with the entire mess. She'd returned to Sinful long enough to pack up her personal belongings and ship them to her new place in New Orleans, sell Gage's old truck and boat, and then give her keys to Graham, probably ready to wash her hands of the entire Babin family.

Graham had, in turn, packed up his mother's personal items for storage at his own home, then donated all the contents to charity. He also signed the deed to the house over to Jenny and started making the necessary repairs to get it listed. Given the whole dead body thing, I wasn't sure how fast it would move, but then, Wade had already sold the boat Gage died in, so you could never tell.

I wondered if Graham would end up moving as well, but Gertie said the general consensus among the locals was that he was a good son and had only done what he had to protect his mother. Protecting mothers got you big golden stars in the South, even if someone died.

Carter had been cleared for duty and Blanchet had happily vacated the chair and Walter's house. He was back in his own home and visiting Mudbug to see Maya every chance he got. I anticipated a wedding announcement sometime soon. They'd already waited long enough to be together.

So all had returned to normal. Sinful normal.

We were crossing the lake when I spotted Dean Allard fishing in one of the coves. I motioned to Ida Belle to head his way. Nancy's affair with Gage had become public knowledge, and I knew she was catching grief for it. Hopefully, none of the fallout would land on her kids. But she'd made her bed.

He frowned as we drew up to his boat. "I guess you three don't have any excitement now that all the secrets are out."

"We're not in it for excitement," I said. "We're in it to catch the bad guys."

His expression said he didn't believe me.

"I wasn't out there that night with Gage," he said.

"I know. You were at the dock rigging that exploding seat in Nickel's boat."

His eyes widened a bit but all he did was scowl. "You're scaring the fish off. Go on with your business."

As we headed off, Ida Belle chuckled. "I had completely forgotten about the seat, and I never would have pegged Dean for doing it. Like he said, he's not whimsical."

"He's not, but my guess is he found out about Gage and Nancy. And in a surprise move, he didn't go right for a fistfight. He knew Gage was on thin ice with Whiskey, so he rigged the seat, figuring Whiskey would think Gage did it because of what he did to Twinkie and ban him from the Swamp Bar permanently. Allard didn't know about Nickel buying the boat."

"He better hope Nickel never finds out," Gertie said.

"He won't from me," I said. "There's already been enough dead bodies around here this month."

———

I HAD JUST HOPPED OUT OF THE SHOWER AFTER OUR LONG day on the boat when I heard my cell phone ring. I checked the display and frowned.

Morrow!

"There's trouble over that situation in Iran," he said when I answered. "The DOD investigation has forced Colonel Kitts into a corner, and he's flinging mud every direction he can. You, Harrison, and Carter are going to need lawyers. This is going to get ugly. I'll send you everything I know."

The next morning, I made a trip into NOLA to speak with Alexander. I had called Harrison after I talked to Morrow and filled him in. I hadn't told Carter, but I had a feeling he already knew, given how increasingly troubled he'd become the past few days.

Alexander gave me a big smile and a hug when I walked in his office. "I would love to think you're here just for a chat and

303

a ridiculously high-calorie lunch, but I know you. What's wrong?"

"I need representation."

"You've got it."

I pulled a twenty out of my wallet and slid it across the desk to make it official. Then I told him everything.

When I was done, he leaned back in his chair, silent for several seconds. Finally, he pinned his gaze on me and asked, "How's Carter doing?"

I frowned. "Before I answer that, tell me why—out of all the questions you could have asked—you asked that one?"

"Because it's not the first time that stories of Colonel Kitts coloring outside the lines have crossed my desk. Does the rest of the unit know that Carter ignored orders and called off the mission?"

"I don't think so. If they do, they wouldn't have heard it from Carter. I'm surprised he told me. But they have a right to know. None of them would even be here if it wasn't for Carter."

He raised one eyebrow. "And yet there were no plans to rescue him."

I heard my dad's voice speaking the words Carter had told me.

You weren't supposed to be here.

The implication of everything I knew clicked together and all rushed through me like a bullet. Kitts hadn't made a mistake or pushed the envelope with intel. He'd known all along that the mission should have been scrapped, but he'd gambled with those men's lives to try and get another star on his uniform.

And he'd intended for Carter to take his secret to the grave.

I jumped up from my chair and proceeded to subject

Alexander to a string of cussing that would have made a long-haul trucker blush. I could feel the blood pounding in my head and my short nails digging into the palms of my hands I was clenching so hard.

"This wasn't a last hoorah for a soon-to-be-retiring colonel."

Alexander shook his head. "It's just the last in a long line of high-risk gambles he's made to build his career."

"At the expense of his men and their families. How has he gotten away with it?"

"He's clever and to some degree, untouchable. But he made a huge mistake this time. His scapegoat comes with an attachment that he didn't have a good background on. He couldn't have predicted that you'd plan your own rescue mission, much less be successful with it."

I sank back into my chair and blew out a breath. "You think Carter has already put this together."

"I think Carter is a very intelligent man who, after some time to physically recover and think hard about everything he knows, would have come to the same conclusion I did. After all, he knows more about what happened than anyone."

"No wonder he's checked out a little more each day."

Alexander nodded. "He's probably mentally reviewing and questioning every mission he ever completed. This has called his entire military career into question. Not from a service standpoint, of course. Carter had orders and he acted on them. But morally...now he has to wonder."

I pounded my hand on the desk. "If I could kill that son of a bitch myself, I would."

"You could, of course. Meaning you certainly have the skill set. But I don't recommend sinking to his level. You have a full life ahead of you, and Carter's already paid enough for Kitts's treachery. There's no point in sacrificing your future together for revenge. Especially not when you have a handsome, well-connected attorney who's been itching to take Kitts down ever since the rumors about him started floating through my office."

"Now that you know everything, you'll still take me on as a client?"

He grinned. "I'm taking you *all* on as clients. And this twenty should cover my fees."

WILL ALEXANDER TAKE DOWN COLONEL KITTS? WILL CARTER find his way back to his old self? What mystery will Swamp Team 3 be embroiled in next?

DID YOU KNOW THAT JANA HAS A STORE? CHECK OUT THE books, audio, and Miss Fortune merchandise at janadeleonstore.com.

FOR NEW RELEASE INFO, SIGN UP FOR JANA'S NEWSLETTER AT janadeleon.com.

Made in the USA
Monee, IL
09 March 2024